Deep Seeds

Two Different Past | One Fatal Future

R. Frazier

ISBN Paperback: 978-0-578-37226-6

Prepared by: Ebony Nicole Smith Consulting, LLC | ebonynicolesmith.com

Editor: A.B. Brumfield for Omni Writing and Editing Services

Book Cover Designed by: Ebony Nicole Smith Consulting, LLC | ebonynicolesmith.com

First paperback edition: 2022

Printed in United States of America

To request permission, contact the publisher at: rfraziertheauthor@yahoo.com

Table of Contents

Dedication

This book, I dedicate to my family, to all the people who are struggling to survive, to all the people who are struggling with who they are and with who they want to be.

I say to you all, don't give up and don't be discouraged. It's never too late to do the things you want to do. Keep in mind that diamonds come from the dirt and they go through a process that brings out the best in them and increases their value. So, remember to always shine bright like a diamond and for every dark night there will always be a brighter day. Just keep positive thoughts and keep moving forward toward your dreams and goals.

Beyond our wisdom, we take for granted all the seeds we've unknowingly planted. People have to realize that no matter how deep you plant a seed in the soil, eventually it will grow and sprout through that soil. Even if you don't personally water the seed, that does not mean that no one else will. And sometimes all it needs is what nature offers it to grow, rain and sunlight!

Acknowledgements

This book took me a little over two years to write, with many failed attempts, because life and tragedy was happening to me and around me. However, I had so many positive and supportive forces and people in my life encouraging me to get it done that I was still able to complete it. There were people who had nothing to believe in or who were facing and living in challenging conditions and unimaginable realities, yet they still found encouraging words for me to keep on going.

A simple thank you to my husband, my best friend who always told me that one of the things he loves about me is my ability to accomplish the things I set my mind to. I wouldn't have been able to accomplish any of those things without you and your continuous support and willingness to do whatever I needed help with or needed done. Your ability to love me is amazing. Thank you, my love.

To my children, my three heartbeats, Ra Shawn, Jayshawn and Levi'ya, thank you for growing with me and for challenging me to do something when I wasn't sure if

I could do it or even if it could be done. Thank you for showing me that I am stronger than I ever realized, each one of you changed my life for the better. You've challenged me to be better, to want better, and to want more. I found new strengths and courage that I would never have found without you. I never knew love like the love I hold for each of you. I hope I have been a positive influence and an encourager in your lives. I hope I have instilled the fear and love of God in you. I hope I've shown you the beauty within yourselves as well as the strength.

I want you all to know that the sky is the limit and that you can do anything you put your minds too. Please remember it is never too late to make a change and if at first you don't succeed, get back up, dust yourself off and try it again. Each one of you are a reflection of me, know that I'll always love you and I'm here for you. Thank you for the gift of unconditional love, you all are my heart in human form. From the cradle to the grave, I got ya'll!

To the many children I have helped raise who are not mine biologically but are mine in every other sense. Two in particular, J.Mar and Kwanique.

J.Mar, I love you because you're my sisters' son and because she allowed me to help in your upbringing. Although we have been faced with many challenges, you have overcome them all. From jail to being shot and almost not making it, to being paralyzed because of being shot, your heart never changed. I truly believe that if you put your all into it, you'll walk again. Thank you for my three honorary grandchildren, Ari, Emoni and little J.Mar (Simba).

Kwanique, I love you because how can I love your father and not love a part of him? I am not your mother and never tried to be, I just wanted to be a positive woman in your life, to help raise you and to teach you that you are strong and can do anything you put your mind to. Having children may delay some things, but it does not stop anything if you are determined. You do not have to settle for anything in life, if you want it go get it.

To YaYa's babies who taught and are teaching me about grandparent hood. Cam (BamBam) & Tre you'll be ok, you have a strong team around you.

I have too many siblings, nieces, nephews, aunts, uncles, cousins and friends to name, but know that I love you all and thank you for anything you've done for me. However, to my sister, Sue, words can't express how happy and proud I am of you. We have been through hell and a lot of bullshit. However, you've always been ready to do whatever I ask of you. You have shown and proved to me a million times forward that you are your sister's keeper. Don't change, my pit bull in a skirt.

To my brother, Bigg Dre, you are more than a brother, you're my best friend, more like my twin. When I'm hurt, you're hurt and vice versa. You're willing to do anything to make me feel better. You've helped me with my children, loving them as your own. When I got married you gave me away, but still remained there for me and my husband. I can't describe the love and support you have given me and continue to give me. I will forever be my brother's keeper.

To my sister, Nicole, who helped raise me when mommy was working, it was me you and sue. You taught me how to drive, you taught me that no one will love my children like me, you taught me work ethics. Mommy taught it to you and you taught it to me. You taught me so many things that I could go on and on and on. Even thou we may not always see eye to eye, I don't take away from what you taught me and I let it be known.

To my mother, Miss B (Bonnie), I want to say thank you for giving me life. Also thank you for all you've done for me. Thank you for not allowing me to know we were poor until I was in my late teens/early twenties when you couldn't shelter me from it anymore. Thank you for always allowing me to express myself even when I didn't know that was what you were doing. I remember looking back at pictures of my younger self and seeing that I'm dressed crazy, church shoes with socks and either pants or shorts on, or wearing Sunday dresses on a Tuesday with cowboy boots. I would have the biggest smile on my face standing there with my signature pose.

Then there's pictures of me clean dressed, hair combed with bows and barrettes, looking loved while I was crying or pouting. I later learned that was you allowing me to express myself in those pictures. You let me dress myself and I was happy, thank you for that. You never judged me when I became a single, teen mom and dropped out of school. I know you wanted more for me. I could go on and on about you, but there is not enough time in the world, not enough paper on the planet, and not enough words in the dictionary to say what I need and want to say. So, I simply say thank you for everything and I hope I made you proud. I love you, Ma!

To my pops, Al, you're not a man of many words, you're a man of action. So, I simply say thank you and will continue showing you the things we don't say, after all, they say action speak louder than words.

To my only living grandparent, my grandmother (grannie), Miss Margie or Madea. I want to first start by saying I am her favorite grandchild (insider). I love you, Grannie. You gave me the courage to love my dark skin when I wasn't comfortable with it. You always told me I was beautiful and made me feel beautiful. You introduced me to God, the comfort of His will, and the benefit of knowing Him. You also let me know when you were not pleased with my behavior or decisions. You were blunt and straight forward with me, but you did it with love. I just want to say thank you and I love you, Margie Lee (Ray) Mims.

A few down ass chicks I know, Pumpkin, Maia, Ebony (Nik), Juanita, Kisha, and Lisa H. You all play different but important roles in my life, no explanation needed. Thank you.

To my brother from another mother, my cousin, Frankie. Regardless of whatever, I love you. Nothing else needs to be said!

To my guardian angels in Heaven, Steven A. Austin Sr., Micheal "Bear" (my gentle giant), Austin Quantrell (Peez) Carson, Austin Eric (Blacker than me) Nevins, and our baby, Andra C. Austin, please continue to watch over us!

Last but not least, I want to thank God for blessing me with the ability to be creative, the ability to grow, and the ability to no longer allow what others think of me to affect me. Thank you, Lord, for saving a wretch like me. Thank you!

Chapter One

Cassandra Lisa Edmonds Baxton, sat in her office during an intake interview listening to the latest drug addict tell her all of the reasons why she was ready to be admitted to the facility and get off of drugs. The woman babbled on and on about how she was tired of ruining her life and tired of destroying the lives of those around her. Cassandra, or Cassie as she was called, had heard it all before. She knew when she was looking at someone that wanted to get off of drugs and when she was listening to someone that was dishing out the bullshit. This crackhead was definitely dishing out the bullshit.

She knew that she shouldn't pass judgement on the people that came to the facility seeking help, but after so many years of hearing the same old sob stories again and again, it was hard not to pass judgement on them. However, even though she judged them in her mind, on the outside she showed them nothing but love and understanding. And with each and every one of them she sincerely hoped they defeated their addictions and made better lives for themselves.

"Those drugs have me so messed up," Trixie Waters continued telling her story, "that I even have a set of twins that no one knows about. They're fraternal, a boy and a girl," she informed Cassie. "Would you believe that I actually sold my children because I needed the money to get high?"

"And how does that make you feel?" Cassie questioned. This was the one question that would always separate those that were serious about getting clean from those that were not.

"I mean," the woman said as she began to scratch her arms and legs, a sure sign that she was entering a withdrawal stage, "I never got to know them so I can't feel anything for them. I sold them as soon as I walked out of the hospital with them. Went straight to the church, found a couple that had been desperate to have children, and sold my babies." The look on the woman's face was so matter of fact that Cassie was struggling not to deck her. "The minute I'd found out I was pregnant, I stopped using those drugs to make sure my baby was going to be healthy, so there was no risk of addiction. I even promised myself that I wouldn't use anymore even after they were born. But in my eighth month those cravings hit me so hard that I struggled to stay clean until after I gave birth. And by the time I had them, I was so desperate for a hit that I was willing to do anything to get it, even sell my children, which I did."

Trixie looked to Cassie for some kind of response but got none. Cassie didn't say a word, didn't even blink. She did nothing that would make that woman know how much she truly despised her actions. "But I did manage to stay clean while I breastfed them and until I could sell them," she said as if that was something to be so damn proud of. "I wanted to get top dollar for them and having them addicted to drugs would not get me the money I needed for the highs I wanted."

Cassie kept her hands hidden beneath her desk and balled her fists into tight knots of fury. She wanted to whip Trixie's ass but couldn't, didn't. There were women out there that had made the mistake of giving away or selling their children, women that were so devastated by the mistake they'd made that they would do anything to undo their mistake. But not Trixie, not the woman sitting there talking about her children as if they were a hot commodity and not actual human beings that she loved and missed with every fiber of her being. And that was what told Cassie that Trixie was not serious about leaving those drugs alone.

Yes. The woman was looking to leave the drugs alone, but not so that she could get and stay clean, there was something else, some other reason she wanted to stop the drugs. And since she had ulterior motives, Cassie knew that the woman wouldn't stay sober long. She would just stay clean long enough to get what she was really after and then go right back to using.

"So, tell me," Cassie asked in as calm a voice as she could muster up, "what do you plan on doing once you're clean?"

"Oh," Trixie beamed a smile at her and scratched some more. "I plan on having more kids. And this time I hope I get pregnant with triplets."

"And why do you want more children?" Cassie already knew the plan the woman had but had to let her say it so that the woman could hear what the drugs were doing to her even if she never intended to stop using them.

"Because the couple I sold the twins to want three more babies. And they're going got pay me a lot of money to give them those babies too," she smiled wide. Cassie wanted to choke her until she was foaming at the mouth. "They want all of their children to have the same mother. But this time, instead of having a bunch of different daddies for the kids, the husband is going to have sex with me and get me pregnant himself. They don't want to go through the IVF process and all of that, so they agreed to pay me good money to screw the husband and spit out three more babies."

"If you don't mind me asking, Trixie," Cassie began, doing her best to keep her face impartial through the fury that was washing over her, "how much are they paying you?"

"Eight thousand," she bragged as if she had won the lottery.

"Eight thousand per child or eight thousand for all three children?" Cassie asked for more details.

"Eight thousand for all three to be given to me at the completion of the deal," she said as she kept that sick smile on her face. "And all I have to do to make that much money is get sober and sleep with the husband. They're even going to put me in a nice apartment where the husband can come and fuck me until I give them their three more kids. I get a free apartment, free clothes, free food. And since the husband is a doctor, he's going to take care of me and all of my medical stuff for free. You can't beat a set up like that." The immense pride that covered Trixie's face enraged Cassie, and still she remained professional by keeping her face neutral. "The husband said twins and triplets run in his family. All of his brothers and sister have at least one set of multiples, so he's sure he can get me pregnant with multiples too. Plus, since I already gave them twins, he said he's going to give me fertility drugs. You know, an extra, extra boost, to make sure I have another set of multiples this pregnancy too."

"And how do you feel about this situation?" Cassie asked, fought to keep from gritting her teeth angrily.

"I'm fine with it," Trixie said as she hunched her shoulders. "I mean, I'm as good as any old surrogate, so why not take the deal and make the money? Especially since I can give them a lot of babies at one time," she spoke as if what she was saying was normal. "And I get to do a good deed and help a loving family to have the children they want. Hell, if they wanted five more children, I would have them and sell all five of them to that good couple."

Cassie sat back in her chair and damn near ground her teeth into dust. The headache that had just formed in her head was killing her. Those people were clearly using the woman and she was too stupid and strung out to know it. A surrogate made anywhere from ninety thousand and upwards per pregnancy and even more if she was carrying multiple children. They were suckering her by only offering Trixie eight thousand for all three children no matter how many pregnancies she had to go through to produce them. And she was more than willing to sell her children as if they were nothing. All so she could get the money she wanted to go back to getting high when it was all said and done.

"And what are your plans after you have the babies?" Cassie questioned.

"I don't know," Trixie said as she thought about what had been asked of her. "Maybe get high a little and after that maybe find another couple to do the same thing with."

Cassie had heard enough. She was done with Trixie. If it was up to her, she would deny the woman help. However, the facility never denied a person looking to get clean, no matter what reason they gave for wanting to get off of drugs. They may qualify them for different treatments plans, less intense treatment plans, but they never denied anyone. So, Trixie would be granted entry, but it irked Cassie that she was taking up a space that someone that sincerely wanted to get clean could use.

"Well, Ms. Waters," Cassie said as she stood and extended her hand, "I'll get your plan all set up, get you a room, and contact you as soon as everything is ready for you. And good luck, I wish you the best."

"You're welcome," Trixie smiled and scratched. "And if you know anybody that wants babies, tell them about me, okay?" Trixie said as if anybody in their right mind would suggest a crackhead to be anyone's surrogate.

Cassie simply nodded and escorted Trixie back to the front office. When the woman was out of her hair, Cassie walked back to her office, closed and locked the door, and took a seat in her desk chair where she placed her elbows on her desk, her head in her hands, and proceeded to bawl like a baby.

While his wife, Cassandra, was bawling as she mentally walked through the inner chambers of hell, on the other side of town, Charles Darnell Baxton was moaning as he floated on a cloud in the sky space above Heaven. He sat at his desk, eyes closed, head leaned against the back of his high back desk chair. His legs were spread as wide as he could get them while his heart practically beat through his ribcage and out of his chest. His eyes were closed, and his hands clenched the arms of his chair in a death grip.

"Just like that," he moaned in a whisper, almost groaned as the person kneeling before him swallowed his manhood whole. "Just like that!" He was being sucked off so good that his breathing hitched and his stomach muscles burned. He was close, so close that he moved his hands from the arms of the chair and gripped the back of the head that was attached to the mouth that was blowing him toward an explosive eruption. Then he prepared to bust.

"Grrrrrrrrrr," he growled deep within his chest when his sac hardened and tightened. His grip on that head tightened, squeezed. And his seed, that hot, violently boiling seed flew through his shaft at lightning speed to his bulbous head and into that sweet, sweet mouth. His body froze and jerked and bucked several times as his emissions fired from him. He practically bit his own tongue to keep from making any noises that would let anyone outside of his office know what was going on inside of his office. "Unnhh," he grunted several times as he gushed and gushed. "Unnhh, unh, unh, unh!" Then, "Unnhh," he grunted a final time when the last of his babies exited him and doused the tonsils of the mouth still attached to him. That final sigh that escaped him was sheer bliss.

For the longest time there was no sound in his office whatsoever, just the deep breathing of a man that had been deeply satisfied. When he was finally able to catch and calm his breath and move again, he stood, reached into his desk where he kept baby wipes and handed them to the person he was cheating on his wife with. "Clean me," was all he said as he watched them do just that. Then he tucked himself back into his slacks and let out one final breath of absolute relief. "You may go now," was all he said.

As soon as the door to his office was closed and he was alone in the huge room again, he walked over to the ornate mirror standing in his office, checked his appearance to make sure he was meticulously dressed again, then he headed back to his desk. Sitting down, he looked at the picture of his wife, Cassie, and shook his head as he lifted it. "Sorry, baby," he spoke to the photo, "but there are just some things you can't do for me. And suck me like that is one of those things."

Placing the photo back on his desk, Charles picked up his office phone and called his wife but she didn't answer. Instead, he was redirected to her voicemail. He hated that, but there was nothing he could do about it at that moment so he resigned himself to leaving a message.

"Cassie, don't be late. This is a very important dinner and we need to make a great impression. And you know how much I hate it when you're late." After hanging up, he looked at his watch, saw that his next meeting was happening in less than ten minutes and immediately got back to work.

Chapter Two

The rest of her day had gone much better than the beginning. It had taken her some serious time and effort to pull herself together, but Cassie had finally done so and pushed through the remainder of her grueling schedule. Every interviewee she'd seen after Trixie had been much easier to stomach, but that was because their stories hadn't hit so close to home. It was now time to clock out of the business of drug rehabilitation of which she was the head counselor at the treatment facility, and clock into the business of her marriage.

Grabbing her things from her office so that she could get to her car and rush home from work that evening, Cassie was slightly irritated. She'd gotten the message from Charles and had to pull off a small miracle to get home quickly in the evening rush hour traffic, get out of her work clothes, get showered, and then get into dinner clothes that were designed to impress. Her husband had an important dinner meeting at the *Top Steak House* and whenever he was expected to meet with important people, she was expected to dress her best and be at his side. Charles had left her several more messages that day, telling her to make sure she wasn't late and had informed her that he would pick her up at seven sharp. Cassie wasn't sure she would be ready for seven sharp which she knew would piss him off.

As she finally exited her office and walked the long halls that would take her out of the building and into the parking lot where her car sat, she reflected on the fact that this was going to be another boring ass dinner meeting with a bunch of old, high society, fake ass, sidity muthafuckas that would grate on her nerves. Those dinners were always filled with the kind of people who would pretend as if they cared about her but really didn't. It was all politics to them and being that her husband was one of the top politicians in the city, playing politics was expected even if those politics were as fake as their attitudes toward her.

Cassie knew those people couldn't stand her young, ghetto ass. However, they dared not express their distaste for her because of who her husband was and because of the political connections they would lose if they crossed Charles wrong in any way. She had mentally prepared herself for the evening's bullshit as she sat through her own work meeting that day. She hoped she could put on just as good a front as Charles' colleagues would for dinner. They didn't like her and she damn sure didn't like their asses either. The difference was that she was much better at hiding her disdain than they were.

Climbing inside of her vehicle and looking at the clock as she started it, Cassie saw that it was now five forty-five, she was running later than she'd originally thought. Her meeting had run longer than expected and she would've still been trapped in there if it wasn't for Denise stepping in and taking over. As she practically scratched out of the parking lot, she suddenly remembered that she needed pantyhose.

"Damn," she said as she navigated out of her workspace parking lot and into traffic hell. "If it isn't one thing, it's another," she sighed.

There were no close stores or corner stores in that bougie neighborhood in which she lived, so Cassie's options were limited. She could wait until she got across town to a mall close to her neighborhood and get what she needed, or she could get them in the hood she was currently in. It was a much better idea to Cassie to get them before she got on the interstate than it was to fight through traffic on that highway, get off the interstate, run to a store, and then get back on the interstate and fight that traffic for another fifteen minutes to get home. A store in the hood is what she decided on.

Normally she wouldn't have been caught dead in one of these corner stores, but at that moment she had no better choices. She had to make do with the store that was immediately available to her. "Shit!" she snapped out loud. If the people that worked there weren't so damn rude and had so little regard for customer service, she wouldn't have had a problem with them. And since she already had to deal with rude and bougie ass people for dinner, she wasn't exactly ready to deal with them at a damn corner store in the hood.

The damn traffic that had already started on the road that would lead her to the store was annoying. She was just about to cuss somebody out for cutting her off when she spotted Trixie. Her tirade had been cut off and immediately she was catapulted back to the time in her life that had brought tears to her eyes that morning.

Listening to Trixie had been one of the hardest things Cassie had ever had to do. That conversation had taken her back, way back to a time when she had been in a similar situation when it came to a child. Her own child. One that she'd been forced to give up all because her grandparents believed that she was too young to have a baby. Letting out a deep sigh with tears that were once more forming in her eyes, she had to admit that they'd been right, but the way they went about getting rid of her baby had been messed up even to Cassie's young mind.

And Romel, how the hell Romel could let things play out the way they did was beyond her. Tightening her grip on her steering wheel while slowly navigating her way through the slow as molasses traffic, Cassie's mind took her back to the place she so rarely allowed it to go to, back to a time when life had been easy and good. Back to the time of Romel.

***

Romel Javon Peeps was a nineteen-year-old, six feet tall drink of water. His brown skin and buff body made her twelve-year-old body react in ways that were new and unfamiliar to her. He was beautiful to look at and immediately she found herself experiencing her first crush.

"Hey, you," she said to him one evening when she saw him in the corner store.

"You talking to me?" he asked her as he looked behind him to make sure she was.

"There's nobody else in here," she said with a childish giggle, "so who else can I be talking to?"

"How old are you, lil' girl?" he asked.

"Twelve," she spoke proudly, boldly.

"Well," he said as he handed the man behind the counter the money for his purchase, "anybody ever told you that you shouldn't talk to strangers? Especially grown man strangers?" When the cashier had given him his change, that tall drink of water strolled toward her until he was standing less than three feet away.

Cassie's heart was racing like crazy, but she refused to back down. "I ain't scared of you," her attitude was much older than her years.

"You should be," he told her as he pinched her gently on her cheeks and walked out of the store.

"He's too old for you," the cashier said as he watched Cassie stare after Romel. "You're just a little girl," he warned her.

"All I did was say hi," she defended her actions.

"Mmm, hmm," the cashier said just before he went back to minding his business.

Back at home that night, Cassie could barely sleep for thinking about the chocolate goodness she'd seen in the store that evening. Even she knew he was too old for her, but she liked the way he looked, like the new feelings he made her feel. So she promised herself that she would find him again so she could look at him and feel those feelings again. Three weeks later, she did just that.

"Hey, you," she said once again as she walked toward a house on French Street in her neighborhood and saw the guy from the store sitting on the porch. He was at Mrs. Bernadine's house, just around the corner from her own house.

"You stalking me, lil girl?" he asked as he looked at her and smiled.

"I'm just going to the store," she told him the truth. She had been stalking the neighborhood looking for him for weeks, but he didn't need to know that. Besides, as hard as she had been looking for him, on that particular afternoon all she had been doing was going to the store for her grandmother.

"I bet," he smiled at her.

"Seriously," she said as she took it upon herself to walk up to the porch and take a seat beside him. "My grandmama's making cornbread for dinner tonight and she needs milk."

"Well, shouldn't you be getting that milk?"

He looked over at her with those chocolate eyes and Cassie almost passed out. "She's not home right now, so I have time," she admitted as she got too comfortable next to him.

Romel didn't say anything to her. Instead, he redirected his attentions back to the people and the activities on French Street.

For the longest time the two of them sat on that porch in silence, a silence so comfortable that Cassie didn't even feel the need to explain why she had taken that seat. It felt so good just to be there and be in his company. After a good forty-five minutes had gone by, Romel finally broke that silence by telling her to, "Go get that milk and go home."

Without saying a single word, Cassie did just that. However, the next day she was right back on that porch sitting in that same spot next to him.

"You're not from around here," she told him when she was comfortable again. "I know everybody in this neighborhood, and I've never seen you before. So what are you doing here sitting on Mrs. Bernadine's porch?"

"I'm not from this neighborhood," he admitted. "But my dad is and I'm visiting him."

They were quiet again for a long time as they both sat there watching the activities in the neighborhood. Then, "What's your name?" Cassie asked him

"Romel," he spoke quietly. "Now go home."

And just like that Cassie left. She'd gotten to sit with him just long enough to get her fix for the day. However, she returned the next day and the next day and the next day. In fact, she kept going back each day until eventually the two of them sparked up a great conversation. Before anyone knew what was happening, Romel and Cassie had become great friends and had learned as much as they could about one another.

Over time that summer, Cassie eventually learned that Romel was nineteen years old and had come from an average home. Romel's mom, Rose, had been a single parent for the first eight years of Romel's life. That's when she married Eric, Romel's stepfather. Hating the fact that his mother had married someone that wasn't his real dad, Romel became a troubled child, going in and out of juvenile homes and youth detention centers for fighting and getting kicked out of school. Romel stole things, broke into houses, sold drugs. If it was illegal and you could name it, he'd done it. No matter how many times Eric had stepped in and tried to be a father to Romel, the child had reminded the man that he was not his father and that he was never going to be.

Romel admitted that he'd been acting out because his father hadn't been there for him. Rasheem Peeps was too busy going to jail to be any kind of a father to his own son and Romel had paid a heavy price for that. Eventually, Rasheem had gone to prison one time too many, and that last time he didn't get out for years. By the time Rasheem was finally free, Rose and Eric had moved to Atlanta so that Romel could live in a different environment and have a better chance at life. The change had been just what Romel needed.

When Rasheem started asking to spend some time with Romel, Rose and Eric thought it was a bad idea. They didn't want Romel getting back on that same track that they had moved hundreds of miles away to get him off of. But when Romel decided that he wanted to get to know his father, they realized that he was a grown man and there was nothing they could do to stop him. Reluctantly, they agreed, and because Rose vowed to never stop Rasheem from seeing his son, because she knew that Romel had spent years looking for his dad's love in all of the wrong places and activities, they paid for their son to be on the first thing smoking to his paternal grandmother's house where his father lived for the time being. It was time for Romel to develop that relationship with his father even if Rose knew that Rasheem would never be able to give Romel that same love in return.

By the time she had learned all of that from Romel, Cassie had fallen in love with him and wanted to do everything she could to make him feel the love his daddy couldn't give him. She may have only been twelve, but she knew enough to understand that no one should go without love. So she spent more time that summer being really nice to him and just being there for him whenever he may have needed her. But that all changed in the blink of an eye one early August evening when the summer was almost over.

Chapter Three

Romel had been hanging out with his friends, getting high and drunk, celebrating before he was supposed to return back to Atlanta. When it was almost dark, he decided to go back to his grandmother's house and wait for his dad to get home. He wanted to talk to him about possibly staying with him instead of going back to Atlanta, but no one was home. Deciding to enjoy the last hour and a half of sunlight, Romel took his seat on the porch and prepared to wait for his dad. He was seriously buzzed from the alcohol and in deep thought when Cassie came down the street heading to the store again.

"Where you going?" he called out to her.

"To the store. Grandma's making yams. She needs some sugar."

"Come talk to me, my little girlfriend," he said as he patted the seat on the porch beside him. The blush

that rushed up her body at the fact that he called her his little girlfriend turned her entire face beet red. Immediately, Cassie did what she always did. She sat beside Romel and as usual they started talking.

"Why are you out here this late?" he questioned.

"My grandparents went to the hospital to pray for one of the church members, so she's gonna be cooking late. She just called the house and asked me to go to the store."

"I just bought a bag of sugar for my grandmother a few hours ago. She didn't open it yet, so you can take that one and I'll go get a new bag later. You shouldn't be wandering around out here this late."

"It's not late, Romel. The sun ain't even set yet," she spoke so innocently.

"It's late to me and I don't want you out here this time of evening." Then he stood up all of a sudden and said, "So go on in the house and get that bag of sugar out of the kitchen. Then go in my room and get my keys off the dresser so I can lock up and walk you home before I go back to the store and get another bag."

Doing what he said, Cassie stood and went into Mrs. Bernadine's house and straight to her kitchen where she grabbed the sugar that was still in the grocery bag. Romel hadn't even put the sugar up yet. Then just as he'd asked her to, she headed down the hall toward his room.

Quickly she realized that she had no idea which one of those rooms was his and was about to call out to him when she walked past a room that she instantly knew belonged to Romel. She entered slowly, almost as if she was creeping in, and instead of getting his keys, she stood in there for a moment looking at all of the posters he had on his wall.

Some of them were of rappers and some of them were of really pretty women wearing bathing suits and skimpy clothes. She wondered if that was the kind of woman Romel liked and immediately felt a little embarrassed. As she looked down at her body, she shook her head sadly. Her body was very well developed for a twelve year old and still she didn't look like those women so she knew Romel would never fall in love with her the way she was in love with him. But that was okay, she was just happy to spend all of that time with him before he had to go back to Atlanta and she might not ever see him again.

Then she saw the Tv and her jaw dropped. There was only one Tv in her house and it was in the living room. Her grandfather had refused to let any of them have a television in their rooms. He said the bedroom was for sleeping, not for watching Tv. Cassie hated having to share the one Tv in their house with her grandparents because that meant she never got to watch what she wanted to watch. She was always stuck watching the preaching channel with them which aggravated her because she was missing all of the good stuff.

When she stopped being shocked just long enough to focus on the actual Tv screen, Cassie got a good look at what was playing on it. It was the kind of movie her grandparents would never have allowed her to watch. Without even thinking about it, Cassie sat on Romel's bed and was immediately absorbed in the movie. There was no way in hell she was going to miss an opportunity to see the movie everybody had been talking about except her. She might not have been able to watch all of it, but she was going to catch as much of it as she could. She had instantly forgotten all about those keys.

That was exactly where Romel found her a little while later. "Come on, Cassie," he said when he stepped inside of his room. "I need to get you home and get to the store before it closes," he told her. But when his eyes drifted to his TV screen and he saw the steamy love scene she was watching, he froze. "I can't let you watch this," he told her as he neared the Tv to turn it off.

"Noooo!" she whined like the kid she was. "I never get to watch stuff like this. My grandparents treat me like a baby. Just let me finish watching it, please," she spoke with wide and innocent eyes.

It was so hard for Romel to tell her no, especially since she'd spent her whole summer being nice to him. So, he stood there contemplating for a moment before deciding to return the favor and be just as nice to her. A short time later, Romel was sitting on the bed beside her and watching the movie with her. Fifteen minutes later, he found that he was thoroughly enjoying himself.

The movie was really good, just as everyone had been saying it was. It was action packed and exciting, just the kind of film he liked. To make it an even better experience for him was Cassie's reactions to everything. It was like the kid had never seen or experienced anything in her life. Then he remembered that she was being raised by the pastor and the first lady and realized that she really hadn't experienced anything like that before.

Another love scene came on the screen, a more adult rated one, and everything changed. Knowing that she had never seen anything like what was about to happen, Romel was about to stand to go and turn the television off when all of a sudden Cassie placed her hand on his knee and gripped it tightly. He looked over to her to see what was going on, but her eyes were glued to that screen. The kissing, the serious making out they were doing. Her skin had deepened in color, signifying the blush that was now covering her. He knew he should stop the movie and bring her home, knew she shouldn't be seeing what adults did when they were in their bedrooms at night, but he didn't move. Couldn't move. He just watched her reaction to the movie like he had been doing the entire time they'd been watching. Then she turned to him and out of the blue she kissed him on the lips.

"What's that for?" he asked as a look of confusion came across his face.

"It's for the fact that I always liked you and," she stared into his eyes, "because you called me your little girlfriend."

"Cassie, that's just—" he began, but she cut him off by kissing him again.

He stared at her once more as if trying to figure out some complex puzzle. This time Cassie watched several expressions run across Romel's face, each one more intriguing than the other. She wondered what he was thinking, but she didn't say anything for fear that he would grab her and bring her home. That wasn't what Romel did. Instead, he let the alcohol in his system and the wild feelings in his body cloud his judgement. Before he could even think to stop himself, Romel had taken her virginity. He was having full out sex with Cassandra.

That night, he walked her home and hugged her tight when they got to her door. "Listen, my little girlfriend," he began as he looked down at her, "we can't tell anybody about this, okay?"

"Okay," she shook her head up and down in agreement.

"If anybody finds out, we can both be in some real trouble and I don't want to get you in any trouble because I like you a lot."

"Okay," she said again as she kept watching him, her heart soaring at the knowledge that Romel liked her a lot.

Then, "Go in the house, lock up, and don't come out no more until your grandparents get home."

"Okay," she said once more as she walked up the steps and let herself into her home, a huge smile on her face. "Romel is my boyfriend," she spoke in a dreamy voice and hugged herself when she walked into her room and closed the door behind her. "And one day he's going to love me just like I love him." Cassie was happier than she had even been as she realized that her fantasy was now her reality.

But outside of her home, on the way to the store, Romel was pissed with himself. "How the hell could you allow yourself to do that to her?" he questioned himself. "She's a fucking kid!" he chastised. But no matter how much his mind berated him and let him know that he was scum, his body and his heart were singing a different tune. They liked Cassie a lot and felt nothing but pleasure at the thought of what happened. Romel was a torn and tortured soul. "Fuck!" he shouted angrily as he promised himself he would never do that with Cassie again. However, Romel quickly found that he couldn't keep that promise no matter how hard he tried.

The following day, Cassandra showed up again. Before he could even try to stop himself, Romel had her right back in Mrs. Bernadine's house, in his room, in his bed, having sex with him again. And again. And again. This went on every day for the rest of the summer as Romel had no self-control when it came to Cassandra. Cassie thought she was in love and wanted Romel more than anything. Romel knew he was dead wrong to want her the way he did and to have her the way he was having her. Yet, knowing that he was wrong didn't stop him from doing what he knew was forbidden. That was when he knew he couldn't stay in Buffalo. He had to go back to Atlanta before he really got Cassie in trouble.

The day after he made his decision, when Cassie showed up again at around two o'clock, Romel refused to let her go in the house. He told her to sit down so that he could talk to her. Then he proceeded to tell her that it was time for him to go back home. As much as Cassie wanted to cry, she had to admit that she had known he was going to leave at some point. The point was now and she just had to be a big girl and suck it up.

"Okay," she said as she hunched her shoulders as if his words were not that big of a deal, but they were a big deal, a really big deal.

Romel stared at her, watching her eyes, seeing the hurt she was trying to hide shining in them. "I'm sorr—"

"Okay, well, I'll see you later," she cut him off. As much as she was trying to be a big girl, there was no way

she could stand on that porch and listen to her crush crush her by telling her that he was leaving.

Just as she had walked down three of the porch steps and was about to walk down the last two, she felt herself being grabbed and yanked back onto the porch. "Don't walk away from me like that," he told her as he held her wrists and forced her to face him. Cassie didn't say anything, she didn't even look at Romel because she knew that if she did she would start crying. "So, you're not even going to talk to me now? Come on, Cassie, I thought we were better than that."

Cassie still refused to talk and still refused to look at Romel. Her tears were forming and she was fighting like hell to keep them from falling from her eyes in front of him. She couldn't let him see her acting like a baby. At the exact moment that she'd determined to keep her tears to herself, a big fat one fell and plopped loud and hard onto the floor of the porch. Seeing that made Romel tighten his grip on her wrists and take her into his house. There was no way he could let her go home while she was crying and there was no way he could let her stand on his porch crying, enough for anyone to come by and see and wonder what the hell he had done to her.

The minute he got her into his house, he rushed her to his bedroom, closed the door and locked it. Then he sat her on his bed and held her tight as he let her cry and cry. He hadn't intended to hurt her at all, but he had and that was all the more reason why he knew he should go back to Atlanta. There was no one there he could hurt. Realizing that Cassie had finally grown quiet in his arms, he loosened his grip on her and looked down at her. She looked up at him.

"I love you, Romel," she told him just before she pressed her lips to his.

"I love you too, Cassie," he finally told her when the kiss was over.

And before either of them could stop themselves again, they were doing what they should not have been doing. Only this time it was more real than it had ever been, especially since they both knew it would be the last time.

"I don't want you to go," Cassie told him in the midst.

"I don't want to go," was his very honest response.

Then they stopped talking and lost themselves in what should not have been taking place. When it was all said and done, it was almost night fall.

"I'm leaving next week, so I guess that was our goodbye." He pulled his shirt over his head and bent to put his shoes on.

"I guess," was all Cassie would allow herself to say. There was no way she was going to start that crying mess all over again.

When they were both dressed, Romel pulled her into his arms and hugged her one more time before walking her through the house, out of the front door and onto the porch. Just as he and Cassie stepped outside, Cassie's uncle Jinx was passing by in his car. The minute Jinx laid eyes on Romel and Cassie, he stopped his car in the middle of the street and hopped out, heading straight for them. He knew shit when he smelled it.

"Go home," he told Cassie as he looked at her with a blank face. Cassie looked at Romel and then back at Jinx as she tried to decide what she wanted to do. On the one hand, those were the last few minutes she was going to ever have to spend with Romel again in life. On the other hand, if she disobeyed her uncle there would be hell to pay. Seeing what she was doing, Jinx spoke once again, "This is not up for discussion, lil' girl. Now go home!"

He'd spoken those words with more authority and had Cassie hopping off of the porch and starting her journey home, but not before she had the chance to say a very sad, "Bye, Romel," just before she hung her head and hid her face as tears started again.

And the last thing she heard before she reached the corner to turn it was Jinx saying to Romel, "Stay the fuck away from Cassie. Got it?"

"Got it," she heard Romel reply with a voice that sounded scared shitless when he'd gotten a real good look at that big ass gun Jinx had on his side.

"Good. And if I find out you touched her, I'm going to kill you. Now, consider yourself warned," Jinx said before he jumped into his car and pulled off just as Cassie turned that corner on French Street for the last time that summer.

Chapter Four

Having to slam on brakes in the middle of that traffic was what yanked Cassie away from that summer with Romel and back to her present. Him leaving had been really hard on her, but what followed after had almost devastated her. For a long time she'd thought that maybe she needed to be admitted to a nut house, but she'd fought like hell to get her head back in a good place and to make something of herself. No way could or would she let what everyone had done to her destroy her entire future. So, Cassie had fought and carved out the life she'd wanted after having endured the life not many would have been able to stand.

Just thinking about all she had gone through after her summer with Romel had her feeling proud of all that she had accomplished. She smiled as she thought of the fact that she was so good at life she had succeeded in getting her colleagues to think she was young, educated, and fun. However, that was her professional persona, a personality only shown to those who knew her on a business level. To family and friends, those closest to her, she was crazy and sexy and cool. When she was on the job, she was very successful as the administrative assistant and coordinator at that local drug treatment center. When she was away from work, she was the life of the party. Balance, she always told herself, life was all about balance and she had managed to balance hers very well.

Even though she was only thirty-two years old, Cassie was at the top of her game. Not only was she a beast in the executive world, she was also a force to be reckoned with in her personal life. For starters, she was married to Mr. Charles Darnell Baxton, one of the top and most well-known city officials in the city of Buffalo. As the wife of a politician, Cassie excelled at getting people to do whatever her husband needed them to do to advance his political career. If Charles needed it to happen, Cassie was the woman to get it done.

Because of how hard she had worked to achieve her success, she'd avoided the dreaded topic of children with her husband thus far. That topic always made her cry, in fact it was what made her cry after she had talked to Trixie that morning. She hated the thought of children of any kind. As far as her life and ambitions were concerned, children did not yet fit into the equation of her existence. Maybe children would fit in one day, just not today. Thank God she had married a man that had no children as well and that wasn't even talking about having any.

Getting off of the topic of children in her head, Cassie thought about how she had an amazing ability to draw people in with her bubbly attitude and her amazing eyes. She was a stunner to look at and was more than accustomed to compliments of her physical appearance being thrown her way. Her husband was no stranger to those compliments as well. At fifty years old, Charles didn't look a day over thirty. The brotha was tall and light skinned with a medium build that made women drool. And with that sexy bald head, handsome was an understatement when it came to describing him. Everything about the man was all-out amazing, but just like everyone else, Charles had his share of issues. However, issues was something Cassie was no stranger to as her childhood had come with more than its share of ups and downs.

Her mother, Georgia Lee Edmonds had died of a drug overdose when Cassie was four years old. That was how she'd ended up being raised by her grandparents, Mrs. Lee Edmonds and Mr. Cleo, short for Cleothis, Edmonds. Georgia, a well-known hustler and stripper, had given birth to Cassie at a young age, but a baby had done nothing to slow that woman down. Having parents that were the pastor and first lady of The Tabernacle Faith in God Baptist Apostle Church, Georgia had been raised right. Her parents were a religious power couple that did all they could to keep her active in the church and out of trouble, but church didn't work on Georgia. Partying and sniffing coke were her first loves and she loved them too much to ever give them up for bible study and Sunday school.

Although Georgia had a lot of weaknesses, drugs, men with money and power, and alcohol were the ones that eventually took her out. That left four-year-old Cassie in the world without a mother. As far as her father was concerned, it was well known to everyone except Cassie who he was because Cassie was the spitting image of him. But because Georgia had never spoken a word about him, everyone correctly assumed that he'd wanted less to do with Cassie than Georgia had when she was alive. So, Cassie went through life as an orphan being raised by extremely religious grandparents. That was why she had been so drawn to Romel, he had given her a break from the religious and had allowed her to just enjoy her life for a short while. Just like her husband, she was no stranger to issues, and that's why she was able to conquer and overcome every hardship life threw her way. She had determined a long time ago that nothing could or would stop her and so far so good.

"Shit!" Cassie cursed harshly as she navigated her cocaine white GLC AMG 43 series Mercedes Benz with the butter pecan leather seats through the makeshift parking lot of Chiraq, the little plaza at the corner of East Delevan and Hagen. She knew her vehicle stood out like a sore thumb in the hood, but she also dared a soul to touch it. She worked too hard for the things she had, she'd be damned if she allowed anyone to take her things and get away with it.

Walking into the store quickly and with purpose, she wasted no time going to the section where the pantyhose were and grabbing them. Since she was there, Cassie decided to kill two birds with one stone and picked up a bottle of Pineapple Cîroc, her favorite, as she skipped past everyone and raced to the register. Once there, without even waiting for the cashier to ring her things up, she threw five dollars on the counter and exited the store. She didn't have time to wait in line for one dollar and twenty eight cents of change.

As she rushed to the parking lot, making a beeline for her car, she suddenly heard, "Hey, Ma, I got that fire. I got that smoke." Not caring which one of the many men standing out there it was that hollered at her, Cassie kept it moving. She had no time, neither would she make time for small talk with the damn weed man.

When she had finally and safely made it to her car, she was just about to reprimand herself for making that stop at that hood store when she was stopped by, "Yo, Cassie, come here!"

"What the hell?" she said as the summer of her twelfth year came crashing down on her again.

When she turned toward the sound of the voice, shock and sheer astonishment almost knocked her on her ass, but she quickly recovered and kept her emotions to herself. Nobody needed to know how she felt about anything, especially not the man rushing toward her as if he had a right to.

"I been looking all over for you," he spoke as if it was actually okay for him to talk to her. She cringed at the sound of his voice and the memories it brought up.

It was Romel, the man that she had once loved with everything in her. It was almost as if because she had thought about him most of her day, she had conjured him up, him and all of the feelings he'd stirred in her when she'd been nothing but a child.

"How did you find me? And what are you doing here?" that was all she cared to know. As much as she hated him, he still had that stupid ass effect on her, the same one he'd had when she was twelve.

"I found you by asking around. Even though you live in that big house in that ritzy neighborhood, the hood still knows where you are," he told her the truth. "And they know you're working to better the hood and to get people off of drugs. You did good for yourself," he smiled affectionately at her. When she didn't return the smile, he went on with his explanation. "I was on my way to your job and stopped here to pick up a few things and all of a sudden there you were."

She wanted to cuss him out, wanted to tell him to cut the shit about her doing good for herself, especially after how hard he'd made it for her to do good for herself. Nevertheless, she wouldn't give him the satisfaction of knowing that he still touched her on an emotional level. Not that she was in love with him anymore, but those memories made her wish for the days of that summer, days when she was first discovering what love was. Those were some powerful feelings, especially for a girl that had her first love actually return some of that love to her.

"That answers one question," she tried not to snap at him, but what about the other one. What are you doing here, Romel?"

"I need your help," he said as he sauntered closer to her, "We need your help," he corrected. "RJ is in trouble." At the mention of RJ, Cassie's defenses dropped and for a second all she could do was stand there looking at him. Romel risked walking a little closer to her, hoping she wouldn't do anything to hurt him after everything he had done to hurt her. "Damn, Cassie," he spoke in that deep voice that used to drive her crazy, "you're still as sexy as ever," he said as he looked her up and down and licked his lips at her. If only he could have her one more time, he thought as his nature rose and he had to adjust himself before he was in pain. She'd always had that affect on him.

Cassie fought like hell not to let her mind go back there, to the place she never should have been in the first place. "What are you talking about? What do you mean RJ is in trouble?" she questioned as aggravation ran through her.

"He's in some real deep shit," he got back to the point when she didn't play into his complement. It was clear that she still hated him and still didn't trust him and he couldn't blame her. So he dropped the compliments and got back to the point at hand. "I don't have enough time to explain it all to you right now, but please call me, Cassie. There's a lot we need to talk about."

"Like there was a lot we needed to talk about back then, but you conveniently kept your mouth shut?" she eyed him angrily. Romel said nothing as Cassie angrily pulled out her cell phone. "What's your number?" she asked and began programming in into her phone. When he had given it to her, she glared at him and said, "I'll call you as soon as I get a chance."

"I never meant to hurt you, Cassie," he spoke from the heart.

"But you did it anyway," was all she said.

There was nothing Romel could say since she had spoken the truth, a truth she didn't quite understand yet. But he would explain it to her one day if she ever let him. Watching Cassie get into her car, Romel shook his head at how things had played out between them that summer and all of the year that had followed. He knew he could never make up for what he had done, but he was damn sure willing to try if only she would give him that chance. Because with what they were about to go through, those two would have to lean on one another more than they would ever be able to lean on anyone else. For them, the shit was about to hit the fan.

Without even saying goodbye to her first love, Cassie scratched out of the parking lot heading toward the interstate that would take her home. Romel had taken up time she didn't have and now she was racing through traffic like a stunt woman. Only this time she had a lot more on her mind then being late for some stupid ass dinner with some stupid ass people. Now she had RJ on her mind.

Chapter Five

By the time Cassie made it home, she was twenty additional minutes behind schedule. She was not only on edge because of RJ, she was also on edge because of Charles. Her husband was very anal when it came to being on time. As quickly as she could, she'd stripped, showered, and dressed again. Charles had been so mad when she'd called him and said that she would be later than expected that he'd decided not to wait for her to get home. He just told Cassie to meet him there, hung up on her, and headed to the dinner so that he could be there to greet his guests. As much as it irritated her that her husband had reacted that way and that he wasn't going to escort her like every other husband was going to escort their wives there, she decided to keep her comments to herself. She was the one that was late and it wouldn't look good or be fair if she forced the host to be late as well.

Arriving at the restaurant, Cassie let out a huge sigh of relief. God must have been on her side because the whole party was running late due to a traffic delay on the highway. The relief that poured through her was palpable and she began to relax. Feeling much better, she walked over to her husband in the semi empty restaurant. Her relief from a few moments ago was short lived. She could tell he'd had a few to drink already and that raised the hairs on the back of her neck. Charles wasn't the nicest person to her when he was sober, alcohol always made him worse.

"Hey," she said as she leaned in, waiting for him greet her with a kiss.

Instead of kissing her, however, her husband looked at his watch as a means of letting her know that he disapproved of her being late. Then Charles shifted eyes of disapproval to her before bringing his glass back to his lips to finish his drink. Once he was done, he grabbed his wife by the hand, squeezed it unnecessarily tight, and tugged a little roughly. The way he touched her was just enough to let her know he was pissed without alerting anyone else that may have been watching his violent mood.

After silently and thoroughly conveying his temperament to Cassie, together they moved across the restaurant toward the Imperial Room that had been reserved for them. Once there, they got settled moments before the other guests started arriving. It surprised her to see her husband's assistant, Demetri, among the others, but it didn't bother her. She and Charles agreed that there were to be no more female assistants after she'd caught Charles cheating with Mary, his last assistant. So as long as his assistant was a man, Cassie really didn't care where she saw him with her husband. She may not have liked Demetri because something about the man was off, but she was never stressed when she found that he was with her husband.

Once everyone was seated, dinner was immediately under way. The first portion of the meal was small talk and conversations about everyone and how they were all doing. To Cassie, it was like one long brag session, and she was bored to tears as they spoke of who bought new houses, new boats, new cars. Whose children went to the bast schools, married the best people, made the most money. It took everything in her not to roll her eyes into the back of her head, but she managed. Following the brag session, they finally got down to business and she was equally if not more bored with that. Several times she had to stifle a yawn, but she smiled as if interested, answered when spoken to, and survived the horror flick that was her evening.

Finally the business dinner was over and Cassie couldn't help the sigh of relief that came from her. As she prepared to go home with her husband and listen to him gripe about her being late, Charles stood, turned to her, and said, "The car will take you home. I need to talk to the guys about a few other things."

"Huh?" Cassie began to notice that all of the guys were sending their wives home and informing them not to wait up. That's when it hit her. They had chosen that particular night to have their monthly get together. At least once a month, every month, Charles and those men would have those meetings and not return home until wee hours of the morning. It used to bother Cassie because something about those get togethers didn't feel quite right, but over time she became used to them and couldn't care less about them anymore. Besides, at least with him at that stupid gathering of testosterone she wouldn't have to hear his mouth. However, when she got a chance she would definitely ask him why those meeting were becoming so much longer than normal as of late. "Okay," she happily agreed. Charles then kissed Cassandra good night and walked her to the car that had been waiting for her.

Once Cassie got home, she immediately changed into her night clothes and lay in their big California king size bed thinking about her relationship with her husband. As much as she hated to admit it, things with her and Charles had been strained for a while and she needed to get to the core of it so that they could begin repairing their relationship before things went too far. It had already been over a month since Charles had touched her and she had no idea why he'd become sexually distant. If that disconnect went on any longer she was sure she would begin to suspect him of cheating again. And neither of them needed her thinking that.

Her mind was all over the place as she remembered a time that sex with Charles had been great, amazing, so much so that she would always orgasm with a scream. The man definitely knew how to touch her, how to tap her g-spot and leave her well satisfied. But that had stopped and then sex with her husband had just become weird. All of a sudden, he'd started desiring things that she wasn't interested in, things like anal sex. Cassie had never wanted or experienced anal sex in her life and wasn't too fond of her husband trying to pressure her into doing it. However, Charles pushed and pushed and pushed until she finally decided to give in.

The first time they'd done it, it hurt like hell. She'd gritted her teeth, balled her hand into tight fists and told Charles she wanted to stop. He'd gotten angry and hadn't spoken to her for almost a week. Then he started pressuring her again, this time with urgency, and she gave in again. The second time it still hurt just as bad as it had the first time, but she kept quiet and endured it and her husband had come harder than he had since they'd been married. Now, whenever he was in one of those moods, Cassie just did it. She didn't like it, but to keep him pleased she stopped resisting altogether and simply grew accustomed to it. Being married is a bitch when you have to compromise on things you hate, she thought.

When she'd calmed her thoughts about her husband and their marital issues, she started thinking about RJ and Romel and the deep shit Romel said RJ was in. She wasn't sure what that deep shit was or even if she should believe anything Romel said, but at the same time she didn't think he would lie about RJ. He may have played with her but she thought RJ may have been too important to him to play those kinds of games.

Thinking about the whole Romel situation and what he could possibly have to tell her, she wasn't sure if she should call her grandparents and tell them about her conversation with him. She was especially unsure since they despised him and since she knew they'd tell Jinx that Romel had reached out to her. And seeing as though Romel had been paid handsomely by them to stay far away from her, Cassandra knew that situation could get out of hand fast and horribly. Choosing not to bring that kind of drama into her life again, she decided that she would call Romel in the morning and see what was going on before she decided what she would do one way or the other.

After lying there for so long with her mind racing, she was unable to sleep. Try as she might, sleep would not allow her to catch it that night. Looking over to the clock, Cassie realized that it was 3:45 a.m. and her husband still wasn't home. Struggling not to become angry and willing herself to go to sleep, she finally drifted off. It was 4:20 a.m. when Cassie finally heard the house alarm being shut off and Charles' keys opening the door. A sigh of relief escaped her at the knowledge that he was alright, but the relief quickly disappeared when he walked into their bedroom smelling of alcohol and a scent that wasn't his. Without a single word to her, Charles undressed, climbed into bed, and immediately went to sleep.

At five that same morning, Cassie's alarm began ringing, signaling that it was time for her to get ready for work. As she cut the alarm off, she got out of bed and walked into the bathroom. Her mind began to focus on her husband and the terrible state of her marriage. Even with that being the case, she refused to begin her day worrying about what she could not fix at that moment, so she got off of the toilet and turned on the shower. Going over to the electronic system that Charles had paid to have installed in their bathroom, she turned on her daily motivational speech. It was the inspiration she listened to every morning before work. She dealt with some seriously messed up people every day and she needed something to keep her sane before dealing with them each morning.

In addition to helping her to make it through her crazy days, that speech was the closet Cassie had been to church in a long time. Since her grandparents had shoved religion down her throat when she was younger, Cassie had practically steered clear of it as an adult. In fact, Cassie no longer even knew if she believed in God anymore. She knew that if her grandparents ever found that out they would be highly disappointed and do all they could to make her get her mind back on the God they served. So, to keep the peace in the family she loved with her whole heart, she kept her struggles with her faith to herself. That was between her and God, if God was real.

Stepping out of her shower refreshed, she strolled her naked body over to her massive closet to choose her attire for the day. There were some very important people she would be meeting with. Turning to the panel in her closet, she changed what she was listening to from the speech to her favorite music artist, Beyoncé. There was something about that woman's music that always made her feel better. Cassie was a proud member of the Beyhive and nobody had better tell her a damn thing about it.

Deciding on an all-white, sleeveless, linen dress with the matching blazer and white three-inch Chanel pumps with little gold buckles on them, Cassie carefully covered her naked body in style. She accommodated her ensemble with the matching Chanel bag and gold accessories that consisted of small hoop earrings, a gold and white Chanel watch, and a small gold necklace. Then she fixed her hair, applied her make up, sprayed herself with her Light Blue by Dolce and Gabbana and was ready to conquer the world. Finally grabbing her keys and her briefcase, Cassie headed out of the door and off to work.

Just before seven that morning, Charles woke with his head spinning and his stomach churning. Unlike his wife who had bounced out of bed to get ready for her day, he was struggling just to move. He had overindulged in all of his bad habits the night before and was now paying for it. He knew he needed to get up and get his morning started, but there was nothing he could do until the world around him stopped spinning.

Lying there regretting every decision he had made the previous night, Charles hated himself. He wondered why he had allowed the men in his group to coerce him into taking that stupid bet, a bet that he'd lost, a bet that had him sniffing a few lines of coke and indulging in some of the best sex of his life. But it was who Charles had sex with in front of them that had him hating his own existence.

Demetri. He'd had sex with Demetri in front of everyone and had enjoyed it way more than he should have. It wasn't like he wasn't banging Demetri on a regular basis, it was just that no one needed to know that. But something about all of the liquor and all of the drugs he'd been pumped with made him lose his inhibitions and let loose, made everyone in that club let loose. Charles groaned in emotional agony as he remembered witnessing the other men there all having sex with male partners. Normally, they would hire female strippers and fuck them, but last night had changed everything. Those men were pumping and grunting like animals as they did what their wives would divorce them for if those women ever found out.

Now they all had to keep that secret. Each and every one of them had indulged in a man and none of them could say a word or they would all be exposed. His secret was out, but so was theirs, and from the looks of the things that Charles remembered, more than a few of those men looked as if that hadn't been their first time with someone of the same sex. Just like him.

"Shit," he said as he finally sat up on the side of the bed and killed the alarm on his phone that had just started to ring. "Shit," he said again as his head started to pound from sitting up. Last night was definitely what he needed, but he was really paying for it.

Looking inside of his nightstand, he grabbed the bottle of Aleve he kept there and popped four of them. He'd needed those pills badly and he sat there without moving a single muscle for another fifteen minutes after taking them just to give them time to kick in and make his head and body stop killing him. Finally, he was able to move without feeling as if he was going to die. Immediately he made his way to the bathroom to shit, shower, and shave. In the shower, the hot water beating down on his head felt like rain from heaven. It made him feel refreshed and invigorated. Now all he needed to do was get some soup into his stomach and he would be good to go.

Charles stepped out of the shower and went back to reflecting on the previous night. He looked at himself in the mirror and wondered what was happening to him and what had happened to him. He had allowed himself to do the same things that had ruined his life once before, things he had vowed he would never do again. Yet, the minute someone dangled those forbidden carrots in front of him, Charles took the bait and went for the gold. How had he gotten back to that place? In fact, how had he gotten to that place the first time?

As he deepened his thoughts, he slowly came to realize that the first time it had been because he'd become exhausted and overwhelmed with hiding who he was, with hiding his true self deep inside of him and letting the world see the fake character he had created. Day in and day out he had to pretend, to hide, and it had taken a mental and emotional toll on him. That's when he had resorted to drinking and using to escape the torture of his life and to try and make himself forget that he could never be who he truly was. That plan had completely backfired because those escapes hadn't done what he'd intended them to do. Those escapes had been the things that led him to let down those inhibitions of his, to free himself, and to let out his true desires, his true natures. And that was how his life had gone down the drain.

Now, he was in a new space, had a new life, a great life, had reinvented himself. He was a powerful man with connects all over the world. He had top politicians in his pocket. He, himself was a top politician. He had a beautiful wife, one that was sexy as hell and that catered to him the way he wanted her to, one that he could control. Then there was the money. He wasn't poor by any means, never had been since he'd grown up with wealth, but he'd earned his own money now. Charles had money falling out of his pockets and could buy whatever and whoever his heart desired. So why, if he had the life of his dreams, was he once again on the road he knew would eventually lead to his downfall? Simple. Because he was still trying to hid the person he really was from the world and it was wearing him out.

Chapter Six

Before Charles could reflect on his realization any deeper, his phone began to ring. Grabbing it, he stared at the screen, confusion crossing his face as he was not familiar with the number it was displaying. Not yet ready to talk to anyone, especially some stranger, he hit ignore. Immediately, it rang again and the same number appeared on his display screen. Charles hit ignore for the second time, but when that same number called him once more, he knew that whoever was calling was intentionally trying to get in touch with him, specifically him.

"They can't even let me get dressed in the damn mornings," he said before he spoke an irritated, "Hello?"

His heart began to race in chest when he heard a weeping woman saying, "Charles, is this you?"

"Yes, it's me," he was confused. The voice sounded very familiar, but because she was wailing uncontrollably he could not place it. "Who is this?"

"It's your ex-wife." Immediately, Charles was at a loss for words. He hadn't heard from Carrie in years. "Are you there?" she asked when he said nothing for the longest time.

In total shock, Charles managed to let out a confused, "Yes."

The next words she spoke took Charles from shocked to devastated. "Terrail's been shot. He's deeeaaadddd!" she wailed even as she fought to try and hold it together.

Charles was even more confused than before. He responded with a disoriented, "What? When? Where? How? Why? Who?" His mind was now racing, running all over the place, trying and understand what was happening.

Carrie didn't help the situation at all when she responded with, "I don't know."

"Then how do you know he's dead? How do you know that our son is no longer alive?" he was getting his bearings back a little, trying to make sense of what she was telling him.

"I just identified his body," she confessed, still unable to accept that she had just seen her lifeless son lying on a cold metal table in the morgue of a hospital.

"Shit!" Charles replied as it hit him that he needed to be in Atlanta as soon as was humanly possible. "Is this a number where I can contact you?" he asked as he rushed to dress himself.

"Yes," was her depleted reply. Charles could hear the tired in her voice.

"Okay, hold tight, Carrie, and let me call you back." Wasting no time, Charles hung up with his ex and called his assistant. Demetri answered on the second ring. "Cancel all my appointments and meetings for the next week and book me a flight to Atlanta right now."

"And just why are we doing that?" Demetri cooed into the phone, still reeling from the goodness of his time with Charles last night. He had loved having sex with the man he loved in front of those people so much that he was struggling to come down from that sexual high.

"Not now, D," Charles snapped at him, yanking his lover from last night and straight into the current moment. "Just do what I'm paying you to do!"

Demetri's reply was a very hurt, "I'll get right on it, boss man." The moment the phone line went dead, Demetri immediately did what was commanded of him, but everything in him wanted to know why he had been commanded to do that.

He loved Charles even if he knew Charles did not love him in return, and because of that love he needed know what the hell was going on. Demetri felt entitled to all of Charles' business and hated it when his boss tried to keep him at a distance. Yes, Charles had made it more than clear from the very beginning that all he wanted from Demetri was sex and nothing more. He had gone into great detail telling Demetri all about the lines that were never to be crossed. No interfering in his personal life, no showing up at his house, no telling his wife anything. No showing up uninvited anywhere Charles was, no catching feelings, no public displays of affection of any kind and definitely no falling in love.

Demetri heard every word Charles had spoken and had obeyed every word except for the feelings part. Demetri had fallen in love with Charles and had fallen hard. Charles had also broken one of those rules now, the previous night when he had fucked him so damn good in front of everyone at their monthly play meetings. Charles had let the cat out of the bag, and since he had done so, that gave Demetri all the right in the world to break a few rules of his own. As far as Demetri was concerned, the moment they started fucking, he deserved to know everything that was going on with Charles at all times. Now that Charles had changed the rules, Demetri was going to do the same thing. He was going to start digging into that business that he now considered his own. All of Charles business was now all of Demetri's business.

***

After hanging up with his assistant, Charles started packing. He needed to go and check on his son, on his ex-wife. He had to come up with a lie to tell Cassie that would explain why he was gone. She knew his schedule like he knew his schedule, so he needed something unexpected to all of a sudden pop up that he needed to tend to immediately. Cassie might have been naïve, but she was far from stupid. The minute he said he had to go, she would want all of the details, especially since she'd found out that he used to take unexpected trips out of town to fuck his last secretary. There was no way she would allow him to get away with that again. This time he had to come up with something that would keep his wife in the dark about his son, a young man she knew absolutely nothing about.

"Shit!" Charles said again for the millionth time as he raced through his bedroom and his closet packing everything he thought he would need. "Why doesn't the past ever stay in the past?"

Sitting in her office, Cassie waited for her team to come in so that they could go over monthly, plans, inventory and numbers. As she sat there preparing for the boringness of their meeting, Romel popped into her head. It was at that moment she decided to shoot him a text.

Cassie: *Hey, at work, but can meet after around 4:00pm?*

Romel: *Fine, where you want to meet?*

Cassie: *Wherever.*

Romel: *Brown's café?*

Cassie: *That's good.*

As she finished the text with Romel, her mind was going to her husband and her marriage, but before it could get all the way involved in those thoughts, the team walked in and Cassie started the meeting with her power point presentation. The team was impressed as usual because Cassie knew her stuff. She had covered all the ins and outs and had eased each of their worries. Cassie was mindful enough to know that those sitting in front of her were major contributors and sponsor's and the facility really needed their backing and support. She had to bring her A game, it was needed to convince them to continue pouring money into the facility that they all entrusted her with.

"And that's everything," she smiled as she made eye contact with each and every one of them. "Any questions?"

They all shook their heads no, smiling as if they had won a grand prize. "As long as I can see where my money is going and the good it is being used for, I'm satisfied," the top contributor said.

"I think you're doing an amazing job of not spending on things that are unnecessary. As long as you continue in that direction, I will continue to contribute."

"Thank you, sir," her smile was big and beautiful.

"Don't smile at me like that," the youngest one said to her. "Otherwise, I might want to forget those rings on your finger and ask you out on a date."

Cassie kept the smile on her face but shook her head no, "I can never forget these rings on my finger."

"I was hoping you didn't say that," the more than stunning man said as he gripped her hand and held it while staring at her with those gorgeous hazel eyes. "But since you did, I have to respect it. However, if you're ever in the mood for not being so married..." he allowed his words to trail off as he exited her office along with everyone else.

"Well, damn!" she said when she was finally alone. He had gotten to her with his flirting, had shaken her with desire. However, she loved her husband and had made vows to Charles that she intended to keep even if her marriage was shaky at the moment.

Gathering her raging hormones, Cassie smiled at her pretty reflection in the mirror. She had always been a knockout and as a result, was accustomed to men flirting with her, trying to get in her panties. She had been rejecting offers from men, both young and old since she was thirteen years old with a very well developed body. This time was just more of the same. They flirted, she rejected. Except when it came to Charles.

She could remember the day she'd met him as clearly as it was happening at that exact moment. She'd been in the gym working out, sweating like crazy, and Charles had strolled up to her looking like a sexy, vanilla piece of eye candy. He stood an easy six feet two inches tall with muscles everywhere and had caught her eye immediately.

"I've made dinner reservations for you and me at Sky Line for nine o'clock tonight," he began in a sexy, hypnotically deep voice. "I've taken the liberty of buying you an outfit, shoes, and accessories included, to wear tonight so that you don't have to scramble to find something on such short notice. You can pick that up tonight at Ibarri's Boutique. Even if you choose not to accompany me to dinner, the outfit is still yours. I'll see you there," he said as he turned and walked away from her. "Oh, he said when he stopped and turned back in her direction, "I'm Charles by the way. And don't be late." Then he walked off, leaving her standing there on the elliptical machine stunned and dazed.

Cassie smiled as she remembered showing up to the boutique and finding the outfit paid for just as he'd said. The amount of money he'd spent on her before he'd even known her name had shaken her. In her mind that meant he thought he was entitled to her body, but that was nowhere near the case. Charles had not only shown her that he hadn't spent money on her to gain access to her body, but that he was excellent company.

That night the two had talked and talked. Cassie had learned that Charles was rich, had been born into money. She'd learned that he was one of the top political officials in Buffalo and that his career was on the rise. She'd learned that he was college educated and that he had his stuff together. He'd been funny, smart, and seriously sexy. That's what had kept her going on dates with him until he'd eventually proposed and had given her the wedding of her dreams. Everything between them had been wonderful until she discovered that her perfect husband had been cheating on her with his secretary. From that moment on things between them hadn't been quite right and now they were strained.

Suddenly remembering that she had a meeting scheduled with Romel, she began to hurriedly pack up her stuff. Time was not on her side, it never really was because there she was running late yet again. She was rushing her way out of the door, not playing attention to where she was going when she banged her whole body into something rock solid. It was the hard chest of a guy. Cassie almost fell and all the stuff in her brief case spilled onto the floor just as the man reached out and gripped her strongly, holding on to her securely to keep her firmly on her feet.

"Thank you," she said as her eyes drank him in. Unable to help herself, she stared him up and down, her mouth instantly watering.

The man staring back at her was sexy as hell. A tall, dark-skinned brother with muscles bulging through his clothes everywhere. His eyes were the bedroom and dreamy, his smile was killer and almost made her wet her panties. Immediately she felt guilty. Cassie hadn't been that attracted to any man since Charles and she was fighting to get herself together. She had thought a few men were attractive over the years, but she hadn't been attracted. At least not until now. And his smell, his hypnotic smell was putting some kind of sexy spell on her that had her immediately intoxicated as he bent to retrieve the contents of her briefcase.

When he had gathered all of her belongings, he put them neatly back inside of her briefcase and handed it to her. "I'm sincerely sorry," he spoke in an erotically deep and sexy voice. Cassie was mesmerized as she pulled herself together. She wasn't a cheater, but if she wasn't married she would have gone for him in a heartbeat.

"Hello, I'm Mazoo," he said as he stuck out his hand while eyeing her up and down the same way she was doing him.

Without thinking, Cassie accepted his outstretched hand and he gripped hers firmly. The electricity that shot between them had her feeling aroused and extremely ashamed of herself. She was a married woman and needed to get her hormones together. "Hi," she squealed, "I'm Cassandra and I'm running late. Please, excuse me." Immediately, she released his hand as if it had just burned her, and intentionally focusing on the fact that she was married, she sped away from him. It seemed Mr. Mazoo was just sexy enough to be the first man that aroused her since she'd married Charles.

Chapter Seven

As he watched Cassandra rush away from him, Mazoo was equally as mesmerized by her as she was by him. It was like lightning had struck him and left him in awe of the woman that had just whizzed by him. That feeling led him to want to know more about her. Redirecting his thoughts, he took his eyes off of her as she made her speedy exit and proceeded into the facility in search of getting his wife, Tameka, some help. Her drug addiction was tearing them apart and this was his last attempt to keep them together. If he could just get her interested in helping herself, maybe, just maybe they could fix their marriage. Mazoo loved Tameka, but at this point he needed Tameka to love herself enough to get better. Then and only then could they work on their quickly failing marriage.

Mazoo walked up to a desk where a lady sat looking as if she was slightly hung over. The name plate in front of her read Lakara Keys.

"Good morning, Ms. Keys," Mazoo said, which caused her to look up from her phone and directly at him.

The smile she put on her face was big and as bright as the sun. "Hi, handsome," she cooed sexily at him, "how are you?" As she talked, her eyes roamed his entire body up and down and the look in them made Mazoo feel as if she could see through his clothes and was seeing him naked. "And how can I do you?" She licked her lips at him, letting him know that all he had to do was say one word and she would be his. "I mean help you, how can I help you?" She flirted boldly with him.

Mazoo was nowhere near impressed when he calmly stated, "I'm here for my wife's assessment." Lakara blinked once as if shocked that he seemed uninterested. As far as she was concerned, all men were interested in her so it kind of hurt her feelings that he wasn't catching what she was so eagerly throwing to him. "I spoke to someone earlier this week about getting her into treatment here," he went on, completely focused on why he was there and not on Lakara the way she wanted him to be. "I think her name was Miss Denise Jones."

Seeing that he wasn't paying attention to her flirting, Lakara got her act together and spoke professionally, "The person that normally takes care of the assessments is gone for the day. However, if you'd like, I can get your assessment started."

"That's fine," was his casual reply.

"Please have a seat then," she gestured her hand toward the couches in the waiting area.

Mazoo took a seat and tried his best to get his focus back on his wife, but that other woman, the one that had bumped into him was clouding his mind while her scent invaded his nostrils. It felt strange to him to be so attracted to someone other than his spouse, but he understood it. Had his wife not been an addict and their marriage not falling apart, Mazoo would have never thought twice about the beauty he'd helped that morning. But since Tameka was strung out and seemed to want everything but him, it made perfect sense why he would start longing for attention from somewhere else.

About twenty minutes had gone by before Lakara finally lead Mazoo to an office where she could conduct an assessment to get his wife into the treatment center. "I don't normally do the assessments, those are handled by Denise and Cassandra, both of whom are out the office for today. So, you're stuck with me," she gave him a flirtatious smile as she proceeded with the start of the assessment. Her ego was crushed once again when she saw that Mr. Mazoo was still not interested in any of her advances. That still didn't stop her from hoping that by the time she was done she'd have changed his mind.

Cassie got inside her car and realized that she smelled amazing. The scent of the guy she'd stumbled into was all over her and lingering. It was Gold By Jay Z, a smell she loved and it made her smile all the way through the traffic until she got to Brown's café. She arrived just in time to see Romel sitting there looking at his watch as if he was contemplating leaving.

Cassie walked into the café looking damn good. She was overdressed for a local eatery but that didn't stop her from turning heads as she walked in and rushed over to Romel. Immediately, she took her seat across from him in the booth he'd chosen. Romel was stunned at how beautiful she was and for just a brief moment he was struggling to say a single word.

Finally, he was able to speak the words, "Hey you, how are you?"

"I'm fine, Romel. What's going on with RJ?" Cassie got straight to the point.

Following her lead, Romel go straight to the point as well. "He's in jail.

"What?" she couldn't help but to shout.

"Lower your voice," Romel tried to hush her as he looked around to see if anyone noticed or was looking their way. The last thing he needed was someone from the neighborhood to see those two together and word get back to Momma and Poppa Edmonds or Jinx, especially Jinx. That dude was dangerous and definitely wasn't playing with a full deck. Cassie stopped speaking when the waiter came over and they placed their orders but the moment the waiter left them along again, Romel spoke once more. "He's in jail for murder."

Cassie's heart began to pound and her eyes filled with unshed tears. Quickly she put her head down so that no one would see. "I need help getting him a lawyer as we don't have much money. Me, my moms and Eric, plus my grandma Bernadine are all chipping in what we can to help out, but it's nowhere near what we need to get him a good lawyer. And since this is a high profile case, we need the best lawyer we can get."

"Why is it a high profile?" she stared at Romel wide eyed and sad. "Who in the world did he kill?"

"He killed a couple of guys that were dressed as girls. They're calling it a hate crime."

"Why?" she wanted details, every detail she could get.

"Because those guys were transgender and didn't make that known before RJ and the guys he was with engaged in some kind of sex with them. Once they all realized that they'd just had sex with boys, they were pissed and well, they killed them." His words were serious and somber. "Now we need at least fifty thousand to retain and pay for the lawyer he's going to need to represent him in his case."

Cassie was so upset that she could barely breathe. Her son was in jail for murder, and not just any murder, the murder of three transgender girls. The case was very high profile and he needed a good lawyer that would cost him at least fifty thousand dollars. She sat back in the booth and rubbed her hand over her temples. Although she hadn't seen him or raised him or had anything to do with him in any way since he was born, RJ was her son and she needed to rectify her absence by doing something for him now. Fifty grand was a lot of money but she would definitely get the money to defend the son that she didn't really know and that didn't know her.

She didn't agree with the fact that her son played any part in the murder of those girls, she did not agree with that at all. She also didn't agree with the fact that those girls weren't up front with those guys. In this situation, everyone involved was wrong. Nobody made any right moves that night and everybody paid a heavy price for it, but the deceased girls paid the heaviest price of all.

"Give me some time and I'll get the money to you," she spoke in a voice that was small and hallow. She was shocked down to her core and struggling to keep it together.

"I can do that," Romel replied as he watched her, saw the genuine hurt on her face and instantly felt bad. He knew that part of her pain was due to her not being a mother to the child she had given birth to and that was partly his fault. Every adult around Cassie had made the decision to take her child away from her back then, including him, and she was, still after all of this time, paying for it tremendously.

"Thank you," he said as he reached his hand across the table to grip hers.

Cassie looked up at him. Romel could clearly see the look in her eyes and knew what it meant. He'd spent an entire summer seeing that look and over time it shocked him to learn that he'd started to feel the same. "Despite it all, Romel, I never stopped loving you or RJ," she began.

Romel cut her off. He knew she'd loved him, she just never knew that he'd felt the same about her. "Listen, it's ok. The whole situation was fucked up back then. But know this, even though I never told you, I love you too, Cass. I loved you back then and I still love you now. I've never stopped and I never will stop. You'll forever be in my heart, my little girlfriend."

For the longest time, neither of them said a word, they couldn't. Too much time had gone by, too much had happened, much of it things that had scarred Cassie for life. As much as she wanted to hate Romel, she just couldn't. He was her first love, the father of her only child, and that meant something to her. So she could forgive him, she could even love him, but trusting him was something she wasn't sure she would ever be able to do again.

Cassie broke their silence by asking, "Does RJ know who I am?"

"No," he was immediately honest with her. "My mom told him that your mom was his mother, so he thinks his mother is dead."

"What?" her heart was breaking at those words.

"I'm sorry, Cassie. I just never felt a reason to fix the little white lie my mom told him." He kept looking at her, could see her facial expression go from that love she expressed a moment ago to hate. "I really wanted to say something, it's just that—"

"Save it!" she snapped as she glared at him. She didn't want to hear another word about other people making decisions about her child and leaving her out of those decisions as usual. Cassie was so done with letting everyone else decide how her relationship with her son was going to go.

"I'm going to visit him when I get back and tell him everything. I promise," Romel assured her. It was about time he started looking out for Cassie the way she had always looked out for him, the way she was going to look out for him now by giving him fifty G's.

"Good, because I want to see him," she spoke truthfully. "I don't want to barge into his life, but I definitely want to make my presence known and develop a relationship with my child." She took a deep breath as she watched Romel, "I can't change what was done, but I can do something about what happens from here on out."

"Okay," he said as he shook his head yes. "I promise you I'll fill him in on everything." That was the least he could do for her after everything he had done to hurt her that summer and beyond.

After leaving the café with Romel, Cassie focused her mind on how she was going to get her hands on the type of money needed to help her son without Charles, her grandparents, or Jinx finding out. Her husband had no idea that she even had a child, so asking him for the money or even taking that much out of their bank accounts would cause major problems. There was no way she was going to add on to the problems she already had with Charles, so he needed to be kept as much in the dark about the situation as possible. Her grandparents and Jinx couldn't stand Romel since he'd gotten her pregnant. They all felt as if he'd taken advantage of a child and each of them would lose their minds if they knew she'd even had a conversation with him. Asking any of the was a no go.

"This is too much," Cassie said as she decided that she couldn't handle going back to work under the circumstances. Instead, she opted to go home and take a nap, to clear her mind and hopefully wake up better able to process everything Romel had told her. To say she was overwhelmed would have been the understatement of the century.

Reaching for her stereo, she put on some Mary J. to relax her mind. "I'm not in love, it's just some kind of thing I'm going through," she sang along as she sat at a red light waiting for it to change.

Belting out the lyrics to a song she loved, she glanced over at the gas station and was shocked to see guy she'd nearly knocked over at her job staring right at her as he pumped gas. The eye contact they made shot little sparks of electricity through her that caused goosebumps to pop up all over her arms. Her heart began that familiar race and her mouth dried as if she had eaten a plate of sand. She wanted him and her body was letting her know that in a huge way. Then the light changed colors and the moment was gone as she had no choice but to drive away.

"Damn," she said aloud. "If only..." Cassie let her words trial off. The guy was fine as hell, sexy as sin, but with all the drama she now had going on in her life, there was just no room for fantasies about him even if her body was thirsty and in need of being quenched.

Chapter Eight

Spending her entire drive home with her thoughts torn between the Greek god she didn't know but wanted to and the son she didn't know but wanted to, Cassie's mind was all over the place. Her son was a murderer. Although she understood why he had done what he had done, she didn't agree with it. But he was her son, a child she had carried and given birth to even if she didn't know him, even if she knew nothing about him. Except that he had murdered someone else's child. How the hell was she supposed to process that? Life could be pretty fucked up at times.

Finally making it home, Cassie kicked her shoes off and took a seat on the side of her bed as she replayed the day's events in her head. Romel, RJ and the Greek god. She was overwhelmed with everything and decided that for now, she would have to put the god on the back burner of her mind. She had a son to think about, something that was so unfamiliar to her. Then there was the issue of the money. Cassie wondered how she could get the money needed to help her child, a child she had never been allowed to help before. This was all so new and staggering to her that it zapped her of all energy. In no time at all, Cassie found that all she had the strength to do was lie back on the bed and fall into a very deep sleep.

As her body gave into the exhaustion that had taken over, her mind found a way to relax. It was tired of the stress and wanted a stress reliever of its own. So it took Cassie to a worry free place, a place where it gave in to sensational thoughts she had no business thinking.

She could see herself coming out of the conference room as she tried to lock the door with her hands full of papers. Suddenly, she dropped those papers and they flew everywhere. She dipped back into the conference room and set down the few items that managed not to fall out her hand. Then rushed back into the hallway to retrieve the things she had dropped. Moving too quickly, she somehow lost her balance and almost fell on a piece of paper. Thank goodness her stumbling was stopped by something hard and brick solid. When Cassie looked up, she was once again staring into the face of the Greek god.

"Sorry," she said as embarrassment washed over her, as he helped her regain her balance. Too ashamed of her clumsiness, she looked away from his intense eyes and focused extra hard on those papers at her feet. Quickly, she began to kneel so that she could pick them up when she noticed his beautiful, million dollar smile.

Then he was stooping down to the floor with her, helping her to pick up her papers. Once she was done, she stood, walked to the table with him following close behind and put yet another pile on it. He wasted no time doing exactly the same.

"Thanks," she said when she turned around and extended her hand. "I'm Cassandra."

Ever so gently, the handsome stranger took her hand into his own and once more flashed her that seductive smile. "I'm Mazoo," he spoke in a very deep and very sexy voice.

The attraction between the two of them was so strong that the moment he touched her it felt as if a million volts of electricity slammed into her. She looked up and into his eyes and something in them made her heart race and her center throb unmercifully. Cassie was immediately aroused. With no words, Mazoo tightened his grip on her hand and gently began to pull her to him. When she was firmly pressed into his chest, he lowered his mouth to hers and kissed her. Gently at first, then passionately, then hungrily.

"Mmmm," she moaned when Mazoo deepened the kiss so much that Cassie thought she would explode.

Her hands began to roam his chest through his shirt, his tongue delved deeper into her mouth, exploring every inch. She could feel herself melting into him, so much so that she was becoming lost in him. This shouldn't be happening, she told herself, this cannot be happening. Something deep inside of her tried to remind her why kissing Mazoo was wrong but she couldn't quite remember what it was.

"I'm sorry," she said when she stopped the kiss and began pulling away from him. She walked over to the door and put her hand on the knob.

"Don't walk away from me," Mazoo gently spun her to face him. "I'm not ready for this to end."

He started that kiss all over again. Hotter this time, more passionate this time. Cassie was so hot, so turned on that she was all over Mazoo, trying to get as much of him as she could. As she kissed him back, she gave as good as she was getting. Her mouth seared his, her teeth gently nipped his lower lip. She could feel his sex hardening against her stomach, stabbing into her flesh like a heated sword.

In a heartbeat she closed the door without ending the kiss. Mazoo, as inflamed as she was, pushed her up against the door as he took the kiss to an erotic level. Ready for her, so much more than ready for her, he slid his hand under her dress, moved her panties to the side. Then he slid two fingers easily into her already wet hot box. Cassie was like Little Caesars, hot and ready.

"Aaaahhhh," she moaned when his fingers filled her. It was no more than a second later that she began to ride his fingers as if for dear life.

"Fuck," Mazoo said when he felt how tight and heated she was. Quickly, he lowered his head to her chest and began to bite her nipples through her dress.

Now it was Cassie's turn to say, "Fuck!" Her breathing deepened, her blood thickened. Her core throbbed and clenched hard. And still Mazoo tried to give her more. They were going at it hot and heavy when he picked her up, pushed her against the door and used his body weight against her to hold her there. Eager to mate with her, he hiked her dress up and pulled his engorged beast from his pants at the same time he used his other hand to move her panties to the side. He then lowered her until she was fully impaled on his dick.

"Oh god!" she almost screamed when she felt him inside of her going deeper as he seemed to get bigger. "Oh, god!" she moaned again.

"Fuck!" Her tightness gripped him and almost had him cumming on the spot.

Cassie was experiencing a fine line between pain and pleasure. She hadn't had sex in so long that her pussy was hungry for the intrusion, was greedy for the ache between her thighs.

"More," she said as he looked him in the eyes.

Deciding to give her exactly what she wanted, Mazoo gripped her by her hips, spread her legs as wide as he could get them, and began guiding her up and down on him as he started a sexy bite into her neck.

Cassandra loved the way he felt thrusting in and out of her, tapping her back wall to a rhythmic beat. His deep and heavy breathing was music to her ears, the feel of his hands on her lower thighs, digging in, forcing her legs to stay apart had her losing her mind. Her pussy clutched, clenched, ached for the release that had started to build in her.

After a few intense minutes of fucking Cassie against that door, Mazoo gripped her and held her to him as he walked her over to the table. There, he lay her down on the edge, spread her legs even wider, and began to plunge deeper and harder and faster into her heated abyss.

"Aaaahhhh," Cassie moaned as her blood boiled. She could feel an explosive orgasm coming, knew she was going to soak him when she came all over his dick.

They were both in Heaven and Mazoo was doing his best to take them higher. "Turn around," he said and helped Cassie to get up and bend over the conference table with her dress up. He ripped her panties completely off of her and swiftly entered her from behind.

"Damn!" She moaned as her body began to melt under the intense pounding it was receiving. "Awwmmmm," she moaned again as she began to throw it back on him, bouncing her ass onto him as he plowed into her.

"Pussy so fucking good," he said as he thrust and thrust and thrust.

Mazoo was on the verge of a huge climax and Cassie was close to the same. He thrust harder, faster, deeper. Only seconds went by before Cassie reached her full peak and let out a scream just as she began to cum and cum and cum. Immediately following, Mazoo let out a grunt then a groan as his body jerked once and Cassie could feel his semen skeeting deep inside of her.

"Fuuuuccccckk!" Mazoo growled as he emptied himself into her while she poured onto him. His cum was hot and shooting out so hard that it was stinging her back wall. "Fuck!" he groaned again as he pumped her full of his seed. When Cassie felt his cum hitting her back wall, that made her cum even harder, made her pussy pour all over his thick shaft and all over his balls. "Damn," he said when he felt her pussy clamp down hard on him and start basting his meat in her hot juices.

Beep beep beep, beep!

Still cumming hard, Cassie's eyes flew open and she tried to jump up to shut that noise off. Recognizing that it was her alarm clock that was buzzing, she went to reach for it to turn it off, but her orgasm was hard and refused to let her move. Her pussy thumped and throbbed and pulsed as her heart banged and raced. Her hands gripped her sheets and her back arched. Her toes curled and her mouth formed that silent O as she came so hard that her center began to pour all over her sheets. And she remained frozen still in that position until finally she was done cumming.

"Shit!" she said when she was able to move. She had never in her life had an orgasm like that in a dream, especially not one that kept going when she woke. She lay still for a few more moments as her heart began to slow it's racing and her breathing returned to normal. She looked around her room to make sure she was actually at home as the dream felt so real that she wasn't sure if she was still in it or not. She was home, in her bedroom, in her bed.

And just why am I dreaming about another man like that? She pondered that thought for a few seconds when it hit her that her marriage had been dead in the bedroom for a while. All of a sudden, it made perfect sense why her mind was so willing to give her what her body wasn't giving her. But she had to keep those dreams exactly where they were. In her head. There would be no sleeping with any man in real life except her husband, no matter how desperate she was to be fucked the way Mazoo had banged her in that dream. And Cassie was sure that had she been getting sexed regularly by Charles, she would never have dreamed about any man that vividly. In fact, she knew that as soon as her marriage was back on track, Mr. Mazoo wouldn't even be a slight thought in her head anymore.

"Shit!" she said again when she came back to her reality and finally got a look at the clock.

It was 7:30 p.m. She couldn't believe she'd slept that long. Her alarm went off every day at that same time as a reminder for her to take her meds so she needed to get up and get to her medicine. Reaching over, she shut off the alarm and allowed her mind to come back to normal. Immediately, her thoughts went back to the events of the day, back to Romel and to RJ. Mazoo and the dream were instantly gone.

Chapter Nine

Sitting all the way up, Cassie looked around for her phone. Remembering where she'd left it, she got up, got out of the bed, went into the living room and retrieved her cell phone from her purse. Then before she looked at her phone and forgot, she took her meds.

When she'd completed that task, she looked at her phone and was shocked to find nineteen missed calls and fourteen voice messages. She was surprised that six of those calls were from her husband. Immediately she called him but was sent straight to voicemail each time. Deciding to call one last time, when she was directed to voicemail yet again, she left a message

"Hey, babe, I'm so sorry I missed your calls. When I got home I was exhausted. I left my phone in my purse on the table in the front room, came straight in the bedroom and went to sleep so I had no idea you were calling me. Again, I'm sorry. Call me back when you get a chance. I love you and I'll talk to you later. Bye."

After hanging up, Cassie then decided to listen to her voicemails to see if her husband was okay or if he had been calling for something serious. The very first message she had received was from him.

"Hey, baby, I really need to talk to you. Call me back as soon as you can." After deleting that one she moved on to the next message and it was Charles again. "Baby, I really need to talk to you, it's important. Call me back."

"What the hell?" she said as she began to worry, to wonder if he was alright.

The next message came from her husband as well, *"Hey, honey. I really didn't want to tell you this via voicemail, but I had to take an emergency business trip. This was not by choice and I'm sorry I couldn't talk to you about it before I left. You know how demanding my job is and this trip is a really important one for my career. I'm headed to Atlanta right now and you probably won't be able to reach me as I'm about to board the plane. More than likely I'll be gone for a few days. Once I land, I'll touch bases with you and fill you in on all of the details. Sorry about the short notice, I'll talk to you later. Love you, bye."*

Cassie sat back for a moment as she processed what her husband had said. An emergency business trip?

One that he had to take immediately? What the hell was so important that he had to just up and leave in the middle of a workday with no notice? Cassie hoped with everything in her that Charles wasn't up to his old shit. Ever since she'd found out about his last infidelity, he'd been good. She hoped he was still being good.

Normally, she would start investigating to see what was going on, but since she had so much stuff of her own weighing her down at that moment, she just didn't have the energy to deal with investigating her husband. If he was doing something, it would come out eventually and when it did, Cassie had already decided that she would leave. Before she could give her husband anymore thought, Cassie heard Romel's voice and her mind was immediately redirected.

"Hey, Cassie, it's me, Romel. I've caught a flight back today. I need to be there for RJ and get things straight with him. I'll be keeping in touch to keep you updated, and yeah, let me know when you get the money. It could help us out a lot. Talk to you later." To Cassie's surprise, the very next message that came through was from Romel as well. "It's me again, just want to say that I'm really sorry about how everything went down back then and thank you for everything." He paused for the longest time as if trying to get his thoughts together. "Anyway, I've always loved you. A lot. Even when you didn't think I did back then." There was another pause before he said, "Well, yeah, I got to go. Bye."

Cassie kept still for a moment and allowed his words to really sink in. She believed that Romel really loved her, but the hurt he'd played a part in inflicting upon her back then still knocked her on her ass today. It was easy to forgive, it was hard as hell to forget. Before she could allow herself to think too deeply about Romel and his confession of love, the next message began to play.

"Cassandra, this is Grandmaw. I haven't heard from you today. Is everything alright? Give me a call and let me know. Love you, grandchild. Bye." That message brought the first genuine smile to Cassie's face. She loved her grandmother and always looked forward to phone calls from her and her grandfather. The next message made her smile even more as it was from her grandmother as well. "Oh, yeah, Cassandra, will you and Charles be joining us for dinner this Sunday? Let me know so I can decide what to cook for y'all. Bye, baby."

As much as Cassie enjoyed the sound of her grandmother's voice, her words made the smile disappear as it took her back to thoughts of Charles. She had no idea if they would be attending dinner on Sunday because her husband had taken a last-minute trip to Atlanta for God knows what. However, before she would allow that thought to bring her to an ugly place, Cassie shifted her focus once more to the messages she had missed.

"Hey, Cassie," she heard the familiar voice of her friend Sam. "Haven't heard from you in a while, give me a call when you're free."

"That's because you've been missing in action for weeks," Cassie spoke out loud, annoyed that her friend seemed to have disappeared off the face of the earth. Everyone had been worried about Sam and she was just now calling to say that she was fine. "What the hell?" she said as that annoyance she was feeling clouded her voice.

"Girl, some guy came into the center today for an assessment for his wife and giiirrrllll, he was super fuckin cute!" said the next voice. It was super high and speaking and very fast. Cassie immediately began to shake her head at her friend and coworker, Lakara. She would be the one to be all excited over a man, even one that she didn't even know. "I was definitely trying to get with him, but he must be gay because he wanted no parts of me. He was fine, though, so you know I got excited. I wish you would have been here to see him, you would have loved to do his assessment. Good eye candy for you, girl. Anyway, call me."

When she had successfully deleted that message, the next one came through and it was from Lakara as well. "I finished up his assessment. There's only the intake interview left to do. He left a deposit to hold a bed so you'll have to process that when you return. But for real, girl, you got to see him. He looks so damn good," she said and Cassandra could practically hear her drooling into the phone. "Okay, for real this time, bye."

The next recording was from another friend and coworker, Denise. "Sorry, girl, I had to take Alexa to the doctor because she was running a temp, so I never made it into work. I did take Mr. Martz's info, inputting everything in from my home computer and uploaded it to the system. I scheduled him for an assessment, but then I got so busy with Alexa that I forgot to call you and give you a head's up. I'm so sorry, call me, okay. Bye.

Just as Cassie selected the calendar app on her phone, the last and final message came through. "Hey, sis" she heard the voice of a man that was like a brother, a real brother to her. "I haven't heard from you in two whole days and I'm not sure what to do about that. I don't know if I should find you to see if you need protection or if I should come over and beat that ass for leaving me worrying about you like this. "You better call me later, baby sis. Today," he spoke seriously. "Love you."

Cassie sat still as her mind replayed and organized all of those calls in her head. There was a lot of work she needed to take care of in her professional life and a lot of important things she needed to deal with in her personal life. From the looks of things, Cassie felt as if she would be busy for months. She had no idea what was going on with her husband and she needed to take care of that. She had every idea about what was going on with her son and she needed to take care of that. And the father of her son and the feelings he had confessed, what was she supposed to do about that?

"Shit!" she said as a thought made her stand to her feet in shock. "Both Romel and Charles were headed to Atlanta that day, it was highly possible that they could end up on the same flight. "It's a good thing they don't know each other," she said on a relieved sigh. "Because that would have been bad for everyone involved," she said aloud. And it could ruin my marriage even more than it already seems like it is, she thought.

As she sat back down and prepared to return those calls, she realized that she had no idea who she should call first. On the one hand, work was important and she needed to get in touch with her coworkers. She was the woman in charge and they moved at her direction so they needed to hear from her. On the other hand, she needed to get in touch with her husband to find out what the hell was going on with him. Thinking that through, she decided Charles would be her last call. If she talked to him and he pissed her off with his explanation about his sudden trip, that would ruin the rest of her night and the rest of her phone calls. She didn't want to be pissed off so she decided to go with calling her grandmother first. There would be no anger there.

"Hi, Momma," she said as soon her grandmother answered, "how are you and Poppa doing?"

"Hi, Cassandra. We're ok, baby, but your grandfather has this nasty cough he can't seem to get rid of," Lee Edmonds said.

"Really?" Cassie asked, concern coming into her voice. "How long has this been going on?" she inquired. "Because he wasn't coughing the last time I was there."

"He didn't cough the last time you were here," she said. "He tried to hold it in so you wouldn't worry, but he's been coughing since before that. It's been going on for a while now."

"Well, Momma, you know he smokes a pack of cigarettes a day and on top of that, he drinks a six-pack of Pepsi. He doesn't have the healthiest of habits."

"I know, sweetheart, but he's been slowing down on that stuff lately. Hopefully, that helps him."

"Even if he's slowed down on that stuff, we still need to take him to the doctor to get him checked out. A prolonged cough could be a sign of something bad and we need to find out if that's the case before it's too late."

"I know, I know, Cassie. And we'll get to that," Lee assured the grandchild she'd raised as her own. "But that's not what I called you for earlier."

"I know, Momma, I was taking a nap."

"Are you ok?" Now there was concern in Lee's voice.

"Yes, Ma'am. I'm fine," Cassie assured her grandmother. "I had that dinner meeting with Charles last night and didn't get home until late, so I didn't sleep much." She told her grandmother the truth, just not all of the truth. Besides, she would only become upset if she knew Cassie was dealing with Romel and the child they'd made her give away, so there was no way Cassie was going to mention anything about that situation.

"Okay," Lee replied, seemingly satisfied with Cassie's answer. "Well, make sure you get some good sleep tonight so you won't be so tired tomorrow."

"I'll definitely be doing that," Cassie promised her grandmother and herself. She had too much on her plate at that moment, she needed all of the rest she could get.

"Are you and Charles coming by for dinner on Sunday?"

This was shaky ground, but rather than rock the boat and have her grandmother asking a ton of questions she didn't yet have answers to, Cassie decide to give her as little information as necessary. "I'll be there, but Charles won't. He's out of town, had a work emergency come up," she said. And before Lee could ask any more questions, Cassie finished up with, "He didn't have enough time to give me all of the details, so I don't know if he'll be back in time for Sunday dinner. I'll let you know if he's going to be there as soon as his flight lands and he calls me."

"He sure takes more out of town trips than a little," Lee commented and the truth of her words grated on Cassie's nerves. She already had her issues with this sudden trip and it irritated her that someone else had issues with the trip as well. Especially when that someone was the woman that loved and raised her.

To keep from engaging in this particular conversation, Cassie acted as if she hadn't heard her grandmother. "Huh?" she said as she feigned ignorance.

"I just hope everything's ok with him and the job," Mrs. Edmonds said as she decided not to repeat herself and vocalize her concerns about how much her granddaughter's husband seemed to travel. Although he had slowed down some in the last year or so, it still seemed as if that man found ways to be out of town and that bothered her a little. But for Cassie's sake, she wouldn't say anything. She didn't want to make something out of what might be nothing.

"Yeah, me too," Cassie replied quietly. Then. "Well, I got to go, Momma. I have a lot of phone calls to return. But I love you, I'll call you later, and I'll definitely see you Sunday, okay?"

"Alright, baby. And I love you too," Lee said just before they ended their call.

After making the rest of her calls and still getting no answer from her husband, Cassie decided to call Romel next. When that call went to voicemail as well, she left him a message.

"Hope you have a safe flight. Please talk to RJ and get things straight with him because I really would like to meet him. I'm working on the money, just give me a few days. Talk to you later."

Deciding to text Lathom instead of playing phone tag with him and waiting for him to return her call, she went to the text app on her phone.

Cassie: *Hey, I need to talk to you. I'm all over the place right now and I really need my brother. It's not a 911 but it is an emergency.*

Cassie hit send, got up and tossed her phone on the table. Then she went into the kitchen looking for something to snack on. She hadn't eaten anything since the rice ball earlier and her stomach was protesting that involuntary fast. After thoroughly searching her kitchen, she realized that there was nothing there she wanted to eat, so she decided to order her favorite dish from a little spot around the way. Realizing that she was over dressed for where she was about to go, she ran back in her bedroom, threw on some biker shorts, a tank top, and some Chanel slide ins. She didn't look a mess, but if Charles had been home, he would never have allowed to walk out of the house dressed like that.

After grabbing her phone, Cassie ran out of the house and headed straight to her car. Less than five minute later, she pulled up to her favorite spot and went inside. To her surprise, it was pretty crowded considering it was the middle of the week.

"Pick up for Cassandra," she said to the man behind the counter.

"Did you call ahead, or did you order it online?" he asked her.

"Called ahead," she responded.

"Okay, hold on." The young man left the counter, went to the window, and began speaking in a foreign language. When he returned, he asked for the phone number associated with her order which she immediately gave him just before he walked away again. By the time he returned the second time, he had her food. "That will be seven dollars,"

When Cassie went to take the cash out of her pocket, that was when she realized she'd left the money at home on the table near her front door. "I'm sorry," her voice expressed the sincerity of her apology. "I forgot my money, let me run to my car and get my credit card."

Immediately, the people behind her grew angry and began to protest. "Ahh, come on lady!" someone voiced.

Cassie, extremely embarrassed, apologized as she headed toward her car. When she reached it, she got inside and realized that she had accidentally left her wallet at home. "Shit!" she shouted in frustration. Frantically, she began to search her car, looking for any money she may have left inside of it. When she could only come up with five dollars, she went back inside, hoping the young man would accept the five and let her come back to pay the remaining balance later.

When she made it back in the restaurant, the first thing she noticed was that the line was gone. "Thank God!" she whispered to herself as she approached the counter where she began to explain her situation. But the man cut her off.

He stopped her mid-sentence and said, "It's ok, my friend. The gentleman paid for your food." Then he handed her the food, smiled at her and said, "Thank you, and come again."

"What gentlemen?" she wanted to know.

"He's not here anymore."

Confused as ever, Cassie began to search the restaurant, but saw no one that was even remotely familiar to her. Still confused, she reached for the door of the establishment, stepped outside, and that's where she saw him. It was the guy from her job, the same guy she'd seen at the gas station earlier. He looked over to her and smiled as they made eye contact. Then he winked at her just before he hopped into his car and pulled off.

Cassie was so embarrassed. Not only had she left her home looking any kind of way, she left it without any money. And to make matters worse, the sexiest man alive had seen her looking like that, seeing that she didn't have any money, and was kind enough to pay for her food. This was the same man that had given her the most amazing orgasm earlier. "Well, shit!" she said again as she shook her head at the shock of it all, got into her car, and made her way home.

Chapter Ten

On the ride home, her phone rang. It was her brother, Lathom. Rushing to answer the call, she almost dropped her phone on the floor of her vehicle. "Hey, I been looking all over for you. I really need to talk to you," she rushed the words out. "So much has happened, I don't even know where to begin."

"Slow down, Cass," he told her. "Catch your breath." When he heard her breathing even out, he spoke again. "First of all, where are you? And why are you out this late?" he asked when he heard the sound of her driving.

"I ran to the store to get something to eat and—" she stopped speaking because he cut her off.

"What?" he asked, shock and anger in his voice. "Wait! Where is Charles?" There was no reason why his sister should have been out that late trying to get food for herself when she had a husband.

"He flew to Atlanta on a business trip."

"Oh, ok." The sarcasm and annoyance was more than clear in his voice. "So, you just out here huh?"

Realizing he wasn't pleased with her behavior, Cassie immediately began to explain. "No, listen, I had a really, really long day." She let out a deep sigh when she realized that her words were rushed and wouldn't explain anything. She started all over again. "It's just that so much has happened in a short span of time."

Hearing her frustration with the situation, Lathom decided to take it down a bit. "Ok, listen, I'm about to slide to this shorty house right now. How about you take some time to calm yourself and we can do lunch tomorrow?"

"Ok," this time her sigh was one of relief.

"I'll pick you up from the office and we can go wherever you want for lunch. Now, Cassie, take ya ass in the house and stay there! And the next time you want something to eat this late and ya man ain't home, call me and I'll get it for you."

"Alright. And I'm on my way home right now."

"I love you, sis."

"I love you, too."

They ended their call and Cassie did exactly what Lathom told her to do. She made her way back to the house with the full intent of staying her ass inside.

As she drove home, instead of listening to her music as she normally did, Cassie thought about Lathom and just how he had become such an important part of her life. Although they were not biological siblings, no one could tell either of them that they weren't real brother and sister. Cassie and Lathom had loved one another like family from the moment they'd met. Lathom had been there for her in ways that no one else had and she had done the same for him, nothing and no one could ever sever the bond between them. Their friendship was genuine and one that Cassie was sure would last a lifetime. Their connection was deep, much deeper than her connection with her own husband.

Lathom Todd Dennings was her protector, had been from day one. Standing a very tall six feet five inches with an extremely muscular build, there were not many people that would step to him with the dumb stuff. Lathom was a beast with the hands, but his size made it so that he rarely had to use them. Men looking for trouble would take one good look at him and immediately get their minds right without Lathom having to say a single word.

While the men did all they could to avoid trouble with him, the women did all they could to get into trouble with him. It was his looks that had them hooked on him. Lathom had a solid caramel complexion with hypnotic, light gray eyes. And if that wasn't enough to have the women chasing him, his very long, very soft, jet-black hair that he kept braided to the back gave him an exotic look that had those women searching for him in the daytime with a flashlight.

The man had gotten his looks mostly from his mother who was from India. Lathom's father, Larry, met Martha when he was in the army on a tour of duty. It didn't take long for them to fall in love and for Martha to become pregnant. When Larry realized she was carrying his child, he married her and brought her back to the states. Everything was good for them until Martha began to want more than to be stuck in the house all day taking care of a child.

After five years of playing house, it wasn't long before she lost complete interest in both Larry and Lathom. Martha wanted to be free to do as she pleased with no baggage. She'd watched the life her mother had lived in India, day in and day out doing nothing but taking care of a husband and a lot of kids. Martha had promised herself that she would never be stuck living that life, so the minute Lathom was old enough to start school, she left Larry and Lathom and they never heard from her again.

Although Lathom had been young, he was old enough to mourn the loss of his mother and for a long time there had been an empty void in his heart for his mom. Larry did his best to raise his son to be a man, but Martha had been Larry's true love and he was hurting just as bad if not more than his son at her departure. She'd left a matching set of holes in both their hearts.

In addition to his mom abandoning him and his father, Lathom had other issues as well. As a preteen, he was tall and skinny and the kids would tease him. They made fun of his eyes, his hair, and his height. Being that he was a mixed child, he looked different from the other kids and they tormented him for his different appearance every chance they got. The fact that they had been dirt poor and he didn't wear the best clothes made things even worse for him, but none of that lasted too long.

When Lathom turned twelve years old, his life suddenly changed. He and his dad weren't so poor anymore. All of a sudden they were living much better than they'd been living before. The house he'd grown up in had been completely renovated and filled with new everything. It wasn't the greatest, but it was the best for them. There was no more missing meals which was what had him so skinny. Now there was more than enough food, more than enough money for food, and Lathom began to swell up in the weight department. He went from tall and skinny to tall and built, and the brand of clothes he wore went from being no-name brands to much better brands. Suddenly, he was teased a lot less and instead of everyone making fun of him, everyone was trying to be his friend, especially the girls.

Then there was Monique, the one girl that had fallen hard for Latham. Monique had genuinely liked Lathom because he wasn't like all the boys their age. He wasn't an asshole like them, he was actually nice and he wasn't wasting his time like the other boys his age. At twelve he'd gotten an after-school job. He got into landscaping and would cut and rake some of the neighbors' yards in the summer, and shovel those same lawns in the winter. He was always saving his earnings and when he did spend any money it was usually to buy Monique whatever she wanted, Since her parents were poor and couldn't get certain things for her, Lathom made sure to make up for it.

Time went on and Monique and Lathom went from puppy love to high school sweethearts. They had a relationship that was so rock solid, a lot of people envied them and wished they could have a relationship as good as the one Monique and Lathom had. Then one day Lathom went to cut the yard of the pastor and his wife and that's when he met Cassie. Soon those two became the best of friends and Lathom was envied by his peers even more because he not only had the best relationship, but he also had the best friendship. In fact, he and Cassie had grown so close that they were more like brother and sister than anything else. Lathom was on top of the world.

At the age of seventeen, Monique and Lathom finally gave their virginities to one another, and almost immediately Monique became pregnant. Larry wasn't happy about Lathom becoming a parent at such a young age. However, that was his son, his only child, and Larry chose to support him no matter the situation. He refused to allow his son to be a young father without any help and advice from his dad.

Although Larry knew about the pregnancy because he and Lathom were close and he told his dad everything, Monique hid her pregnancy from her parents. She started spending a lot of time at Lathom's house and a lot less time at her own. After a while, Monique could no longer hide her pregnancy from anyone and she finally had no choice but to tell her parents. Monique's parents were heartbroken, angry, and livid to say the least.

Monique's mother, Florence, was so disappointed that she took Monique to the doctor in hopes of it not being too late to get rid of the baby. Her parents had no idea how far along Monique was until that trip to the OBGYN where they found out that their daughter was six and a half months pregnant and that she was having a girl. Her mother was furious but Monique was excited and couldn't wait to tell Lathom the news.

While Monique and Lathom were celebrating, Monique's mother was not. She was so distraught about her seventeen year old daughter being pregnant that she slipped into a semi-depression. She wanted so much more for her daughter than for her to be a young mother, but it was too late to do anything to stop that train at that moment. Monique was going to be a mother whether Florence wanted her to be or not.

Monique's father, Frank, had tried everything he could to get his wife out of her funk. When nothing worked, he planned a trip, a family trip to get everyone away from reality to a place where everyone could just relax for a little while without Lathom being around. The weekend was fast approaching and Monique had a really bad feeling about the trip. She didn't really want to go, but she had no choice.

As much as Lathom didn't want her to go because he had that same bad feeling about that trip, he understood that she had to obey her parents and go whether she wanted to or not. She lived with them so she had to obey their rules, but Lathom planned to change all of that. By the time they returned from their trip, he planned on having an apartment for him and Monique to live in. Then she would never again be forced to do anything she didn't want to do.

To keep Monique's mind off of Lathom while they were gone, her father made arrangements for his wife sister, Ester, and Ester's daughter, Shell, to meet them there. The vacation would give his daughter and wife a break and people they could talk to instead of spending the entire trip bickering with one another about the baby.

The day finally arrived for them to leave and head to the campground. Lathom was outside of their house early that morning to say goodbye to his girlfriend.

"I'll have a surprise for you when you get back," he whispered in her ear as he hugged her goodbye. "I love you," he said as he kissed her on the cheek. He would have given her a deeper kiss than that, but since her parents were there and since they were already pissed that he'd gotten their child pregnant, Lathom decided not to push that envelope. "I'll see you in a few weeks," he told her as he helped her into the car.

"I love you too," she said as tears began to form in her eyes. "And I'm really going to miss you."

"I'm going to miss you too." He reached into the car and hugged her once more. "But after this trip, you'll never have to miss me again," he reassured her with another whisper that her parents couldn't hear. Then he closed the door and stood there watching them drive away until he couldn't see their car anymore. After that, Lathom got busy with completing his plans to have an apartment ready for his girl when she returned.

Several hours later, Monique and her family finally made it to their cabin and got settled in. Shortly after they arrived, Ester and Shell arrived as well. There was a lot of excitement at first, a lot of small talk. Then, just as he knew would happen, Frank watched in silence as Florence took her sister Ester in one room and

Monique took her cousin Shell in the other room and the ladies began to spill their guts.

Things were going exactly as Frank had planned.

Back at home, Lathom was excited about the plans he'd made for him and Monique. He loved that girl more than anything and she was about to have his baby girl. They would both be done with school at the end of that school year and could then start on their careers as they raised their child in their own home. Life was good, better than good, and Lathom planned on marrying Monique the moment they were both eighteen in a few short months.

After spilling her guts to her cousin, Shell and Monique realized they needed to make a store run for some feminine hygiene products.

"Okay," Frank said when they told him. "Let me get my keys and we can go right now."

"Come on, Daddy," Monique said as she pouted just a little. "We have a lot of things we're talking about right now and we can't talk about that stuff if you're there."

"Yeah," Shell chimed in. "That'll just be weird, Uncle Frank."

Laughing and agreeing with them, Frank relented and decided to let them take the car, but not before saying, "Be careful, ladies. Go to the store and come straight back, no extra stops."

"Okay," they called out simultaneously as they took the keys he handed them and left.

"You drive," Monique said as she tossed the keys to her cousin. "I don't want to drive on these country roads."

"Okay," Shell spoke excitedly as she caught the keys in mid-air and hopped into the car alongside her favorite cousin.

It didn't take them long to reach the store. Still talking a mile a minute, they walked through the store picking up what they needed and a few extra things to snack on. It was only a very short while later before they were back on the road and on their way back to the campsite. Monique was in the process of telling Shell all about Lathom and how much she loved him when a drunk driver ran the stop sign and smashed his vehicle head-on into theirs. Both Shell and Monique died instantly.

When word got back to Lathom, he was crushed. His whole word had fallen apart and he felt that he had nothing left to live for. Even though they too were grieving, seeing how hard Lathom grieved the loss of their child made Monique's parents decide to allow

Lathom to name the baby so that they could have a name to put on the tombstone along with Monique's. Lathom named their daughter Latrice Monique Martha Dennings.

After that, Lathom fell into a deep depression and as much as Larry hated to see his son like that, there was nothing his father could do. So he showed his son understanding because he really did know what Lathom was going through. Although his wife hadn't died, he'd felt the same heartache when she walked out that Lathom was feeling at the loss of Monique and his child. And when Lathom confessed that he felt like every woman he truly loved was gone, his mom, his girl, and his daughter, Larry could do nothing but hug his son and cry with him.

Cassie did everything she could do for her friend. She was there for him in every sense of the word and then some, but there was no luck in getting him out of that depression. He was so deep in it that it was scary. For a long time, Lathom just went through the daily motions of life, doing the bare minimum. He barely finished high school, but he did graduate, he just refused to attend his own graduation. After that, Lathom up and disappeared and no one seemed to know where he was or what happened to him, not even Cassie. That hurt Cassie a lot, but she understood. Lathom was hurting and he needed the space and time to heal.

Periodically, Cassie would receive a postcard from him with no return address. All the post cards would say was that Lathom was ok, that he'd be in touch, and that he loved her. That went on for years until one day Cassie looked up and Lathom was back and back on top of the world. She was so happy to have her brother back and the two of them picked up their friendship as if they hadn't missed a beat. The only thing that was different was that Lathom never, under any circumstances, spoke of his past.

Chapter Eleven

Back in Atlanta, Romel's flight had finally landed. It had caught him off guard to see Charles on that plane with him and Romel had spent their entire flight watching him, battling with the thought of introducing himself. His assumption was that Cassie had already told Charles about him and RJ, but since the man had looked in his direction several times and didn't seem to know who he was, Romel thought twice about doing what Cassie may not have already done. However, he didn't stop watching him, didn't stop paying attention to every move the man-made.

Once the plane was completely empty and everyone went to baggage claim, Romel approached Charles. "Excuse me, Mr. Baxton," he said and then extended his hand for a shake. "I'm Romel."

Charles cut him off with a very rude, "Hi. I don't have time to do any interviews or sign anything or take any photos." Then he shook Romel's hand and pat him on his back.

As Charles retrieved his bag, there was suddenly the sound of a woman's voice calling out to him. Immediately, he turned around. Then seeing her, he walked over to her and they embraced as tears began to fall from the woman's eyes. The entire time Romel was standing there with his mouth open, watching the whole thing.

"This arrogant bastard is up to something," he whispered to himself as he decided then and there to keep his eyes on Charles even more than he'd already been doing throughout the years.

He already didn't like the man Cassie had married and now it seemed like he had good reason to hate him. Romel knew his disdain for Charles stemmed from the fact that he believed Cassie was and would always be his. It didn't matter if he had done her dirty when they were younger. He loved her when she was twelve and he loved her now. That was enough for him to hate the man she had married even if that man had done nothing to him. Romel despised Charles and he would make sure it stayed that way. Now all he had to do was find one thing about that bastard that he could use to make Cassie leave him for good. Then maybe, just maybe he could make her his again, the way it should have always been. And he would start by finding out all about the woman Charles was heading out of the airport with.

As soon as Romel grabbed his own luggage, he turned on his cell phone and called for his ride. The car pulled up almost immediately. "I got a name for you. I want you to find out everything you can on this person for me," he told the driver the minute the doors were closed and they were on the move. He then handed the man a piece of paper that read Charles Baxton. "It should be easy since he's a politician."

The driver responded with only one word, "Okay," as they finally made it out of the maze that was Hartsfield-Jackson International Airport.

The minute Romel got home, he began to prepare himself for the big day ahead of him tomorrow. The first thing he had to do was visit RJ's lawyer. After that he had to go to the jailhouse to visit RJ so that he could finally tell him the truth about Cassie. Romel had never been so nervous about anything in his life except for the time Jinx threatened him, but he would have to get over that nervousness and let his son know that Cassie was alive and fully intended to have a relationship with him. When he had everything he'd need for the following day packed up and ready to go, Romel then focused on his other task. Charles Baxton.

Immediately, he started making phone calls. He needed to find out what Charles was up to in Atlanta.

When he'd gotten in touch with the right people and had gotten the ball rolling on that, he put business aside and decided to relax. The very next call he made was to his new fling, Kelly.

After declining to stay with Carrie at her house, Charles checked into the really nice suite Demetri had booked for him for the week. He wasted no time going to the bar and making himself a drink and then hopping into the shower. As the steaming hot water ran down his body, he let out a sigh of contentment. The water felt almost as if it was washing away the stress from that day. Shit was happening too fast and he needed to get control of it. There was no way it could leak to the media that he'd had a son that he'd kept hidden from the public eye for all of those years. He was a politician, his reputation had to be sterling or his constituents would rake him over the coals.

"I've got to work this out," he said as he stepped from the shower and wrapped a towel around his waist.

At that exact moment, there was a knock on the door of his suite. Charles wasn't in the mood for room service or dinner or anything, so he stormed over to the door still dressed in his bath towel, and flung the door open with the intent to dismiss whoever it was. However, he got a shock when he saw that it was his ex-wife standing there.

"What are you doing here?" he asked her as he stepped aside and allowed her into his suite.

"I didn't want to be alone, Charles," she confessed. "I'm struggling with the fact that I've lost my son," she began to cry.

Charles didn't really want any company at that moment, but seeing the struggle she was going through in her eyes and in the stiff way she held her body, he really felt for Carrie. "Have a seat," he said as he went over to the bar to make her a drink. Then he walked back to the couch and handed it to her.

"What is it?" she looked up at him with sad eyes.

"A shot of Hennessey straight. It'll calm your mind and help you to relax a little."

"Okay," she began to sip from the glass.

"It'll go down easier if you down it all at once," he told her.

"Okay," she said again as she put the shot glass to her lips and downed it as he suggested.

When she was done, Charles took her empty glass and sat it back on the bar. Then he took a seat on the couch beside her. "Now, start from the beginning, I want to know everything."

Carrie began by saying, "All I know is that I was contacted by the police, asking me to come down to the station. I was questioned because my credit card had been used to book a room that is now the center of a murder investigation."

Charles sat quietly, listening to every word Carrie spoke. He comforted her when she began to cry, held her, hugged her, wiped her tears away, supported her. She leaned into him, resting her head on his chest, the sound of his heartbeat familiar and very comforting to her. It felt like old times, like when they were married and Carrie liked that very much.

"Can I have another drink, please?" she asked her ex-husband when the first drink had her feeling much better.

"Sure," Charles went back to the bar and poured her another shot of the strong liquor.

This time Carrie downed it without hesitation and paused for a moment as the smooth brown alcohol began to relax her and give her a nice little buzz. She went back to telling him everything, every sordid detail she could.

"Almost two hours of interrogation later," she went on, "I was finally told that Terrail and three of his friends had been murdered," she said as the tears began to fall down her face once again. But this time she wasn't hysterical the way she had been earlier, the alcohol had worked and she was simply allowing the tears to run down her face.

Charles was speechless as a very emotional Carrie told the story of how their child had been murdered. He moved as close to Carrie as he could get and held her. As much as she needed to rely on him in that moment, it shocked Charles to find that he needed to rely on her. She was the only other person in the world that could understand what it was like to lose Terrail. He had been so busy trying to console her, but he was heartbroken as well. Heartbroken and disappointed in himself and the fact that he'd walked away from Carrie and Terrail and had missed out on the life of his son, his son that was now deceased.

"Fuck!" he said as his own eyes filled with tears of pain and sorrow.

Carrie looked up at him and was surprised to see the tears shimmering in his eyes. It touched her so much to see how much Charles loved their son, to know that he was grieving much harder than she thought he would at the loss of Terrail. "I should have been there for him."

"You're here now," she comforted him. "And that's what matters at this moment."

"Fuck!" he said again as his heart shattered in his chest and the tears fell from both of their eyes as they sat on that couch, held one another, and cried for a long time.

Then Charles' phone began to ring. "I have to take this," he said as he stood. "It's my wife." He walked away from his ex-wife and went into the bathroom to take the call from his current wife. "Hey, bae," he said after he'd cleared his throat and made his voice sound as if he had not been crying. "I was just about to call you. I made it to the hotel room literally five minutes ago."

"Good," she replied. "Is everything okay? What was so important that you had to leave in a hurry?"

Charles knew he had to handle this carefully or Cassie would be suspicious and pissed. That was the last thing he needed at that moment.

"Yeah, everything is okay. Apparently, I've been summoned because our current district is going to be in need of a congressman real soon and they're looking at me to run."

"What?" was all she said.

Charles could hear the shock and excitement in her voice. He hadn't told her about the congressman retiring and it was a good thing because now he could use that as his alibi.

"Yeah, I was shocked when I got the call. I don't have all of the details yet, but as soon as I do, I'll let you know. Right now I don't know what my schedule is going to be like for the next couple of days, but I know it'll be pretty hectic with the meetings I'm going to have. But if all goes well, I just might become the next congressman for our district, baby."

"Are you ok, Charles?" Cassie surprised him by asking.

"What do you mean?" He was confused, wondering why she would ask him that.

"Because you just gave me great news but you don't sound too excited about it. You sound a little down."

"Yes, of course, I'm excited about it," he quickly lied. "I'm just tired from all the traveling on such short notice, that's all. When I hang up with you, I'm just going to lie down and get some rest, especially since I have a big day ahead of me tomorrow."

"Do that, baby. Right now, and just call me when you wake, okay?" She spoke in a voice filled with genuine worry. Her wifely concern made her blind to his deceit. She believed the lie he'd told her and that made him let out a silent sigh of grateful relief. "Get some rest and call me tomorrow, okay?"

"Alright, baby. I love you." Charles was happy to have dodged that bullet.

"I love you too," she replied.

"Bye," he said and they hung up.

Going back into the living room of the hotel suite where Carrie was, Charles was happy that he didn't have to deal with his wife and her suspicions for the moment. He needed to take care of his ex-wife and make sure she was okay. As of now, Cassie was still in the dark. He was unsure of how long he could keep her there before he had no choice but to tell her about his past life, a life he'd kept completely hidden from her. That would be hard enough when he had to do it, but he still had some time before that would even be an issue. The last thing he needed at that moment was to make trouble with Cassie now when Carrie needed him most. It was a relief not to have to be a husband to Cassie right then.

What Charles didn't know though, was that a few hundred miles away, his wife, Cassie, was as relieved as he was. She was actually happy that Charles was gone as she had so many things of her own to figure out without him being there to harass her. She was happy that he needed rest and that she didn't have to talk to him for very long. She needed her own rest and she got the best rest when Charles wasn't there to make her life a prison hell.

Going back to the couch and sitting next to Carrie again, Charles picked up the conversation where they had left off. "Is that everything about Terrail?"

"That's all I know right now," she admitted when he sat next to her once more. The sight of his chiseled, naked chest and that towel wrapped around his waist had Carrie's mind going in the wrong direction. She fought like hell to get control of her thoughts. "May I have one more drink before I leave, please?"

"Sure," he said as he took her glass, went to the bar, and made her one more."

When he returned and handed her the glass, she downed that one and relaxed a little more on the couch. "Thank you so much for coming. I don't know how I would have made it through this without you."

"I know I haven't been here, but Terrail is my child, of course I would come for this."

"Thank you," she said again as the alcohol had her staring at his chest once again. It took everything she had in her not to reach out and touch it. Just thinking about touching him made her remember the feel of Charles' hands on her, made her remember how well he used to lay it down in their bedroom.

Seeing the hungry look on her face told Charles exactly where Carrie's mind was. She was thinking the wrong thing because of where her head was with their son. She needed comfort, but not of the sexual kind. However, she didn't know that, she was hurting too bad to realize that. She was just looking for anything that would make her feel better than she did at that moment.

Not wanting to take advantage of an almost drunk woman, especially when she was in a vulnerable state, he grabbed her hands and said, "Go home and try to get some rest, Carrie."

But Carrie ignored Charles. Instead, she leaned into him and kissed him, really kissed him, and it shook him down to the bone when he realized that he was just vulnerable enough to want her too. That's why he kissed her back. That's why he allowed her to remove his towel and take him into her mouth. That's why when she had him on the verge of cumming like crazy, he put his face between her legs and devoured her.

"My god, Charles!" she moaned when he'd eaten her so good that her legs were shaking. Old feelings were sparked again, reignited again. Familiarities resurfaced, old touches, sensual memories. And when Charles lay her back on that couch and entered her, filled her with his thick manhood, Carrie allowed the tears to fall from her eyes as she spread her legs and gave into to the comfort that only Charles could give her. "My god!" she said again when he began those familiar slow and sensual thrusts.

"You feel so good," he told her as he kissed her tears away. "I missed you, the feel of you, the touch of you, the taste of you."

"I missed you, too," she moaned, spread her legs, gave all of herself to him. She knew what she was doing was wrong, but at that moment Carrie didn't have it in her to care. She was hurting too bad, in extreme emotional pain. She wanted Charles to take it away, to make it all just go away even if it was only for a little while. So she gave to him, took from him what he was offering, and hoped God would forgive her when it was all said and done. "I missed you so much."

Together they spent the better part of an hour comforting one another through the tragic loss of their son.

Sometime later, Charles woke in bed with Carrie wrapped in his arms. In the silence and the darkness, he could hear her light breathing as she slept. That whole scene was so familiar to him, took him back to when they were married and things were good between them. There were times he missed that life and would have given anything to go back, but he only wanted to go back for a little while. Not permanently. He could never go back to that life permanently because that life with Carrie back then had been a lie. He'd been hiding his true self from her, from the world to be exact. And she'd busted him, caught him in the middle of the best blowjob he'd received up until that point in his life. She'd freaked out, completely lost it, and then told him to leave and never come back. So, he didn't, and now he couldn't.

He could never go back to that life again, especially not after the one he'd built for himself was everything he wanted and so much more. He was still hiding, but not from everybody. There were some that knew him, knew what he liked and how he liked to get down. He'd even gone as far as to carve out time once or twice a month to be who he really was so that the pressure to pretend wasn't as bad as it had been when he was with Carrie. He was happy now, really happy. Going back to Carrie was never something he could do again. The sex he'd just had with her had been great, so much more than wonderful, but that's all it was. Sex. An amazing trip down memory lane. But now the memory was over.

Deciding not to wake her and send her home in the middle of the night, Charles let Carrie sleep. She needed it, hell, he needed it too, but there was business to be handled before tomorrow. Getting out of bed, going into the living room, and grabbing his phone, he began making calls. He needed more information about what happened to Terrail than what Carrie had given him. The only way to find out what was really going on was to call in some favors from some people he knew could get the job done and keep quiet about it.

After about an hour, he'd talked to everyone he needed to and exhaustion was gripping him hard. Stepping back into that bedroom, he crawled back in bed with the woman he used to love and fell asleep as soon as his head hit the pillow. Sometime during the middle of the night, Carrie had awakened and decided to go home. Charles woke again and walked her to the door.

"I'll help in any way possible," he said as he hugged her tight. "I'll also pay for the funeral."

"Thank you," she kissed him on the lips. "We'll talk. And get some more rest if you can, you look exhausted." Then she walked out. Once the door closed, Charles immediately headed to the bar and poured himself a nice, stiff drink. He downed that and he poured another one. He downed that and poured another one and another one. Then he went to his room and sat on the bed looking around the room just before he broke down again.

Although it was Carrie that had ended their marriage by leaving him when Terrail was young, as a result, he hadn't been involved in Terrail's life. Charles felt solely responsible for Terrail's life being what it was. He was so distraught about his failures as a father that he spent the rest of the night crying and weeping for his recent actions, for the son he'd had and lost so many years ago, and for the daughter he never wanted.

On the other side of town, Carrie had made it home and lay in her own bed sobbing for the son she'd lost and the mixed feelings she now had about Charles. She'd known that sleeping with him would spark those feelings again, but she hadn't expected those feelings to be so deep. It amazed her to find that she still loved him so hard even though she blamed him for Terrail's lifestyle and somehow for his death. Now, in addition to grieving the death of her son, she was going to have to get over the love she had for Charles once again. She shouldn't have slept with him, but at that moment she'd needed him and he'd needed her. She didn't regret doing it, but she did regret what it would do to her heart now that she loved him again.

That one thought made her cry even more.

Chapter Twelve

Even though it was a little late, Romel had made plans to get up with Kelly. Although she was a little older, she was an excellent stress reliever. Things between them weren't serious or anything, Kelly wasn't his girl. She was just something to do until he could be with the girl he really wanted.

Once he made it to Kelly's house, he quickly realized that they wouldn't get straight to the fucking that night. She was seriously upset and instead of fooling around, he understood that she needed to be consoled. So he did that in the only way he knew how. He and Kelly sat, talked a little, and smoke a lot. After he'd gotten her to relax, she finally told him that she was upset because earlier that day she'd found out that her niece had been killed.

"I don't really know the details, but I do know that she was murdered along with some of her friends.

"Damn, bae. I'm so sorry to hear that."

"Me too," she said as she reached for the smoke and took a few more hits.

"Do you want to talk about it some more," Romel asked as he pulled her to him for a hug.

"Not right now," she shook her head no and reached for him. "Right now I just want to forget."

"Then let me help you forget," Romel said as he consoled Kelly with his dick. They smashed, hard and loud, so loud that Romel thought the neighbors were going to come banging on the door or they were going to call the cops.

"I needed that," Kelly said when it was over and her body was good and relaxed.

"I'm glad you feel better," Romel told her as he went to get them some snacks.

For the longest time, they snacked and chilled as Kelly showed him pictures of her niece that were stored in her phone.

"She was a very beautiful young lady," he continued comforting her. However, after getting a really good look at her pictures, Romel was shocked shitless. Kelly's niece was one of the girls that had been killed by his son. When the realization hit him, he kept quiet and let Kelly do all the talking just as she had been doing.

There was no way in hell he was going to tell her and no way he was going to give her any information that she may have been able to use against his kid. So Romel kept his mouth shut and kept looking at those pictures she was determined to show him. He kept comforting her, kept consoling her, kept being there for her. He chilled with Kelly some more and when she wanted to fuck again, he fucked her again until he knocked her out.

When Kelly was deeply asleep, Romel eased quietly out of her bed, out of her house, and headed straight home.

"Damn!" he said when he'd used his keys to let himself inside. "This shit is crazy. I mean, how the hell can my son have killed Kelly's niece?" He was still shocked at the discovery he'd made and had to figure out what he planned on doing about it. Did he leave her alone, just ghost her and disappear on her? Did he stick around and maybe gather information he could give to his son's lawyer that would help to free RJ? Did he tell her the truth and see where shit went from there? He had no idea what to do and his head began to pound as he grew more stressed about the situation. "Damn!" he said again as tired himself of those thoughts and headed for the shower.

Washing his body, he allowed his thoughts to go in another direction. Cassie. He reflected on his feelings for Cassie. It was hard to believe that after all of that time he still loved her and still wanted her. Seeing her in that restaurant made him realize that he had never gotten over her, he'd just been forced to leave her alone. Jinx hadn't been playing when he told him to stay the fuck away from Cassie, and that big ass gun Jinx had shoved in his face made sure Romel did what Jinx had said.

Now, years later, he was paying a price for letting her go. Cassie had moved on to some rich bastard that Romel had a newfound hate for. She was married and living the good life and she looked damn good doing it. To Romel, that was so fucked up because if he had been given the chance he would never have left Cassie. He'd have made a way for them to be together and to raise RJ together. But what could he have done when her grandparents, who really didn't want him to go to jail, had threatened to have him sent to jail if he didn't stay away from their underaged grandchild? And what could he do when Jinx was ready to take his life? Not a damn thing. So he'd let them take her child from her, then he took the money Jinx had paid him to stay away from her and lost a good love in the process.

He knew no one would understand how he could love her when she was at such a young age, but no one had been there that summer except him and Cassie. No one could possibly understand what had developed between them or even how it had developed. Hell, he still struggled to understand just how that love had emerged. He knew everyone thought he was a pervert, but he wasn't. He didn't go around messing with young girls, he'd never done that shit before in his life. As a matter of fact, he hadn't intended to do that with Cassie, but there was just something about her, something that made him let her keep coming around him. Something that had made him fall in love with her as she was falling in love with him even though he'd known it was all wrong.

"Fuck!" was all he said when he was done thinking about what he couldn't change. Getting out of the shower, he dried himself and headed for his bedroom. "Everything is so fucked up right now!"

As mental exhaustion settled over him, Romel went over to his bed and climbed in. Moments before he closed his eyes and settled into a deep sleep, all he could think was, if it wasn't for the weed and liquor in his system, the millions of thoughts running through his mind would never have allowed him to get any sleep.

Back in Buffalo, Cassie was up for the day and going through her morning routine. She was still a little groggy as she turned on the shower so the water could get hot, sat on the toilet, and turned on Marco's motivational speeches. She selected the one she would listen to as she showered and stepped into the steaming water.

Everyone in Buffalo was fully aware of the fact that in one day all four seasons of weather could be experienced, so Cassie needed to dress for the crazy weather. She settled on a nice, hot pink blazer, a white fitted tee, flower pants that were hot pink, dark orange, teal green, and tan. Gold accessories and a pair of gold flat sandals complemented her ensemble as it was a cool day, not too cold. At least that's what the weather was predicted to be. To top everything off, she styled her hair in a jet black, shoulder-length bob with a bang.

When she was done dressing, Cassie grabbed her clutch and briefcase. Then she looked in the mirror, giving herself a one over, and approved of how good she looked. Then she grabbed her keys from the table in the living room and strolled out of the front door of her home, heading to work.

Although she had a hectic schedule ahead of her, she was excited about the day because she was having lunch with her brother, Lathom. There was so much she had to fill him in on, so much that had happened. In addition to all of that, she needed to ask him something significant. She hoped he wouldn't be too pissed with her for asking, but if there was anyone she knew she could count on, it was her brother.

Pulling into the parking lot of her job, Mrs. Baxton realized she'd forgotten to stop and pick up her coffee. There was no way she could make it through her entire hectic day without the caffeine to give her a boost. Quickly, she dialed Denise's number, hoping to reach her before Denise reached the job.

"Hey, girl," Denise answered.

Cassie was so grateful that Denise had picked up the phone that her words rushed out of her mouth. "Please do me a favor and stop by Tim Horton's and grab me a XL coffee with a shot of hazelnut, six creamers and ten sugars."

"Girl, no problem. Your timing is perfect because I was just about to drive past it on my way to work."

"Thank goodness, you know how I am about my caffeine in the morning," she sighed with relief. "Oh, and good morning. Girl, I'm sorry for being rude."

"It's cool," Denise responded with a chuckle. You haven't had your coffee yet, so I understand."

The two ladies laughed for a minute before they ended their call.

As Cassie made her way through the building, she noticed that none of her girls were there yet. Then she looked at the gold watch on her arm and realized that she was a little early. As always, she entered her office and synced her phone to the stereo system. Immediately, Mary J's version of 'I'm Going Down' started to play. Opening her briefcase, Cassie removed the contents and sat them on her desk. She then took a seat and looked at her calendar to see what she had scheduled for the day and what time it was all scheduled for.

As she sang along with her music for a few minutes, Denise popped in with her coffee. "Thank you so much," she spoke gratefully as she handed Denise the money for the coffee.

Girl, please," Denise kindly refused the money and instead took a seat as Cassie paused the music.

They began their weekly morning ritual of catching one another up on everything that was going on in their personal lives. After only about five minutes, a knock sounded on the door. Neither of the ladies were surprised to see Lakara open the door and step through it, and just as Denise had done, Lakara took a seat and joined the conversation.

"You look cute today," Denise said to Cassie as they talked and laughed until the time for them to start working began to approach.

"Thanks, and so do you," Denise replied.

Both ladies then turned and looked at Lakara as they simultaneously said, "You look cute too."

"And why are you extra dressed up?" Denise added.

"Y'all remember that super fine guy, Mr. Martz, that I was telling y'all about." Both ladies shook their heads yes in response to her question. "Well, he's coming in with his wife for his second intake visit today."

Cassie and Denise both said, "What?"

Lakara smiled big. "Yes, so you know I have to look good."

"Damn, I forgot. Is that today?" Denise asked.

Cassie looked confused and Denise looked apologetic. Lakara, on the other hand, was excited. "Yes, and I can't wait," she said with a sexy look on her face.

"I'm sorry, Cassie, I totally forgot, please forgive me," Denise said, knowing that Cassie was going to have to complete the intake work she hadn't done.

"Don't worry about it," Cassie waved her hand in a dismissive manner, letting Denise know that it was no big deal. "What time is their appointment?

"Nine-thirty," Lakara piped in with a look of sheer satisfaction on her face. "And I'm ready."

Denise looked at Lakara and laughed while shaking her head. "Didn't you say that he was married?"

"Yes," Lakara looked at her seriously.

"And didn't you say his wife was coming with him?" Cassie spoke.

"Yes," Lakara licked her lips as if starving for the man.

"And you still dressed up for him and plan on flirting with him?" Denise pressed.

"Yes," Lakara's face was as serious as could be. "What's wrong with that?"

Both Denise and Cassie burst into laughter.

"If you don't know, we're not going to tell you."

Lakara hunched her shoulders and smiled. "All I know is that he is sexy and I'm going to try as many times as it takes to get him." Then she smiled bigger and walked out of Cassie's office to get to her desk before any clients entered the facility.

"Girl," Cassie said when Denise looked at her. "You know that girl comes from money and entitlement. She thinks everything and everyone is hers."

Denise shook her head and chuckled. "I guess that's what happens when Mommy and Daddy make life easy for you."

"I heard that," Lakara shouted to them. "And I don't give a shit!" Then they all burst into hearty laughter, Lakara included.

As the ladies dispersed to their designated areas to begin preparations for the intake assessment with Mr. Martz and his wife, Cassie pressed play on her phone and the song finished. A few minutes later, when Mary sang, "Sleep don't come easy. Boy please believe me. Since you've been gone everything's going wrong," Charles instantly popped into her mind.

Cassie cut the music off in a heartbeat, the thought that she hadn't heard from Charles that morning weighing on her mind. What hit her even harder was the next thought that flowed so easily through her. She didn't miss Charles at all. In fact, unlike the lyrics to the song Mary was singing, she'd slept great the night before. The sigh she let out was a deep one, a hurt one when she came to the realization that they actually needed that time apart.

"When did I get to the point that I need time away from my husband?" she asked herself as she shook her head in despair.

Just then her office phone rang. It was Denise calling to inform her that Lakara was finishing up her part of the intake with the Martz's and that they would soon be coming her way.

"Thanks for the heads up," Cassie said before she hung up, grateful for the team she worked with.

She was in the process of finishing up the last of her paperwork when her phone chimed, letting her know she had a text message. Cassie picked it up and opened the message.

Charles: Hey, Cassie. Sorry, I didn't call you before you went to work, I had a long night, very restless. However, I'll call you after my meetings are over with later tonight. Love you.

Cassie: Ok. Love you too. Have a good day. TTYL.

When she was done with her response, she pressed send. As soon as the message went through, there was a knock on her door.

"Come in," Cassie called out.

"Hey," Denise said as she peeked her head in. "I have Mr. Martz and his wife. Are you ready for them?" As Cassie and Denise made eye contact, Denise mouthed, "Oh, my God. He is super fine!"

The two ladies shared a silent laugh just before Cassie said, "Yes, send them in."

The moment Mr. Martz and his wife entered her office, Cassie's heart skipped several beats and she fought like hell not to let her mouth fall off of her face. "Hello," she spoke politely as she recognized the man that had given her an orgasm the day before. He'd infiltrated her dream, fucked the shit of her, and had her cumming both in her dream and in real life as she rose from her sleep. "I'm Cassandra Baxton." She extended her hand and shook each one of theirs. When the pleasantries were done she spoke once again. "Please have a seat."

"So, Mr. and Mrs. Martz, can you guys—"

"I'm Tameka, my name is Tameka, you can call me Tameka," she cut Cassie off and spoke almost angrily as she got as look at her husband and the way he was staring at the woman sitting behind the desk dressed in those expensive clothes.

Mr. Martz looked completely embarrassed. "Please excuse my wife." Then he gave Tameka a warning look, one that was clearly meant to make her act as if she had some kind of class and sense. After clearing his throat, he turned back to Cassie. "You can call me Mazoo and her Tameka."

No sooner than he'd spoken those words, Cassie got a whiff of that Gold by Jay Z and instantly the juncture between her legs started punching at the seat of her panties. As Cassie was fighting her reaction to Mazoo, he was catching a whiff of her Dolce and Gabbana Light Blue and it was making his dick throb so hard it pained him. He was ridiculously attracted to that woman and would have said as much had his wife not been there. So he played it cool, kept his mouth shut, and respected the woman he'd married.

While the two of them were trying their best to keep their attraction to one another from surfacing, Tameka was seeing it all. She may have been on drugs but she was far from stupid. Her husband wanted that woman and she knew that the moment he got a chance to have her, he would take her. That pissed her off and she decided then and there that she would deal with Mazoo when the time was right.

As Cassie went over forms, paperwork, rules, occupancy, and requirements, she noticed Tameka seemed absolutely uninterested. Cassie did her best to remain professional, stay focused, and to not be disrespectful to the woman that was being disrespectful to her. The entire time that was happening, the little woman in her pants was acting a fool. She clearly wanted Mazoo and was not ashamed to thump and throb and let Cassie know. It appeared her womanhood remembered that dream and wanted Mazoo to do more of what he'd done to her in that dream.

Tameka, bored out of her mind, pulled out her phone and began to play on it. Cassie tried not to roll her eyes at Tameka and instead directed her attention to Mazoo. Mazoo, staring so hard at Cassie, caught Cassie's look and said, "I apologize for my wife's behavior."

Tameka, pissed and tired of her husband doing everything but drooling over Mrs. Baxton, sucked her teeth but never looked up from her phone. She was furious and knew that if she looked at him lusting after that woman one more time she was going to start world war three in that office. Feeling the tension in the room, Cassie finished up the meeting with Mazoo and Tameka as quickly she could.

"There's one last step that needs to be completed before the process can be finished and Tameka can get a bed." Then she explained the remainder of the details to the couple before concluding the meeting. "Well," she stood from her desk, "that's it for today. All you have left to do is call and schedule the last step to the entry placement. Any questions?

"No," Tameka spoke rudely as she hopped out of her chair and headed straight toward the door.

"Will you calm down, Tameka?" Mazoo said to his wife, frustration in his voice. "We're leaving in a second."

"How about you calm down!" she snapped at him.

"What?" he asked, confusion on his face.

"You know what," she snapped again. "Don't play me like I'm stupid."

Mazoo was seriously puzzled. He had no idea what Tameka was talking about. "What the hell is your problem?" He turned to face her, tried to keep from glaring at her.

"You're my fucking problem!" she started to go off on him but cut herself off. Letting out a deep breath she said, "You better be glad I came to this stupid ass meeting. I'll be waiting in the car." With no more words, she turned away from them and left the office.

"Well," Cassie said after a few moments of silence. Mazoo said nothing, he only stood there looking defeated and embarrassed. "Okay," she spoke once more. "It's looks like you have your hands full, but it'll be okay. This is actually normal behavior for an addict. We'll be able to help once she's accepted into the program," she tried to reassure him.

Mazoo looked at Cassie and shook his head. "She wasn't always like this, she used to be really sweet."

"Let us help her. Give us a little time and you'll have the woman you married back in no time."

"I hope it's not too late," he opened the door to leave.

"I know it looks like that, but I promise you, it's not too late."

Mazoo gave her no words, just a look of gratitude as he stepped outside of her office. "Thanks," he said and turned to walk away.

"Thank you for coming," Cassie replied. "And don't forget to make your appointment before you leave. The quicker you get this done, the sooner we'll be able to help her. Mazoo turned back to her, looked at Cassie and just stared. He was simply mesmerized by her, by her beauty. "Thank you," she said again as he flashed that million dollar smile and almost made her orgasm from just that.

"I'll see you soon," he said as he finally walked away and toward the desk to make that appointment.

As Mazoo walked out of Cassie's office, Lathom walked in.

"Hey, I'm here to take you to lunch, baby girl. And oh," he said when he got a really good look at her, "you looking sexy."

"Oh, Lathom!" Her eyes widened in surprise. "I'm sorry, I forgot. But let me grab my purse and I'll be ready."

It only took her second to be ready for that lunch with her brother.

Chapter Thirteen

After the meeting, Mazoo was so confused. Tameka had been rude, uninvolved, and uninterested. She'd said she was going to do the treatment, accept the rehab, but all of a sudden she was no longer interested. What the hell happened that made her change her mind? Letting out a sigh of disgust, he walked through the parking lot and toward his car. This shit was getting old. He'd already threatened Tameka with divorce more times than he could count and he was tired of issuing those threats. At some point, he was going to have to turn those threats into a promise.

Mazoo knew that leaving Tameka wouldn't be hard at all, especially with the way she had been giving her body to anybody that would give her the money to get those drugs. She hadn't been faithful to him since she'd become an addict and he'd lost interest in physically touching her for the same amount of time. He was sticking with his wife because he'd made vows to her, but the fact that Tameka had been wildin' out lately had him reconsidering everything about those vows. And why should he keep them when she had stopped keeping them long ago?

"I'm tired of this shit," he said when he reached the car. Then, just before he opened the driver side door and took his place behind the wheel, he straightened his face. There was no need in letting Tameka know just how much he didn't want to be married to her anymore. That little revelation would only start a war and he was just too tired to fight with her again.

"Took you long enough," she looked at him and rolled her eyes the moment he was in the car.

"Don't start that shit, Tameka. You know damn well I had to stop at the front desk to schedule that last appointment for you."

"Mmm, hmm," was all she said as she picked up her phone and started playing on it again.

"What the fuck is that supposed to mean?" Now it was him that snapped.

"It don't mean nothin'" she spoke in a disinterested voice. "It don't mean a damn thing!"

"That's bullshit and we both know it!" He was fighting so hard not to get loud with her, but she was pushing his buttons as she had done too much lately.

"You clowned in that meeting and now you're clowning in this damn car. What the fuck is going on with you?" When Tameka kept her mouth shut and just kept playing whatever game she was playing on her phone, Mazoo said, "Fuck it!" Then he started the car and drove off. He didn't have time for Tameka and her shit. Besides, he had other things that he would rather think about at that moment.

Cassandra Baxton. She was the woman that had invaded his mind and wouldn't leave. The woman was beautiful, she had an amazing body, and those eyes of hers were alluring and driving him crazy. Although she was classy, Mazoo could tell she had a little hood in her too. As ironic as it was, she was almost like Tameka used to be, classy and sexy with just a little ghetto riding beneath the surface.

Between Cassandra's eyes and her scent, he wasn't sure which one had him the most captivated. To be honest, he really didn't care. All that mattered was that the woman had made him have many a wet dream over the last few days and if he didn't get some real soon, his balls were going to explode. And who the hell was that man that had walked past him and into her office? Was he the reason she was wearing that big ass rock on her finger? Was that her husband? If he was, Mazoo now wondered if she liked the debonair street type.

Not knowing what she liked made him realize that he wanted to know much more about her. He needed to know what made her smile, what turned her on, what stimulated that mind of hers. He shook his head as he realized he was caught up in another woman when he shouldn't have been. He had never been interested in any other women other than his wife before, but that Cassandra lady had his uninvited attention and he couldn't seem to shake her. Something about her was pulling at his heart strings and Mazoo couldn't believe the position he found himself in. Just thinking about her made him smile and he wasn't even aware that he was doing it.

"Over there thinking about that bitch, huh?" Tameka spoke and yanked him firmly out of his thoughts.

"What?" he turned to look at his wife.

"You fucking heard me. But it's cool, Mazoo. Do you and I'ma do me," she spoke with venom in her voice.

"Tameka, you've been doing you," he reminded her. "You've been doing you for a long time now."

Mazoo saw the anger surrounding his wife like a thick cloud of the blackest smoke. She was so mad that her body started shaking. "Fuck you and that bitch. I saw the way you looked at her. You want her? Huh, Mazoo? You want that bitch?" Tameka yelled.

"What I wanted was my wife, my clean and sober wife," he almost yelled right back at her but found a way to keep his voice much calmer than Tameka managed to keep hers. “And I've wanted my wife the whole time you've been on these damn drugs. But since my wife let me know that she gave up on herself in that office today, I realized that I do want to move on. I do want something else,” he told her the God's honest truth.

“Well, guess what?” she was still yelling. “From the size of that rock on her finger, your broke ass can't afford that young, high-priced bitch. In her eyes, you're just a low class, struggling ex con.

As calmly and as deadly as could be, Mazoo said. “Is that her eyes we're really talking about or yours?

Tameka never answered and her silence told Mazoo the truth. The second he realized what Tameka really thought of him, that was the second he made up in his mind to leave her. He was going to help Tameka, but it was over. The marriage was officially over. Tameka may have thought he was broke, but he was far from that. The minute she'd started using, he'd been smart enough to keep his finances from her so that she wouldn't snort, or shoot, or sniff them all away feeding her addiction. Between the gym he owned, being a personal trainer, and working at the plant, Mazoo knew he would be more than financially stable.

“Do you fucking hear me?” Tameka screamed, snapping Mazoo out of his deep thought.

“What?” he looked at her, confusion all over his face.

"I said I'm sorry," she spoke in a much softer and much calmer tone than before. "And I'm going to go. I'm going to go to the center. I'm going to do better, I promise, Mazoo. I'm going to get clean. Okay?"

Mazoo's voice was dry as hell when he said, "Okay."

He Knew Tameka was full of shit, he recognized that voice, knew it was the one she often used to win him over. However, that voice wasn't working at that moment. In fact, it hadn't worked in a long time. Now, all that voice did was make him sick.

Pulling over to run into the store, Mazoo was happy to put some space between him and his soon-to-be ex-wife for a few minutes. He just needed to breathe and gather his thoughts before he got back in that damn car with her. However, he wouldn't be getting back in the car at all with her that day or for the next three days, because by the time Mazoo walked out of the store and back to his car, Tameka was nowhere to be found.

"Here we go with this shit again," he said as he let out a deep, annoyed sigh.

After finally getting some rest and waking for the day, Charles was in a much better frame of mind. He was in the process of stepping from the shower when suddenly there was a knock on the door. Since he wasn't expecting anyone, he was surprised. Then he remembered how Carrie had surprised him by just showing up last night and he assumed it was her doing the same thing again. When he opened the door, he was even more surprised to find Demetri standing there.

"What are you doing here and how did you get here?" Charles asked as he yanked his assistant into his room and looked around the hall. Then he closed the door and turned to Demetri. "And did anyone see you?"

"No," Demetri gave him a gorgeous smile while walking further into the hotel room with his bags.

"You know you can't stay here." Charles was doing his best to hide his anger.

"Listen, boss man, I came to help you. After all, I am your assistant, right? So, I'm here to assist," he said with a spreading of his arms. "Besides, my room is next door, it's adjacent to this one, but I can't check in until three p.m.

Charles let out a deep, annoyed breath. He really didn't want to have to deal with Demetri and his clinginess at that moment, but he couldn't think enough to see any other choice. "Fine, but I have to go. There's a lot going on, I'll talk to you when I get back." Then he strolled back into his bedroom where he dropped the towel that had been around his waist and was about to get dressed.

Demetri followed suit, walking in just when that towel hit the floor. "You look like you can use a massage to get your day started," he said as he eyed Charles' naked body.

Charles looked over to Demetri when he heard the lust in his voice and clearly saw the lust in his eyes. "Not right now, Demetri. I have a lot to do. I don't have time for you and this right now."

"It'll only take a second," Demetri said when he'd walked up to Charles. Then, before the man could put up a single protest, Demetri was on his knees and Charles was in his mouth. And Demetri was giving Charles what he promised him, a massage. Only it was his balls he was massaging as he sucked the shit out of his dick.

"Fuck!" was all Charles could say as he gave into what he knew was going to be the best blowjob on earth. With Demetri, he thought as he sighed deeply and contentedly, it always was.

Chapter Fourteen

Forty-five minutes later, Charles finally left his hotel room. He pulled out his phone and called Carrie to let her know he would be at her house in an hour to go over the funeral arrangements. Then he sat back in the car and prepared for the long drive. He couldn't believe the things that were happening all around him. First, his son was dead. Then there were the terrible decisions he couldn't seem to help making.

There was the sex he'd had with his ex-wife and then the sex he'd just had with Demetri. There was the lying to his wife and the sneaking around Carrie's back to get information about what really happened to Terrail in that hotel room. His demons were resurfacing, and he needed to get his stuff together before everything he was doing blew up in his face and ruined the life he'd spent so many years building. Just like it had the last time.

As Charles drove the new and unfamiliar path to Carrie's house, he thought about his son, thought about all of the ways he had failed Terrail, all the times he had failed Terrail, starting with his name. When Charles and Carrie found out they were having a son, Carrie instantly wanted to name him Charles Junior. However, Charles was firmly against that, he wanted nothing more than for his son to be nothing like him. To ensure that, he refused to allow Carrie to name their baby after him. It had hurt her feelings, but because Carrie loved her husband, she agreed.

It was Charles that had named him Terrail Dexter Baxton, not Carrie. Carrie knew that Dexter had been Charles' childhood friend, a friend that had gotten killed before she met him, so she said nothing when Charles named him Terrail Dexter after his friend. She was also well aware that Charles believed he was too messed up to give his son his name. She'd known about the issues he had very early in their relationship. When they'd met, he was in counseling and drinking heavily. She'd known that he had demons that tormented him on a daily basis, however, she chalked those demons up to him having issues from being in the army. Charles hated himself and Carrie knew it, that was why she understood about naming their son even if she absolutely hated the fact that she couldn't give her son his father's name.

Charles knew what Carrie thought and never told her anything different. His demons were much deeper than anything she could possibly understand, so he let her believe what wasn't the truth. He didn't want anyone that deep in his business, knowing the monster he was, the monster he could become at any given moment.

Over the years, things inside of his mind had become so bad that his drinking became heavier, so heavy that it was too much for Carrie and her young son. Charles had been violent with Carrie a few times and he'd done it in front of Terrail. Even though he was scared to death, Terrail, had still tried to help his mom and ended up on the wrong side of Charles' fists. The child was no match for the big strong man he called Dad, and it tore Carrie apart to see that Charles had escalated from just abusing her to now abusing their child as well. She had to do something, but at that time she'd had no idea what that something was.

Thinking her marriage was salvageable, Carrie stuck around, hoping Charles would eventually see how much his wife and child loved him and that he would get his act together. That never happened, things only got dangerously worse, so much so that she no longer even knew who she was. So, she'd planned to leave him. Then she found out that she was pregnant with child number two. She knew that trying to leave Charles with another baby on the way would be difficult. Nevertheless, she still worked toward getting everything set up so that her transition would be smooth when she finally left.

Almost as if Charles had been trying to prove how much worse he could make things, one day Carrie came in from work early and got the shock of her life. The pregnancy had her feeling sick that day and she decided to leave work, go home, and get some rest. The drive home had been sheer torture and her stomach was churning like crazy. She knew that the moment she got home she was heading straight to the bathroom to empty the contents of her gut.

Wasting no time getting out of the car when she arrived at the house she shared with her husband, Carrie walked inside and closed the door. In her haste to get to the bathroom, she didn't notice the sound of water running until she was halfway there. No one was supposed to be home, so Carrie, as quietly as she could, grabbed one of her son's bats and began to creep quietly down the hall, following the sound of the water. Whoever was in her house was going to get their ass kicked with a plastic baseball bat while she threw up all over them when she got in that bathroom. It would serve their asses right for being where the hell they weren't supposed to be.

Quietly reaching her destination, she stopped at the bathroom door where she now heard serious moaning in addition to the running shower. Unable to believe her ears, Carrie slowly and quietly opened the door, only to find Charles in the shower, his head thrown back and his eyes closed while he was getting his dick sucked. Carrie was crushed. That was not the first time she'd caught Charles cheating. However, it was the first time she'd caught her husband cheating with a man.

There would be no forgiving him this time, no taking him back and hoping things would get better.

"You son of a bitch!" she shouted as she threw the bat into the bathroom before turning to leave and slamming the bathroom door behind her. Her eyes were wide, her heart was racing. She was completely shocked at what she had seen. Crying and running, Carrie moved as fast as she could away from her house, her husband, and her dead-end marriage.

Charles was instantly pulled from his indulgence and immediately snapped back into the harshness of his reality. Carrie had caught him once again, but this time was different he realized. He too had known that his marriage was over. That didn't change the fact that he was going to do all he could to talk her out of leaving him. As fast as he could, Charles jumped out of that shower and tried to catch his wife, but by the time he'd made it out of the bathroom, it was too late. Carrie was already gone.

Once Carrie got outside the building, she lost everything that was in her stomach. She was so hurt and so devastated. He'd promised her that he would never cheat again, promised her that there would be no more infidelities, but not only did he cheat again, but this time was also so much worse. What she had seen was too much.

After weeks of not speaking to Charles, Carrie finally decided to call him and she told him everything, every detail of how she had found him that day and every detail of how she was done with that marriage. She told him that she was moving and taking their son with her. She told him that she was getting rid of the baby she was carrying and she advised him to not contact her or their son. She informed him that she had taken the hundred grand out of their savings account and had only left him with twenty thousand, which she felt was more than generous. She also told him that divorce papers would be in the mail and that all he needed to do was sign them. The last thing she told Charles was that if he tried anything to stop her from getting that divorce or if he contacted her or their son, she would do everything in her power to destroy him.

By that point, Charles had just gotten into politics in Atlanta and could not afford a nasty divorce, especially one that came with the scandal of a same sex affair and domestic violent charges. So Charles chose Carrie's only option which was to go away quietly. He'd known she would take the money which was why he'd left it in their joint account. Besides, Charles had come from money so a hundred thousand was a small price to pay for hurting Carrie and their son the way he had.

He had convinced himself that she was right to leave him and that young Terrail would be better off without him and the demons that plagued him. Charles thought it was all for the best if that child never saw or heard from him again. Carrie, true to her word, went on with her plan and her life and the two hadn't spoken to one another until Carrie called him to tell him that Terrail had been killed. And what did he do in response? He fucked her. He'd allowed those demons to make him spread his ex-wife's legs and fuck her as if he still loved her.

While they had been making love, Charles had seen the moment the love had shown up in her eyes, letting him know that she had never really gotten over him. She had kept her promise to stay away from him, but that had been easy for her to do when there was the distance between them. However, the moment they were in the same city, in the same building, she had gone at him like she'd been starved for him and he'd let her. He'd done nothing to stop her and in fact, had gone at her the same way. Now there were feelings involved and he hoped with everything in him that he wouldn't have to help her get through them. He hoped for all of their sakes that she would forget what happened, get through the funeral and the trial, and let things go back to the way they were. Him in Buffalo with his wife and her in Atlanta with whomever.

An hour and fifteen minutes later, he pulled up to Carrie's house. Before getting out of the car, he took a few deep breaths and gathered his thoughts. He didn't want any repeats of the night before and he needed to be focused and not emotional to make sure it didn't happen. When he was sure he was able to keep his shit together, he exited the car, went up to her house, and knocked on the door.

Carrie opened the door in an instant. "Hey," she said as she looked at him with a smile and invited him in. Then she walked over to a table where she'd been sitting with pictures and papers everywhere, trying to figure things out. "I'm still in the air about how to dress him."

"What?" Charles asked, not quite sure of what she was talking about. "What do you mean?"

"I mean, should I dress him as Terrail or as Tee Tee?"

"Tee Tee?" he asked, having an idea of what she meant but not quite sure. He needed clarification.

"He was transitioning, Charles." She looked him directly in the eyes when she spoke those words.

Charles was instantly upset, it seemed as if some of him had rubbed off on Terrail after all. He didn't like where the conversation was about to go. There was no way he wanted his son lying in a casket dressed as a girl, no way he was ready to face in his son what he still hadn't faced within himself. But he hadn't been a part of Terrail's life, so what the hell could he say or even do about it? "What's to decide?" he spoke the words casually although he was feeling anything but.

Carrie spoke very simply when she said, "Everyone knew him as Tee Tee, we're the only ones who knew him as Terrail."

Immediately he began clenching his teeth so hard he was unable to form another word. He looked down to try and refocus his thoughts and, on the table, he saw tons of pictures of them as a family. Terrail's baby pictures, different pictures of him throughout his childhood. There were pictures of Terrail as he began to transform into Tee Tee. It had started off simple, just a few girly accessories here and there, but then his son had gone from a few girly accessories to wearing a full face of makeup and fully dressed in female clothes. The transformation had been stunning and complete. Had he run into Terrail on the street dressed like that, Charles would never have known that was his son.

Then he noticed pictures of his own twin sister, Kelly, with Terrail and then with Tee Tee, as they called him. Charles stared at the pictures, thinking how much Terrail looked like him as a boy and how in his transition he began to look just like Kelly. "I take it that Terrail and Kelly were close," he spoke softly.

"Yes, very close," Carrie informed him. "She's always been there for him, always been very supportive of him even when I struggled with it."

Unable to take looking at the pictures anymore, Charles said, "Well, to make things easier on yourself, how about you do not struggle with how to dress him. You're already dealing with enough so maybe you should just dress him as Terrail."

"Would that be for me or for you?" Carrie said as she looked at Charles, saw the struggle in his own eyes.

"Both," he looked back at her. "I think it would be easier on both of us."

She was about to say that Terrail's transition no longer bothered her but decided against it. She and Charles were in a good place at that moment and she didn't want to do anything to rock that boat.

"Okay," she spoke quietly, and with that issue settled, the two of them moved on to the other issue at hand. They'd decided on the time and the place and all of the arrangements for the services. Then they moved on to discussing the wording on the program.

Chapter Fifteen

"Charles," Carrie began in an apprehensive tone. "I've been thinking, and I've decided not to list you as his father." Charles was both glad and pissed, so pissed that he was speechless. On the one hand he wanted to be listed as the father of his own damn child, but on the other hand, the life he'd built could be destroyed if it got out that he'd hidden a child from the public and from his wife for all of those years. His feelings were all over the place and Carrie saw them and mistook them for anger at her. "I'm not doing it to hurt you," she quickly assured him. "I just don't want to interrupt your life. I'll list you as a special friend of the family, a person who's been in his life since he was born."

"Okay," he began, still unable to process his thoughts or his feelings about the situation. "I want you to do what you feel is best." He refused to voice his thoughts to Carrie, refused to let her know that he was torn between being pissed and relieved. The last thing he wanted to do was piss her off or argue with her at a time like that. "Whatever is easiest for you is what I want."

"Okay, then it's settled," she told him. "Now, all I have to do is get these printed and we'll be done with this part of things.

"My assistant just flew in this morning. If you need help with the printing or with anything, let me know and it'll get done whether I do it or he does it," Charles told her.

"Your assistant is a male?" She looked at him, tried to keep her suspicions to herself.

"Yes," Charles saw where her thoughts were going and needed to stop them before they were screaming at each other like old times. "After catching one of my female assistants flirting with me, my wife was uncomfortable with women assistants and made me promise to only have male assistants from here on out," he rolled his eyes as if annoyed with that whole situation.

"I see," was all Carrie said. Then, "Okay, if I need help, I'll let you know."

Desperate for a change of subject, Charles asked, "Did you speak to Kelly yet?"

Knowing that anything dealing with Charles and his twin sister, Kelly, was a taboo subject, Carrie debated her answer. She could tell him the truth about Kelly, but she could never tell him the whole truth. She could never verbalize to him that she and Kelly were very close, had been close even while they were married. She had told Kelly every detail of everything that had happened in her marriage to Charles. Kelly hadn't just been her sister-in-law, she was her best friend, hell, her only friend.

"Yes," she was honest with him. "She knows and she will be in attendance at the funeral. I'm assuming that since you had to ask, you and Kelly are still not talking to one another.

"No, we're not," was all he would volunteer. There was no way he would tell her that he didn't have time to deal with Carrie and the grudge she'd been holding since their parents died in that car accident.

His sister had accused him of giving their parents a shitty funeral so that he could skimp on funeral costs and run off with the remainder of the insurance money. Kelly had been so mad that she'd vowed to do everything she could to destroy Charles one day. That had been years ago and the twins hadn't spoken since. As much as that should have hurt Charles, it didn't. He'd moved on with his life and didn't care to think about his vengeful sister. She was the past and he had every intention of leaving her there.

"Charles," Carrie spoke gently, "you need to make it right."

"Things are fine the way they are. No need to change them." Seeing that the conversation would get nowhere with him, Carrie decided to change the subject. "Okay, well, will your wife be attending the funeral?"

"Huh?" was his confused response. He hadn't been expecting her to ask about Cassie and it had caught him off guard.

"Will your wife be at the funeral?" she repeated herself.

"No, Carrie, she won't."

"Why?" She asked. "I would love to meet her."

"Her grandfather is very sick, so she's helping out with him right now." That was a half-lie and half-truth. Mr. Edmonds was ill, but not as bad as he was making it seem and Cassie didn't need to help out with anything. However, Charles preferred to lie than to tell Carrie that Cassie had no idea he'd ever been married, that he had a son, or even that he had a twin sister. He had really left the past in the past.

"Will she be here for the trial?" Carrie asked innocently, but Charles could hear the curiosity in her voice. She wanted to know what Cassie was like because she had ulterior motives. Carrie wanted to size up what she thought was the competition and that confused him to no end. She'd divorced him. She'd told him to stay away. Why was she trying to see if there was a chance to have him again?

Rather than answer her, Charles simply replied, "Carrie, just let me know how much everything is when you find out, okay?"

"Okay," she replied, the disappointment clearly evident in her voice.

Deciding that he should leave before things became awkward, he looked at Carrie, "I'm going to go back to the hotel and catch some rest. I didn't get much sleep and I really need some."

Reluctantly, Carrie agreed. "Okay," was her disappointed response. "But if it's possible, I would like to spend some more time with you before things become too hectic to do so."

Charles knew what Carrie was doing and he wanted no parts of it. He decided then and there that he needed to let her know that. "Carrie, last night we were both drinking and really emotional. I don't want to take advantage of those emotions and start something that we can't finish. I don't want either of us to get hurt. Neither of us are in a good frame of mind under the circumstances."

"I know," she admitted. "I know, but I just really need the comfort and being with you last night really helped to comfort me."

"It comforted me too," he told her the truth, "but with our history, things can go bad between us real quick and I don't want that. I like where we are and I'd like to keep it this way. Especially since all we have is us now."

"I know you're right, but that doesn't change the fact that no one will be able to understand what I'm going through like you can. We both lost a son. We're both grieving the loss of that son. We both can console each other like nobody else can."

"I already cheated on my wife once, I don't want to do that again," he told her.

"But it was okay for you to cheat on me multiple times?" She couldn't help the anger and the jealousy that was welling up in her.

"You just proved my point," he told her as he walked toward the door. "So, it's best that I leave. And don't forget to let me know how much everything is."

"Okay," was all Carrie said as Charles walked out of her house.

As much as she hated to admit it, everything he'd said about them was absolutely right. Knowing that still didn't make her desire his consolation any less.

On the other side of Atlanta, Romel was just waking up. He had a lot of things to do that day, so he quickly hit the shower, got dressed, and headed downtown to speak with RJ's lawyer. Michael Leadman was a great defense attorney with an amazing team and that made Romel feel pretty good about his son being found not guilty. All he had to do was come up with the money to pay the man. He had already given him the retainer, but Michael needed the rest.

While in his office, Michael talked to Romel about the case. He let his clients' father know that the case was very high profile, that it was a tough case to fight and that he would do the best he could considering.

"My services are going to cost twenty-five thousand. And as of now RJ will be facing the death penalty. I'm going to do my best to try and get that taken off of the table. If I do, he'll be facing life in prison if convicted. But because both myself and the prosecutors have just gotten the case, they will be screaming for the death penalty. I need you to be prepared just in case they refuse to take it off of the table."

Romel looked hurt and angry, but he understood. "I hear you," he told the attorney. "And here's ten thousand, he said as he pulled out a bag filled with the bills. I'm working on the rest. Just please help me save my boy." Leadman took the money and called his assistant so that she could count it up and print up a receipt.

"I'll do everything in my power to," Leadman spoke honestly.

Romel left the attorney's office with receipt in hand. His next stop was Atlanta County Jail. It was time to see RJ. As he drove toward the jailhouse, he thought about Cassie again. He knew it was fucked up that he was asking her for fifty thousand, but he had just given that attorney his life savings. He needed that money back. Once Cassie gave him the fifty grand, he would give the lawyer the remaining twenty five grand, get his ten grand back and will have gained another fifteen thousand.

"Shit, it ain't her money, anyway," he tried to convince himself that he was justified in stealing from her. "It's that bitch ass husband of hers. And that muthafucka owes me, especially with the way he treated me in that damn airport. Arrogant son of a bitch!" His hands clenched the steering wheel of the car. He really hated Charles and it amazed him just how much.

Once he arrived at the county jail, Romel put all thoughts of his hatred for Charles aside. He needed to focus on RJ and his wellbeing. Emptying his pockets of everything, he made sure to leave his belongings in the car, except for his ID. The last thing he wanted was to have to throw something important away or to have to come back to the car to drop something off because it might have been contraband and jailhouse security wouldn't allow it inside.

About forty minutes after he arrived, Romel had finally completed the process to get in and see RJ. When he stepped inside of the visiting room, Romel sat at a table and waited for deputies to bring his son down. Only five minutes had gone by before RJ was brought in. Immediately he went to the table at which his father was seated and they embraced before he took his seat.

"I went to see the lawyer before I came here," Romel said, "I gave him the ten thousand retainer fee. I'll come up with the rest."

"How much is the rest?" RJ asked.

"We need another twenty-five thousand."

"That's a lot of money. How are you going to come up with that?"

"About that," Romel began, his voice a little apprehensive. "There's something I need to talk to you about pertaining that."

"What's up pops?" He saw the apprehension in his father and began to worry just a little. When Romel took too long to speak, he said, "Spill it."

"It's a lot, son. But first, let me say that I haven't always been there for you like I should have been and I'm sorry for that."

"Come on pops, what's the deal?" RJ's nerves were starting to get the best of him. He just wanted his father to stop procrastinating and get on with it. He had enough to be stressed about, he didn't need his father adding to that stress.

"Okay," Romel let out a deep breath in preparation of letting his son know what the real deal was. "You know how my mom told you that whole story about Georgia Lee being your mom, and how she died and that's how you came to live with us?"

"Yeah," RJ did not like the way the conversation had started.

"Well, son, that's not the truth."

"What do you mean that's not the truth. Georgia Lee isn't dead?" His heart began to be a little faster.

"No, she's really dead, but she wasn't really your mother. Georgia was your grandmother, your mother's mother." He paused for a moment to see how RJ was taking the news. When his son kept his face straight and blank, Romel figured he was okay and went on. "Your mother's name is Cassie, well, Cassandra. She's alive and I've been in contact with her recently."

RJ sat across from his father absolutely speechless. There were so many emotions flowing through his body, so many questions going through his head. Romel took his son's silence as his cue to continue.

"Your mother and I hooked up years ago. At the time she lied to me about her age. She was twelve and I was nineteen."

Part of what Romel said to RJ was a lie, but there was no way he was going to tell his child that he'd voluntarily had sex with a minor. Especially one that was as young as Cassie had been when he'd gotten her pregnant. He was ashamed of what he had done and he'd already had enough people judging him about that situation. He lied because he didn't want his son doing the same.

Chapter Sixteen

"What?" RJ looked at his father like he was crazy, complete shock was running through his body. Had he heard right? Did he really say what he thought he said? "What did you say?"

"I said I got her pregnant," he went on, embarrassment filling him as he saw the judgement he had been trying to avoid clearly present on RJ's face.

"You got a twelve year old pregnant, dad?" RJ was stunned at what he was hearing, couldn't believe what Romel was telling him.

"Yeah, but she didn't look nowhere near twelve and she lied about her age," he said it again, making sure his son didn't come to see him as a bad guy like everybody else did. He was determined to cover his ass with RJ. "And her grandparents, who were raising her because her mother, Georgia Lee, had died, decided not to send me to jail. But that was only under the condition that I left her alone.

They made me promise to leave her alone and never contact her again."

Romel decided to also leave out the part where he had been paid handsomely to stay away from her and to provide for the baby. "But like I said, once they found out she was pregnant, they sent her out of town. She had the baby, you, and then my mom and Eric picked you up, brought you home, and raised you as theirs. Even though I was there, I wasn't allowed to say that you were my child because your mother was a minor and nobody wanted to explain that. So that's why I kept it hidden that I was your father for a long time."

RJ was pissed. "All this time I got a mother out here and she didn't even check on me or for me?"

"Calm down, son. It's not like that. She was—"

"Fuck that!" RJ practically shouted. "That's some bullshit and you know it!"

"It's not like what you're thinking," Romel tried to explain.

"I had a mom, she didn't give a fuck about me so she didn't have anything to do with me. What else can it be?" RJ was so angry that his body started to shake.

"Well, she wants to be here for you now. I went to Buffalo to tell her the situation and that we need help and—"

"We don't need shit from her!"

"Yes we do."

"Maybe you do, but I don't! I don't need shit from her!"

"Son, you're just upset, but when you calm down you're going to realize that you do need her. The lawyer wants another twenty-five thousand dollars, I just gave him ten thousand. That's my whole life savings and I don't have another dime. Neither do you for that matter, so yes, you do need her." Romel let his words sink in for a minute. Without Cassie, it was a guarantee that RJ would spend the rest of his life in jail, or even possibly be sentenced to death. They needed Cassie and Romel needed to make RJ see that.

"Hmph," was the only sound RJ made.

"She's willing to give you the rest of the money."

"So she's caked up like that? And she couldn't bother to make some room in her comfy life for her own son?" RJ was pissed and becoming more so the more his father talked.

"Her husband is caked up."

"Oh, so she married? Got a whole other family with kids and shit?" RJ was on the verge of exploding with rage as he wondered how she could take care of children with her rich husband but abandon him.

"She's married, but she doesn't have any other kids, son. And she wants to meet you, she wants to help."

"Why? Why after all this time does she want to help or even meet me?"

"RJ, it's not like what you're thinking," Romel said again. "She was very young when she actually gave birth to you, and the choice to keep you or give you up was not hers. It was the adults around her that took her choice away from her and made the decision to give you to my parents. It was never her decision. And she was told not to ever speak to me again or to ever speak about you. None of this was her doing because she was only twelve when she got pregnant and thirteen when she had you."

"Fuck!" RJ said.

"Can you even understand the position she was in? I mean how was she going to take care of you at thirteen? She was being taken care of herself." Romel could see his son thinking it through, coming to an understanding. "But she does love you."

"Yeah, whatever." RJ didn't want to hear any more about the rich mother that abandoned him.

"It's not completely her fault how things turned out. I played a big part in it too."

"My life turned out this way all because bitches lie. First my mom lied about her age and tricked you back then, and now because a nigga lied about being a bitch while he was dressed and acting like a bitch!" RJ yelled.

The visiting room became quite as everyone looked in their direction. To try and calm the situation, Romel lowered his voice as he spoke with a very strong and firm tone. "Listen, little nigga, I don't care how old you are or how you feel, you bet not ever let me hear you disrespect your mother ever again in life. If you do, you're not going to have to worry about this case or the death penalty because I'll kill you myself! Understood?"

RJ was completely shocked at his dad's reaction to him disrespecting his mother. Romel had never come at him like that before. Immediately, he realized that there must be some kind of feelings there for him to be so pissed over a bitch that lied to him and got him caught up in some bullshit. But he responded respectfully to his father when he said, "Yes, Dad."

When RJ was behaving like he had some sense, Romel said, "She wants to meet you. As much as I would like you to agree to meet her, the choice is yours. But if you do decide to meet her, I won't bring her here for you to disrespect her. If you do, me and you will have some problems." Romel looked RJ dead in his eyes, letting him see how serious he was, letting him know that he wasn't playing with him. "Now you can take some time to figure out what you want to do and call me when you do. I put money on your books so you can get the stuff you need while you're in here. Then he stood up. "You better figure this shit out, little nigga. One," he said just before he turned around and walked away, leaving RJ even more confused and angry about his life than he was before his dad had arrived.

"Stupid bitches," RJ said when he reached his cell and the guard closed the door.

He was so angry that all he could do was lie down and breathe deep until he calmed down. As he lay there thinking that today was the worst day of his life, his mind went back to the worst night of his life.

He'd gone out with a few of his friends to a spot called Sanctuary Dreams. They were having a good time chilling, partying, getting high and drunk out of their minds with four young ladies they had just met. Once the night began to wind down, they all made plans to go to a hotel. The ladies informed the guys that they already had a hotel room they could all go to and the guys agreed to meet them there.

RJ, Ramp, Cally, and Miles got in their car and followed Tee Tee, Shelia, Lisha and Danique to their spot. The guys were supposed to be meeting up with their crew to do a job, but they decided that the girls were too fine to leave them for some crazy ass job. So they ditched the fellas for the bitches. On the other side of town, their crew members, Holiday, Tool, Rito, Mar Fezzy , Pnells, Bucky, Dead Eyes, C.E.O. and Teck 8 all stuck with the plan to pull a caper.

Ramp got a call from Tool asking where they were because shit was about to go down. "This is supposed to be the lick that gets us all the motherload."

"We're not going to make it," Ramp replied.

Tool flipped the fuck out. "Y'all pass up some money for some pussy? Y'all young boys got life twisted."

"I feel you, but these bitches is bad as hell." Then he gave his brother a serious visual description of the bad bitches they met.

Just as Tool was about to go in on his brother, his other line began beeping. "Hold on, nigga," he said to Ramp, then clicked over to take the incoming call. It was two of his henchmen, the one everybody called The Deacon and the other, YG. The Deacon was calling to let Tool know who his little brother had been in the club with and to let him know they had all just left with those broads a little while ago. Immediately Tool came back on the line and said, "Yo, Ramp, those chicks y'all left with ain't no damn girls. Those are niggas. Get the fuck outta there, man!"

Ramp instantly yelled, "Oh, hell naw, man!" He was pissed. "What the fuck!"

"Yeah, I heard about them. Those are the ones that be tricking niggas into fucking them and then turning them dudes out. That's they hustle and they 'bout to hustle y'all young asses. Get the fuck outta that hotel, man."

"Man, this is some fucked up shit!" Ramp was in rare form as his anger began to get the best of him.

"Yo, man, I told yo ass to be careful. Now, get the fuck outta that hotel before they hustle y'all asses. It's time for me to go, I got work," he said and hung up.

Ramp was so pissed at those dudes for what they'd pulled on him and his crew that he stormed back into the hotel room where RJ, Cally, and Miles were with the girls. If he thought he was pissed before, he was even more infuriated when he saw that Cally and Miles had just finished getting their dicks sucked and were taking off their clothes, getting ready to smash. And he almost exploded when he saw that RJ was bustin' in Tee Tee's mouth at that exact moment.

"This bitch mouth is the business," RJ breathed hard, shot in Tee Tee's throat hard as he spoke when Ramp stormed into the room.

"You bustin' in a nigga mouth, RJ! All y'all just got y'all dicks sucked by niggas!" Ramp yelled.

"The fuck?" RJ yelled as he and the rest of the guys all jumped back in shock.

At just that moment, the one they had been calling Lisha came running out of the bathroom saying, "What's all the commotion about?"

Since Lisha was the one that had played the fuck out of him, Ramp pulled his gun out and shot her in the head. No questions asked.

"What the fuck?" RJ yelled again.

The guys were all shocked and the girls began running toward the door. Realizing that if those dudes got out of that room, they were going to call the cops and him and his boys were all going to jail, Miles pulled out his gun and shot Sheila, the one that had just finished sucking his dick, in the back of her head. When Cally saw Sheila go down, he grabbed his piece and poured lead into Danique just as she opened her mouth to scream. Cally hadn't even given her the chance to let that scram out.

Now all eyes were on RJ and the chick they called Tee Tee. "Look, I'm sorry," Tee Tee began apologizing and pleading for his life. "It was all just fun and games, we didn't mean to hurt nobody." As Tee Tee spoke, the guys were all shocked and surprised to hear a man's voice come out of the person who looked remarkably like a girl. "I don't want to die! Please, don't kill me!" she said as she looked to RJ. "I'm so sorry! I really don't want to die!" she pleaded with him.

All of the fellas were looking at RJ as well, waiting for him to do what they had done. There was no way they could let Tee Tee walk out of that room after seeing each of them kill her friends. She would ruin their lives and they had each determined that if RJ wasn't going to kill Tee Tee, they would.

"I don't want to die!" she said again as tears of fear and extreme regret ran down her face, ruining her flawless makeup.

"And I didn't want my dick sucked by a man," RJ said as he pulled out his own piece and fired one round into her forehead, dropping her in a heartbeat.

That's when they the guys began to panic. Neither of them had ever killed anyone and the shock of what they had just done was hitting them hard. "Calm the fuck down before somebody comes in here!" Ramp told them. Throw them bitches in the bathtub and wipe everything down as clean as you can get it. Make sure you catch everything y'all touched to get y'all's fingerprints off that shit. After that, we gettin' the fuck outta here!"

When they were done and had left the hotel, Ramp called Tool to tell him what happened and to see what they needed to do next, but Tool never responded. What Ramp, Cally, Miles and RJ didn't know was that while they were running from the spot where they'd left those dead bodies, their crew was in a shootout with the cops.

"Fuck!" Ramp shouted and dialed his brother's number again. "He's not answering."

"What the fuck are we supposed to do now?" Miles asked as the guys started to panic all over again.

"Why the fuck did you shoot Lisha?" Cally asked Ramp. "If you wouldn't have done that shit, I wouldn't have shot old girl. Why the fuck did you flip out like that?"

"Y'all mothafuckas not gon' blame this shit on me," he shouted as they began arguing amongst themselves. Deep down they all knew they were about to go on a long vacation and they truly believed it was all Ramp's fault. If he hadn't raged out and killed Lisha, they would never have killed those other girls.

The guys finally stopped arguing long enough to decide that they would go to Ramp's house. The second they made it there, they changed clothes and hid the clothes they'd just shed. Then they headed back to the club so they could be seen and have an alibi. After the club, they went to midnight bowling, again making sure they were seen. When they had finally exhausted themselves, they headed back to Ramp's house to go over their story. When they had their story together, the guys all gave Ramp their guns and let him keep the bag with the clothes. They were banking on Tool knowing how to dispose of their evidence and banking on him helping them fix the mess they'd gotten into. Before they separated from one another, they all vowed to not speak of that night ever.

They each finally went home, planning to act as if that night never happened and move on with their lives. The next morning each of them got a rude awakening. The news was reporting that everybody in their crew, everyone that had been involved in that bank robbery, was either in the hospital or dead. They'd been caught during the robbery and had attempted to escape the cops. That escape lead to a high speed chase and a shootout with the cops. That shootout led to three of them going to the hospital and five of them going to jail. Now they had no one to help them with the murders they had committed the night before. They were in deep shit.

Ramp called all the guys and asked them to meet up at his house. "What the fuck are we going to do?" he asked when they arrived.

They sat around working out a plan while drinking and smoking to calm their nerves. But no matter how drunk and high they tried to get, seeing all of their homies' faces flash across the TV screen kept them straight sober. Ramp was more on edge then any of them because Tool was his older brother and this new crime was his third strike. He knew his brother was going down for life and he would never see him as a free man again. The guys were all figuring out their next step while watching the news when Breaking News suddenly cut in.

The reporter interrupted regular news, saying, "This is Naomi Kingston and we are live outside of Dine's Hotel where the bodies of four young women have just been found dead in the bathtub of one of the hotel rooms. At this time, reports are that the police are trying to identify the victims. Once verification is confirmed, the families will be notified."

The room was absolutely silent as the guys all listened to every word. They were scared shitless and stunned and hard cold, reality was setting into each of them. When the report ended, they were frantic and went back to trying to cover their asses. After once more confirming their stories, they decided to go home and stay away from each other for a few weeks. They knew it wouldn't look good for four guys to be hanging out in a group after four girls had just been killed.

A few days later, after an anonymous tip, the police ran up in Ramp's house and found the clothes and the guns. Ramp had told the guys that he'd gotten rid of it, but the truth was he'd been waiting for Tool to do it and then had forgotten after learning what happened to his brother and the rest of their crew. Ramp had already been on the police's radar because his semen had been found in Lisha's rectum. Ramp hadn't told the fellas that he freaked out the way he did because he'd fucked Lisha in the bathroom of the nightclub after she sucked his dick. He'd been ashamed that he'd been tricked into fucking a man and too pissed to admit to himself that he'd liked it before he knew it was a man. Ramps DNA had been all in and all over Larry, who was in the process of transitioning into Lisha.

Although they had Ramp red handed, he didn't talk. The cops tried hard but couldn't get a word out of him. His DNA already had him going down, so he figured he would take the charge for killing all four and let the fellas have a shot at life. He would agree to plead guilty if they took the death penalty off the table and just spend the rest of his life on lockdown. Besides, his only family left alive was Tool and he was locked up. With it being Tool's third strike, his brother was going to be in jail for life as well. However, Ramp's plan failed miserably when they picked up Cally after getting his DNA off of his clothes and out of Danique's mouth. His bitch ass started singing like a first soprano. He sang so good that anybody listening would have thought his name was Whitney Huston and that he was every woman. Out of all four of the men, Cally was the one that couldn't handle the pressure. He turned out the be the 'do the crime but can't do the time' ass nigga. As a result, all four of them had been arrested, booked, and were waiting to be arraigned.

RJ knew by now that if the cops had found Ramp's DNA in Lisha's ass, and Cally's DNA in Danique's mouth, they would definitely find his DNA in Tee Tee's mouth. He'd been in the process of nuttin' when Ramp had come busting into the room screaming that they were niggas. He'd emptied his gun in Tee Tee's head less than two minutes after he'd emptied his load in her mouth. He was positive that they'd find a hell of a lot of his DNA in her.

"I ain't never getting the fuck out of here!" he spoke angrily. "What the fuck? I'm only nineteen years old and my life is over before that shit even got started. And all over some lying bitches and their bullshit!"

Chapter Seventeen

Lathom took Cassie to a nice Hibachi place called Okoye 3. When they were seated inside and had ordered their drinks, they were looking over the menu, trying to decide what they would eat when Lathom said, "Baby Sis, spill it. Stress doesn't look good on you." He eyed her for a few more moments, seeing in her what others may not have been able to. "You might be able to hide that shit from the rest of the world, but I know the real you. Now tell me what's wrong and who the fuck I have to kill."

Cassie put her head down, let out a deep breath. "It's a long and very complicated story."

"Good, 'cause I have all day." Before Cassie could utter a syllable, the waitress returned and took their orders. Then Cassie sat silently for a minute, not knowing where to begin. "Cassie?" Lathom called out to her in a voice that warned her to get to it.

"Ok," she looked up at him apologetically. "I just don't know where to begin.

"It's me, Cassie. You can start anywhere you want to. You know how we do."

"I got problems, Big Brother," is how she began. "Charles is out of town on what he says is a business trip, but I think he's on a cheating trip. I think he has some hoe out there that he's fucking around with. And the crazy part is that I'm not even mad that he's gone this time." She closed her eyes and let out another deep breath. "I'm actually relieved because he's controlling as fuck and for the first time in a long time he's not around to control me like that. He gets so mad and then—"

Lathom cut her off like an amputated limb. "Has he hit you, Cassandra?" The way Lathom asked that question and used her real name let Cassie know that he was going to really hurt Charles the first chance he got. At that moment, the waitress came back with their order, then quickly left. Cassie immediately bowed her head and said grace over her food. Once she was done, Lathom said, "Amen. Now answer me. Has he hit you?"

"Once or twice," she quickly fixed her statement when she saw Lathom's eyes shift to deadly, "but only when he's been drinking." She lied, lied to calm her brother's quickly building rage. The truth was that Charles hit her whenever the mood struck him and he had been doing it a lot more than usual lately.

"I'm going to kill that nigga!" Lathom calmly informed her. "So you may as well get ready to plan that nigga's funeral. I suggest a closed casket service."

"Lathom, no!" she began to panic. If Lathom said he was going to kill Charles, there wasn't shit on earth that was going to stop him from doing just that. "Please, just listen," she pleaded with him, hoped to talk him out of his deadly intentions. "I don't need you to do anything to him, he doesn't hit me anymore," she lied once again.

Lathom knew she was lying but refused to call her on it, at least he refused for the moment. "Okay," he said to her, "since it was in the past, I ain't gon' touch him," but he made a mental note to handle that nigga the first chance he got. He never liked that bougie muthafucka anyway.

"Thank you!" Cassie breathed out a grateful sigh of relief.

"No prob, Sis," his face was poker straight as he looked at her, did an excellent job of keeping her in the dark about his intentions with her soon to be deceased husband. "All I want to do is keep you happy."

Hearing his words had Cassie relaxing. When she had sipped from her glass and her body stopped shaking from fear of Lathom killing Charles, she proceeded to tell Lathom about the late-night meetings, the time she'd busted him fucking his assistant and how she'd made him fire her. She told him how she threatened to leave him if he hired another female assistant but left out the part about how Charles had choked her up for threatening to leave. "He hired a male after that."

"Mmmh, hmmm," Lathom said as he processed what she was saying while planning his next move.

But his plans were stopped in their tracks when Cassie unexpectedly blurted out, "Lathom, I have a son."

Lathom's fork fell from his hand and clattered on his plate. "What?" he said as his mind struggled to process her words. He went completely blank and just stared at her. "You got a what?"

"I have a son," she calmly repeated herself.

Thinking she was kidding, because she had to be, Lathom laughed before saying, "Cassie, stop playing."

Cassie's eyes watered. "Stop laughing." Her voice was serious and Lathom quickly realized she wasn't kidding.

"You're serious," he said more than asked, looked at her, shock showing on his face.

"Yes, I'm serious. I have a son, he's nineteen now." Then she went into detail, explaining the whole situation about her and Romel and that summer while Lathom sat there speechless. "Say something," Cassie said to Lathom when she had finished her story and he didn't say a word.

"Well, damn," he ran his hand over the top of his head. "I mean damn, Cass." He was quiet for another few minutes as his mind absorbed everything. Then he looked up at her and gave her a warm smile. "I guess I got me a nephew."

"No, you don't."

"Huh?" Lathom was genuinely confused. "If you have a son, I have a nephew."

"There's more," she told him and went on to tell him the rest. "...now, he's in jail for murder and he needs money for a good lawyer because it's a high profile case."

"Well, shit," he went right back into shock.

"Lathom, I know this is a lot to ask, but I need to borrow fifty thousand to help my son pay for a lawyer. I don't want my grandparents to find out that I'm talking to Romel after they made me promise not to, so I can't ask them. And if they can't know, neither can Jinx. Especially since Jinx is the one the one that wanted to kIll him and then paid him off to keep him away from me." She looked at her brother with sad eyes. "Charles is definitely out the question because I never even told him that I have a son and even if he knew, he would say no anyway. He's mean, selfish, greedy, and controlling when it comes to me, he wouldn't want to share me with a son."

"Cassie—" Lathom began, but she interrupted him, fearful that he would say no.

"Please, Lathom, I'll pay you back, I promise."

"Baby Sis, anything for you. You know I'll never tell you no and you never have to pay me back for shit I do for you. Besides, you caught me at a good time. I just sold two of my houses, so when you need it?"

"As soon as possible. And can it be cash and not a check, please? I don't want Charles to be able to trace that to me and start asking questions.

"Safe life all day. I don't play with the banks and I'm damn sure not going to put you in a bad space with Charles." He clenched his jaw as he thought about her bitch ass husband, but said nothing. He would deal with Mr. Baxton later. "But are you sure you want to do this? Are you sure you want to get involved after all these years of not being involved?"

"I'm his mom and I finally get the choice and the chance to be his mom," she said determinedly. "So, yes, I'm sure I want to do it. I have to do it. I need to do it."

"Well, I'm here for you when you need me," he assured her.

"Thanks, big brah. And oh yeah, there's this guy." Cassie's entire face blushed a bright red when she spoke.

"Oh, shit," Lathom said when he saw her blushing over a guy. "There's more. You on a roll today, sis."

"Let me finish," she groaned as embarrassment washed over her. "The guy you saw leaving my office today, I think I have a crush on him."

"Shit just keeps getting better," he smiled at her. "And what do you mean, you think?"

"I mean, I haven't really spent any time with him, but something about him gets to me."

"Sis, what's going on with you? That dude is a drug addict."

"No," she shook her head vehemently, "he's not. He was there trying to get his wife into the program."

"Damn, he's married, too? Come on, Cassie. This is not like you, baby girl."

"I know," she hung her head, trying to figure out what was going on with herself.

"Does he know how you feel?"

"Like I said, I never really spoke with him about anything other than his wife getting into the program. However, I did bump into him at that restaurant last night and he paid for my dinner."

"Hold up," Lathom held his hands up. "Tell me the whole story, I mean everything, Cass. What the hell, girl?"

Cassie explained what happened the first time they met and the time she'd seen him at the gas station. She explained exactly what happened at the restaurant the previous night and how he'd ended up paying for her food. She even told Lathom how her feelings were developing for him even though she didn't really know him and how she couldn't seem to control them.

"Sis, please be careful, and don't keep things like this away from me. You're going through some rough stuff right now, it makes sense that your feelings would be all over the place and that you would be looking for comfort wherever you can get it." He reached across the table and grabbed her hands, "You need someone you can talk to. I've never kept any secrets from you because we don't do secrets, so let's not start doing them now."

"I know. And thank you so much for everything. I feel so much better now." The relief was clearly evident in her voice.

"So, now what? What's your next move?"

"Well, I'm going to get myself together first. Then I'm going to write my son and hopefully meet him. I'll start with that and figure out everything else as I go."

"Slow down with that. You've been out of his life since he was born, so you might want to be open to the possibility that he may not want to meet you or have a relationship with you." Lathom knew the words he'd said were rough ones, but he needed her to be ready for the rough things as well as the easy.

"I know," she said seconds before she broke down crying.

"Don't cry, baby sis. I hate when you cry," he gripped her hands tighter. "Just try and understand and be aware of these possibilities. Try to go into this being open-minded and it'll be easier on you, okay?"

"I will," she gave him a half-smile as he handed her a napkin.

"Good, now fixed ya face." They spent another half hour talking before Lathom finally flagged a waiter down to bag up their leftovers. Then he paid the bill and dropped Cassie back off at the office. "Take it easy. I'll be by in a few days to check on you and to give you the money. And if you need me before then, call me. I'ma be real pissed if I find out you were going through and didn't hit me up. I love you, okay?"

"Okay," she said as she got out of his car. "Thanks, big brother, and I love you too."

Back in her office, Cassie was full and semi relieved. She was determined to get started on developing a relationship with her son. She was afraid he would reject her because he may have felt that she had rejected him. However, before she chickened out and allowed her mind to focus on anything else, she sat at her desk and composed her first letter to the child she had given birth to.

Dear RJ,

Hi. I'm Cassandra Lisa Edmonds Baxton, Cassie for short. I am thirty-two years old and I'm your mother. I'm sure you have a ton of questions about me, any of which you can feel free to ask me at any time. To maybe start answering some of them, I'll tell you about your father and me.

I met Romel when I was a young girl, twelve years old. I fell in love with your dad and as messed up as people thought it was, he fell in love with me. Things happened that shouldn't have happened and I became pregnant. I was thirteen when I had you and your father was twenty. You were immediately taken away from me, I had no say in that. I wanted to raise you myself, but the adults around me wouldn't let that be the case. I wish I could have played a part in raising you, but I wasn't allowed. I know that's not an excuse, but I'm sorry. Sincerely. Especially since I know what it's like to grow up without a mother. I wish you didn't have to experience that.

My mother died when I was just a little girl, it was a drug overdose that killed her. I don't know my father, I don't even know his name. My mother was an only child, so my grandparents decided to raise me along with a family friend named Jinx that I lovingly refer to as uncle.

Because I was so young when I was pregnant, Jinx was pissed and told Romel to never come around me again or he would kill him. My grandparents, being into the church the way they were, sent me down south to have you in secret. When you were born, the only thing I was allowed to do for you was name you.

My grandparents called Mrs. Rose and Mr. Eric, who came and picked you up so that they could raise you. They gave your father a lot of money to take care of you, to stay away from me, and to never speak about our baby. I never saw you again and I never saw your father again until recently when he sought me out to tell me about what was going on with you.

I often wonder about you, how you look, what you're doing. Once I got a little older, I built up the courage to go to Miss Bernadine's house and ask her if she had any information on you. Miss Bernadine told me it was best if I just left things alone, if I left them how they were. She told me that her son was dead because of my fast ass and that just like she didn't have a son, she wouldn't help me to have one either. Then she told to me stay the fuck away from her house. I couldn't tell anyone about that incident because I was told to forget about you.

After that, I never tried to find you again. I always thought of you and how it would have been if I could have kept you. But I was thirteen, too young to get my own house and too young to get a job. I wouldn't have been able to give you a good life at that age. I always loved you and hated the fact that I was kept away from you. Again, I'm sorry for not being a mother to you. I would like to stay in touch with you and I'm hoping that you feel the same. I'm willing via phone, mail, email, visits, whatever, it's all up to you if you allow this or not. I hope you do.

However, if you don't want to be bothered with me or to build a relationship with me, I understand. Either way, it goes and whatever you decide, I have the money and it's yours.

Love always, Cassie.

P.S. I would like to attend your trial. Please let me know how you feel about that.

When Cassie was done writing the letter to her son, she folded it, placed it in an envelope, and put it in her mail tray to be picked up and mailed later that day. Then she sat at her desk and cried like a baby for the life she missed out on with her son.

Chapter Eighteen

When she had composed herself and put a few things into better perspective, Cassie began making preparations for Sunday's dinner at her grandparents' house. She called to see what she needed to bring and to let her know Lathom would be joining them. Then it was time for her to touch bases with her husband as she hadn't heard from him at all that day. That was unusual behavior on his part because he was usually so controlling. That change from the norm confirmed her suspicions that her husband was cheating on her. Immediately, she called him but got no answer. Instead, she was sent directly to voicemail.

"Hey, bae. Just wanted to touch bases with you. Hope all is well. I know you're probably in a meeting but call me when you get a chance. Talk to you later. Love you, bye."

After she had taken care of all of those things, she began the task of setting up the last meeting she'd need to have with Mr. Martz and his wife. The first thing she did was take out her calendar and schedule the Martz's meeting for a week and a half out. Then she set her reminder for an hour prior to the meeting so that she could have everything set up for Tameka Martz to be checked into the facility. When she was done with those tasks, she sent out a group text to Lathom, Denise, Lakara, and Sam, reminding them of the office party at Club Noise.

Cassie: Hey, everybody, we can meet at my house before we hit the club. Charles is out of town so if everyone is there by eight, we should be good since the party starts at nine.

Sam: See you there.

Lathom: Cool.

Lakara: You already know I'm probably gon' be late, but I'll be there.

Lathom: Lakara, your ass better show up on time or you getting left.

Lakara: LOL!

Denise: I'll be on time so I'll see y'all there.

Lakara: Y'all gon' stop clowning me.

Cassie: Stop being late for everything.

Lakara: It takes time looking as good as I do. LOL!

Lathom: Then your ass better start getting dressed now, right there at work at your damn desk!

At that text, everyone responded with laugh emojis.

Lakara: Alright, shit! I'ma be on time, damn! See y'all at eight.

Lathom: Better be.

Denise: Thank you.

Sam: All y'all some clowns! LMAO!

When she was done playing on the phone with her friends, Cassie made her last call, the one she'd been contemplating making all day. She had to call Romel to check on RJ and to inform him that she had the money. However, when she dialed his number, just like with Charles, she was sent straight to voicemail, so she left a message.

"Hey, Romel, it's Cassie. I pretty much have the money; I'm just waiting for a few things to clear. Also, I wanted to know if you talked to RJ, I'd like to visit him. Oh, and please send me his information, I'd like to write him. Thank you, talk to you later. Bye."

Even though she had already written her son and had that letter sent off to the jailhouse address she'd looked up, she still wanted to confirm with Romel that she'd sent it to the right place. If the address she'd found was incorrect, she'd just write RJ another letter and send it to the right place.

Done with her work for the day, Cassie straightened her office, packed up her things and went home. Once there, she sat her briefcase on the table, took off her blazer and heels, and sat down to rest her aching feet. After a few minutes of pampering her feet, she grabbed a bottle of Grey Goose and poured herself a drink. Then she pulled out a notepad and a pen and she began to write RJ another letter just in case Romel told her she'd sent the first one to the wrong place.

When she had penned pretty much the same thing she'd written the first time, she folded that letter, placed it in an envelope and tucked it away in her briefcase. Writing that letter had worn Cassie out just as writing the first one had done, so she downed one more shot before heading to the bathroom to hit the shower. Stepping out of the shower, she threw on a t-shirt and panties with some socks. Charles hated it when she chilled like that, but his ass was gone and Cassie was enjoying herself.

Thinking about her husband made her realize just how much she didn't miss him. She liked the time she was having away from him, liked not having to worry about when he would become upset and possibly violent. She liked not having to be perfect all of the time and how she could do things like lie around the house in comfy clothes and stare at the ceiling if she wanted to. As much as she loved Charles, he was overwhelming, and this time apart was teaching her that life without him wasn't bad at all.

Her thoughts then switched to RJ and whether or not he would be receptive to meeting her. She contemplated telling Charles, but decided there was no reason to until she had firmly established a relationship with her son if that was what RJ wanted. Besides, Cassie knew her husband and she was fully aware that if she told him about RJ before she and RJ had a chance to really connect with one another, Charles would do all he could to put a stop to their relationship. He would go out of his way to ruin it before it even started.

"Why does he have to be like that?" she asked herself aloud. "Why can't he be more like..." she allowed her sentence to trail off because she honestly had no idea who the hell Charles could be more like. She just knew that although she loved her husband, she no longer liked him.

That's when Mr. Martz came into her mind. She liked him, a lot. A small smile spread across Cassie's face as she thought about how fine he was and how nice he seemed.

"And how the hell did he hook up with and marry somebody like Tameka?" Cassie asked. "That woman is rude as hell just not pleasant at all." Then something hit her. "Hell, how the hell did I end up with a cheating, alcoholic, abuser like Charles?"

Cassie knew the answer to her situation. In the beginning, Charles had been charming and sweet. She fell for that and then after they were married, he did the old bait and switch on her. As far as Mazoo was concerned, Cassie believed she had the answer to that question as well. She'd spent years working in her field and that had allowed Cassie to realize that drugs changed people. It changed their physical appearance, it changed their mind, their emotions, their actions. Tameka had probably been a very nice and pretty girl before the drugs took over. Now, however, she was something else entirely.

Just as she was dealing with Charles, Mazoo was dealing with Tameka. In a sense, Cassie felt really sorry for both of them. Mazoo had his monster and she had hers. She chuckled to herself as she wondered what life would have been like if Charles had married Tameka instead of her and if she had married Mazoo instead of Charles. An undercover alcoholic and a drug addict, and a businessman with a working woman.

"That might have been nice," she smiled as she began to drift off to sleep. "Real nice," she said with a smile.

The moment sleep had her, she began to dream about Mazoo.

It was pouring down raining when she got a text from Mazoo.

Mazoo: Hey, beautiful. Can you come out?

Cassie: Yes.

Mazoo: Come.

Cassie: Be there in 15 minutes.

Looking forward to spending time with him, Cassie got up, put on a pair of sweatpants, and hopped into her ride, headed to Mazoo's house. When she arrived, she got out and walked up on his porch in the storming rain. Her clothes and body were drenched, but she didn't care about any of that. All she cared about was Mazoo and it appeared that all he cared about was her as well because before she could even knock on his door, Mazoo opened it and yanked her inside.

He wasted no time kissing her, running his hands all over her wet body. He was in rare form, passionate and primitive, desperate as he stripped every article of clothing off her right there at the door. In the blink of an eye, Mazoo had Cassie standing before him completely naked, nipples hard, core drenched and throbbing. Watching her, desperate to fuck her, Mazoo removed his basketball shorts and boxers, Cassie almost drooled when she saw his manhood at its full potential and aimed at her.

She stepped close to him, gripped his chin in her hand firmly and brought his amazing lips to hers. The kiss she gave Mazoo had him moaning and reaching out his hand to tantalize her breasts. Cassie kept her mouth on his body, her lips leaving his and working her way to his neck and down his chest. She was desperate to taste him, every part of him. She continued her way down until she was face to face with his one eyed warrior.

She was quick to grab his dick, the full length of it, and when she had a firm grip on it, she snaked out her tongue and gave it the wettest and sloppiest kiss possible. Then she eased him out of her mouth and moved her orifice down while lifting his penis up. The next thing Mazoo knew, Cassie had taken his balls into her mouth while she jerked his thickness slowly. And to make sure she broke him all the way down, she was slurping, and licking, and sucking and humming on his balls so masterfully that he almost bust all over her face.

"Ohhhhh, shiiiiittt!" he moaned out loud and hard. "Fuck!" he grunted and gripped her head, holding her firmly in place as she exquisitely tortured him with her mouth. "Daaaammmnnn!" he moaned, almost groaned as his balls began to fill with his life-giving seed.

When Cassie knew Mazoo was close to skeeting, she released his balls and did a face dive onto his throbbing rod. Mazoo growled as Cassie devoured his dick so good, she had him moaning a long and high-pitched soprano note. Cassie kept up the torture by licking and sucking as if she was trying to suck the skin off it. Mazoo was so lost, so caught up in Cassie and what she as doing to him with her mouth that his hips began a slow, sensual and sexy back and forth rocking. He held her head tightly as he fucked her amazing mouth.

Suddenly, Cassie relaxed her jaw muscles and let his bone slide as deep inside as he could get. Then she did an amazing trick with her tongue while still massaging his balls. Seconds later, Mazoo couldn't take it anymore. His stomach tightened, his legs began to tremble, his moans grew louder.

"Aaahhhhhh fuuuuuccckkkkk!" he shouted as he exploded in her mouth, his body jerking and seizing while she kept right on sucking his dick and massaging his heavy balls. "Casssssssiiiieee!" he shot out his seed so hard, gripped her hair so tight that she was almost in pain, and still she sucked until she lured every last drop out of him.

When Mazoo finally caught his breath and could walk again, he gently helped Cassie up and lead her to his bedroom and to his bed. Once there, Mazoo flipped the script on her.

"Lie down," he ordered her and she wasted no time complying.

He eased himself down next to her and went for her neck, sucking, licking, kissing, biting while allowing his hands to roam all over her sexy body. Then his fingers reached her hot box and the heat emanating from it could have singed his skin. Cassie was super hot and ready for him.

With his dick quickly hardening again, Mazoo slid his fingers in and out of Cassie while tonguing her down.

"Oooohhh," she moaned as her hips rose and fell while she rode his fingers. "Yessss," she hissed as her hips gyrated on his hand. With his dick now harder than Chinese arithmetic, he spread Cassie's beautiful legs and moved his face between them. And before Cassie even recognized what was going on, Mazoo was fingering her and licking her so good that his tongue was practically vibrating on her clit. "Ohhhh fuuuccck!" Cassie screamed as an orgasm tore through her and made her entire body freeze.

Still, Mazoo kept licking and sucking her slit, lavishing her core with his tongue. He was eating her, pleasuring her, taking her body to new heights as she cried out her pleasure incoherently. Then she was on the verge, right there at the place of no return. When Mazoo felt Cassie's body begin to tremble, was when he removed his fingers and his mouth and slid into her with his sword. He began a hard and deep thrust, making love to her mind, her body, her soul. His dick felt so good in her, almost like he was writing his name in her; like he was taking ownership of her.

"Fuuuuccckkkk, Maaazooo!" she cried out, feeling as if she just couldn't take anymore. Just then, Mazoo upped his love making by putting his hand on her neck and applying just the right amount of pressure. That move brought Cassie the perfect mix of decadent pain and erotic pleasure which caused her to explode. "Maaazzzzooooooo!" she screamed his name as she came so hard that her stomach muscles burned and her toes curled.

Her orgasm set off an intense fire inside of Mazoo. Suddenly he released her neck and began to pump her pussy until he was on the verge of a massive eruption. "Cassie," he called out her named as he neared his breaking point, and a few pumps later, Mazoo was squirting his essence into her essence. "Cassie," he said again when she clenched her core muscles tight and had him gushing deep in her.

"Keep cumming," she moaned as Mazoo never stopped stroking her even after his climax had passed.

"I'll never stop cumming for you," he told her and had her instantly falling in love.

When they were well satisfied, completely satiated, Mazoo collapsed his body on top of Cassie. They were both breathing hard, trying to catch their breath. When their breathing slowed and their hearts stopped racing, Cassie began to lazily rub Mazoo's back while he kept absolutely still, enjoying the feel of still being inside of her.

"Hey," Cassie called out to him. "I need you to get up, I have to go to the bathroom."

The moment Mazoo raised his body from hers and pulled his manhood all the way out of Cassie, her eyes popped wide open, she woke completely up, and raced as fast as she could to the bathroom.

"I am not falling in love with a man because of my dreams," she told herself as she enjoyed the best pee of her life. Still, out of breath from the dream, she reached her hand up to feel her neck and was surprised to realize that she could still feel Mazoo's fingers there. She looked around the bathroom, making sure she was really where she was. That dream had been so real that she was struggling to believe she was really out of it. Mazoo was infiltrating every single part of her life and she knew exactly why it was happening. "I just cannot be falling in love with him," she repeated herself. However, she knew that deep down inside, she was doing just that. Falling in love with Mazoo Martz.

Chapter Nineteen

Charles was in a mood, he wanted sex and alcohol and drugs and he was losing his mind. He had fought the urge to screw Carrie again and that had damn near killed him. Deciding that his cravings were more than he could take, Charles gave in to his addictions and decided that he would go to one of his old spots just like old times. He knew he was making a big mistake but at that point his craving were greater than his desire to use his common sense.

Before he disappeared for a few hours like he planned to do, he made a few calls, the first of which was to his wife. She picked up on the second ring.

"Hey, baby," he said. "How are you?"

"I'm ok, just swamped with work," her voice seemed distant.

"I know the feeling, these meetings are long and boring," he lied. "Half of them are pissing matches and we get nowhere."

"How long do you think you'll be there?" she inquired.

"I'm not sure, but as soon as I find out I'll let you know." His answer was evasive. He had no idea how long he was going to be there. There was the funeral and the arraignment, and he planned to attend them both. He knew when the funeral was, but he had no idea when the arraignment would be held so there was no way he could give his wife a return date just yet. If it was far enough away, he could just return home and then come back to Atlanta. If it was soon, he would just stay where he was. Either way, he had every intention of being there for both.

"Oh, okay," she spoke cheerfully. If Charles didn't know any better, he would have sworn his wife was happy that he wasn't going to be home. However, he was sure he was mistaken because he had trained Cassie to love the ground he walked on, there was no way his wife wasn't missing him like crazy.

"You miss me?" he asked her out of the blue, wanting to test the ground she was walking on without him.

"Of course, I do," Cassie replied quickly and convincingly enough that Charles believed her.

"Good," he replied. "Now, I have to go, there's a presentation I have to get started on."

"Knock 'em dead, baby," she wished him well.

Charles, taken aback by her choice of words said, "Huh?"

Cassie repeated herself. "Knock 'em dead."

"When did you start saying that?" he asked. "I've never heard you use those words before and I'm not sure how I feel about you saying it," controlling Charles was trying to rule her from thousands of miles away. "You're my wife, Cassie. People expect the best from me and mine, so you can't go around saying things like that. A good luck would have been just fine." He paused, let his words sink into her head. "Now say good luck," he ordered her.

She was hesitant for a minute, waiting to see if he had anything else to say. She was well aware of how he hated when she spoke at the same time he spoke.

Her hesitation had him angry on top of jonesing. "I asked you to tell me good luck," he was infuriated. "So, tell me good luck." That abusive firmness was in his voice.

"Good luck," Cassie said without a single protest. She was so over Charles and his controlling issues.

"That's better," he could feel his body relax and the anger lessen, but now he was fiending even more. "Thank you, and I love you. I'll talk to you later, baby. Bye."

The moment they hung up, Charles made a mental note to investigate who Cassie was hanging around while he was gone. New language meant new people and Charles needed to vet those new people to see if they met his standards for anyone who would be in the company of his wife. When he was done setting that reminder in his phone, he stepped out of his ride and entered the building known as Sin City.

"This is going to be a long night," he said to himself as he stepped inside and prepared to indulge in some taboo pleasures.

Finally stepping out of his car after a long day of secretly following Charles around, Demetri said, "This is going to be a great night." He knew a few people, many of which were in both high and low places. That meant he was very familiar with where Charles was and with what he was about to get into. A big smile spread across his face. Whatever was about to go down in there, he would make sure he could be in it with Charles. And if not, he was going to make sure he got as much proof as he could just in case he may have a reason to use that proof later. Without any further delay, Demetri entered Sin City a few minutes after his boss.

Romel listened intently to his voicemail as Cassie told him she had the money and that she wanted RJ's address. Not yet ready to call her back because he had another phone call he was waiting on, he decided to respond with a text giving her all of their son's information.

Cassie: Thank you and okay.

The very minute Romel was done reading Cassie's text message, Kelly called asking if he could come over to her house because she needed to talk. Romel told her he would be there as soon as he could and ended that call. Before he could do anything else, his phone rang again, and it was just the call he had been waiting for.

"Yo," he spoke calmly, trying to hide his excitement.

"Yo, son, you busy?"

"Not at all. Whatchu got for me?"

"That information you were looking for on ya boy."

Romel immediately pulled his car over and said, "Speak."

"Ya boy is a busy man. I pulled up some background info on him and the shit I found is gonna blow your fucking mind."

"Ok. I'm listening."

"Charles was married to that woman we saw him at the airport with. Her name is Carrie. During that marriage they had a son together, but that marriage didn't last. They divorced some years ago. He also has a twin sister by the name of Kaleya, but everyone calls her Kelly. He's originally from here, his parents died in a car accident, his mom was a nurse and his father was a judge. After his divorce, he got deeper into politics, climbed that ladder fast as fuck, and moved to Buffalo. Then he—" The sound of his phone beeping interrupted his spiel and made him end the conversation. "Yo, I have to go, but there's more. I'll hit you later."

They both say," "One," before the call was disconnected.

"It's like, damn, this dude is a real shitbag," Romel said as he started driving again, heading toward Kelly's house. "Cassie said that muthafucka didn't have any kids, but that shit was a lie. What else is he lying about?" Romel kept talking to himself. "I definitely got to find out more," he said as he drifted back into traffic. "Shit, with everything that's going on and everything I know, should I even be going my ass to Kelly's house? His fucking twin sister?" he asked aloud as his mind went over the excess thoughts in his head.

There was so much happening in his life that he wasn't even sure he should keep dealing with Kelly and her bitch ass brother. He figured it might be better to leave well enough alone, but when he remembered just how much he hated Charles, Romel decided then and there that he was going to keep digging for info on Charles and keep fucking with Kelly just in case she had some info that his man couldn't get.

Pulling into the driveway of Kelly's house, he hit her up on her cell. "Yo, open the door."

Kelly came to the door almost immediately. Her eyes were swollen from crying and she looked exhausted. Romel stepped in, grabbed her hand, walked her into the living room, and sat them both on the couch.

She eagerly lay her head on his shoulder. "Thank you for coming."

Romel could clearly see that she was having a hard time dealing with Tee Tee's death. If he ever revealed to her that it was his son that killed her niece, she would be having an even harder time. Knowing when to keep his mouth shut, Romel said nothing. He just waited for her to speak first.

It felt so good being in Romel's arms. He made her feel safe and made her want to confide in him and tell him all about Tee Tee's transformation, about her and Charles' relationship, even about Charles and Carrie's relationship. She wanted his advice, wanted to unload everything she'd been holding in all of those years. However, she didn't want to run the man away with all of her family issues. Better to leave some things left unsaid, she thought, but needed to talk to somebody so bad that she decided to test the waters with Romel and hoped for the best.

"Romel?" she called out to him.

"Yeah?"

"We been kicking it for a while now and I'm feeling safe with you, like I can trust you."

"Okay," was all he said.

"There are so many things I want to tell you but I'm not sure. I don't want to be judged or looked at as crazy."

Romel rubbed her shoulders gently. "You know you can tell me anything. I know the death of your niece is hard on you and that you need to talk about it. I'm here to listen and to help you in any way I can without judging, okay?"

That was all Kelly needed to hear to get her to pour her heart out. Within seconds she was telling Romel everything. She told him everything about her brother and their beef, about how dirty he did his wife and son who was now her dead niece. And she would have told him much more if she had been interrupted by a phone call.

"Excuse me," she said to Romel as she grabbed her cell phone from the dresser. "Hello?"

"Change of plans," Carrie spoke as if she was in a rush. "The funeral will be the day after tomorrow at Rhymes Funeral Home at twelve-thirty. It's going to be a private affair, that way I can keep the media out."

"Oh, ok," was all Carrie could manage to say as her heart began to shatter in her chest. She was really about to bury her niece and she couldn't handle it. She listened to Carrie give her a few more details before their conversation ended and she hung up. Then she bawled her eyes out.

Romel didn't say a single word, he simply walked over to her and held her while she cried and cried.

"This shit is not fair!" she wailed. "How the fuck could someone kill my niece. She was the sweetest person I know." Then she cried some more. When she had finally gained some control of herself, she asked Romel, "Will you attend the services with me? I'd really like you to." Romel was immediately reluctant, but decided to agree. He had his reasons, reasons that might eventually hurt Kelly, but he would cross that bridge when he got to it.

After spending countless hours in Sin City, Charles was completely exhausted and inebriated. Demetri had been watching him from afar, seeing just the kind of things Charles did when he thought no was watching. Although he had participated in a little of the fun himself, he realized that Charles was a really depraved man. Demetri had watched his boss do some things that if anyone ever found out, his political career would be dead in the water.

Once the night was over, Demetri, still secretly following Charles, made sure he got safely back to his hotel room. When he watched Charles fail many times to get his keycard in the door, he walked up and did it for him. Then he proceeded to help his boss into the room where he undressed him and put him to bed.

He was about to go back to his room and sort out everything he had seen in Sin City, but seeing Charles naked with a semi-hard-on was sexy as fuck to him. That was why Demetri decided to take off his clothes, climb in bed with the intoxicated man he was in love with and suck his dick. Then, when Charles was good and fully hard and desperate for a fuck, Demetri climbed atop Charles and rode him until they were both cumming and screaming like crazy. When they were done, Demetri lay next to Charles, snuggled tightly in his arms, and fell soundly to sleep with him.

It was pretty late, but Carrie decided to call Charles anyway. She wanted to talk to him about the arrangements and about her possibly spending the night with him. Her heart was racing as she grabbed her phone. She knew it wasn't wise to keep sleeping with her ex-husband, especially since her feelings were now involved, but it felt so good with him. The sex had always been good with Charles. And she needed him, he was the only other person on earth that had lost the same child she had lost. Terrail wasn't just her child, he was Charles' child too.

"He's going to break your heart," she told herself. "He broke it before and he's going to do it again." She closed her eyes and let out a deep sigh. "Maybe he's changed. I mean, after all, he was doing his best to be faithful to his wife so that has to mean something. Maybe he's changed," she said it again. At first it had pissed her off to know that he was trying to be faithful to his wife when it seemed that he'd never tried to be faithful to her when they were married, but she chose to let the past stay where it was. Now his actions endeared her to him. It was a new day, Charles seemed like a new person, and she needed him. "It's settled," she told herself as she made up her mind to go for it. Carrie then dialed Charles' number. "The worst thing that could happen is him saying no."

But that wasn't the worst thing that could happen. In fact, the worst thing that could happen was exactly what happened when Charles' phone was answered.

"Mr. Charles Baxton's assistant speaking, how may I help you?"

Carrie was taken aback at the realization that a man was answering Charles' phone at that time of night.

Instantly, her mind went back to the day she'd caught him in the shower getting his dick sucked by that man. She was immediately disgusted. Some things never change, she thought as she snapped a very angry, "Where is Charles?"

"May I ask who's calling?" Demetri asked, a lazy, satisfied sound in his voice.

"It's none of your business who's calling. Where is he?" Carrie was infuriated. She was so angry that she was seeing red.

"I'm sorry, but he's asleep right now. Can I take a message?" came the voice that was irritating the hell out of her.

"No, you cannot take a message. What you can do is wake him!" she all but shouted.

"I'm very sorry, Ma'am, but Charles has had a very hard and very busy day. He's asleep right now and cannot take any phone calls. Unless it's an emergency, I cannot wake him. So, may I please take a message?" Demetri said as kindly as he could, but the woman was working on his last nerve.

Carrie sighed angrily. "You can tell him that the services are the day after tomorrow, twelve-thirty p.m. at Rhymes."

"Services? What services?"

"That's not your business, sweetie. You just do your damn job and relay the message to your fucking boss!" Carrie was so pissed and so hurt that she slammed the phone down and began to wail as if she was dying. "I knew Charles would never change," she cried hard. "How could I have been so damn stupid?" It seemed she hadn't been able to leave the past in the past the way she'd wanted to.

Demetri hung up the phone and rolled his eyes as he looked at the name on the caller ID. "Rude bitch," he whispered and looked over at a sleeping Charles.

It appeared his boss had more skeletons in his closet than he was aware of. That woman was a little too pissed at him answering Charles' phone so that meant he must have been fucking her too, or at least trying to. Demetri planned to put a stop to that immediately. It was bad enough he had to share Charles with his wife, there was no way in hell he was going to share him with a rude bitch too.

"I'll deal with her rude ass," he said. "I'll show her just who Charles really belongs to."

Demetri wondered if she was the woman whose house he'd followed Charles to earlier that day. And what services was she talking about? Funeral services? And if that was the case, whose funeral was it? Demetri shook his head at the confusion of it all. Charles had too much shit going on for just one man.

Now more exhausted than he'd been before, Demetri snuggled back up against Charles and went right back to sleep. Whatever that phone call was about, Demetri decided that he would get to the bottom of it tomorrow. For now, he wrapped himself in the arms of the man he loved and went straight to sleep.

Chapter Twenty

Cassie was getting ready to go into her grandparents' house when a text message came through. It was from Lathom,

Lathom: Hey, sis, I have the money for you. Do you want me to bring it to dinner with me?

Cassie: Yes, please. And thanks for everything.

After putting her phone back into her purse, she sighed deeply. She knew the dinner at her grandparents' house was going to be a long one, and then there was the meet with the crew later on. By the time she hit the sack that night she was going to be exhausted, but she'd signed up for all of it, so she had to suck it up and get a move on. Unable to delay going inside any longer, Cassie finally got out of her car and let herself in the house. The moment she stepped inside, she saw Poppa Edmonds sitting in his favorite recliner, chilling, watching a game.

She walked over to him and kissed him on the cheek. "Hey, Poppa, where's Momma?"

"In the kitchen cooking everything in sight."

Cassie laughed as she sat her purse and keys down on the couch, then she walked into the kitchen to see what Momma Edmonds needed help with. Her grandmother was in the process of finishing up her favorite meal, a meal that consisted of fried chicken, roast and potatoes, mustard greens, baked mac and cheese, baked beans, fried okra, dressing, potato salad, cheesecake, homemade cornbread, pound cake, homemade strawberry lemonade, and coconut tea.

Cassie kissed her on the cheek. "Hey, Momma."

"Don't hey me. Save your hay, you may be married to a mule one day."

Cassie laughed as she replied, "Hello, grandmother."

"That's better, now go wash your hands so you can help set the table."

Cassie did as she was told and returned to the kitchen to get the things she needed to set the table. Fifteen minutes later, the doorbell rang. It was Jinx and Lathom. The minute they stepped inside, Cassie hugged them both. Each man greeted the patriarch of the family before heading to the kitchen to do the same with the matriarch. Once they did that, they retreated back to the living room to watch the game with Poppa Edmonds, while the ladies finished bringing the food to the dining room and fixing the table.

"Dinner's ready!" Momma Edmonds yelled when everything was in place. Like starving animals, all three guys ran to the dining room in their rush to grub.

"I know y'all better go wash y'all's hands." All that could be heard was the sound of grumbling as they went to wash up before finally taking their seats.

Once everyone was seated, Poppa Edmonds lead the blessing over the food. Almost before he was done speaking, "Amen," was quickly said and plates were immediately filled with copious amounts of food. At first it was silent, no sound could be heard except a few moans and groans of pleasure at how good the food was.

When tastebuds were satisfied, Jinx asked, "Cassie, where's Charles?"

"Out of town on a business trip," she said between forkfuls of potato salad.

"That man has more late-night meetings and out-of-town business trips than the law allows," Jinx spoke disapprovingly.

"Exactly," Lathom agreed.

Cassie looked at Momma Edmonds with pleading eyes, she didn't want the conversation to go where she knew it was heading but she respected Jinx too much to say anything. Although he wasn't really her blood uncle, Jinx had been a part of that family since before Cassie was born. She grew up respecting him and his position in their family and she would never dare say anything out of pocket to him. She loved and revered him too much for that.

"Enough, Jinx," Momma Edmonds said, and both men immediately ended that conversation like it had never started and simply began another one.

For the better part of an hour, the four of them ate and talked and laughed. That dinner felt more like a holiday than a regular Sunday night get-together. Old times were discussed, current times were discussed. Future plans were discussed. It felt like family to Cassie and she realized at that moment that she wouldn't trade in times like that for anything in the world.

"I need you to take some of this food home, Cassie," Momma Edmonds said when dinner was over. "Ain't no way your Poppa and I can eat all of this," she gestured around the table at everything that was left.

"No problem," Cassie chimed in cheerfully. "That keeps me from having to cook for a few days."

As Cassie and Momma Edmonds completed the clean-up process and began to fix to-go plates for Jinx and Lathom to take home, she noticed that they had been in deep conversation all evening. As much as she wanted to know what they were discussing, she would never disrespect either of them by intruding on what appeared to be an important and private verbal exchange. Still, it concerned her a little.

Once everything was all tidied up, everyone began to say their goodbyes.

"I'll meet you at your house later," Lathom told Cassie as they were leaving.

"Ok," she replied. "We taking your ride?"

"I ain't riding in your car with a bunch of crazy girls," was his blunt reply. "So, yeah, we taking my ride." Then he stopped in mid stride, turned back to her and said, "Oh, yeah, I almost forgot."

"It's cool," Cassie responded. "Besides, I'd rather get it from you when you come by."

When Lathom and Cassie were done talking and Lathom had driven away, Momma Edmonds spoke. "You need to come by more, baby girl. I've been missing you lately and your grandfather ain't been doing too good. It looks like he's getting older and more tired nowadays."

"Really?" Cassie asked.

"Yeah. That's why I'd like to spend more time with you. We're getting up in age."

That sparked a conversation that was a lot deeper than Cassie had been expecting. But by the time they were done, Cassie promised to come by and spend more time with them. Before she left, she stopped in the living room and gave her grandfather a hug and since Jinx was still there talking with him, she gave Jinx a hug as well.

"I'll see you in a few days Poppa," she told him before she walked out of the door headed for home.

The moment Cassie hit the door of the house she shared with her husband, her phone started ringing.

"Hello?" she said when she saw that it was Lakara calling.

"Hey, girl," it was Denise's voice she heard speaking to her.

"Denise?" she asked as her eyes furrowed in confusion and she looked at her phone again to make sure it said Lakara.

"We're on conference," Lakara said with a laugh. "Both of us are on the line."

"Oh," Cassie began to laugh. "I thought I was trippin' for a second. But what's good?"

"The two of us are going to link up and then we will be by your house," Denise replied.

"Yeah, it doesn't make sense to take two cars to your house, so since we live close by one another we're going to take Lakara's car and leave it at your house when we ride with Lathom to the club."

"Ok, ladies. That's fine with me," she began to undress so that she could shower. "Can't wait to see ya'll."

"Same," Denise and Lakara spoke simultaneously before the call was ended.

Then her phone chimed twice, notifying her that a text had come through.

Lathom: I'm on the way.

Cassie: See you soon.

Standing there stark naked, Cassie decided to make one last call before she hopped in the shower. She was so excited to hang out with Sam, especially since she hadn't seen or heard from her in a while. However, Cassie realized it was going to be a little bit longer before she talked to Sam again because Sam didn't answer. She was just about to hang up when Sam's voicemail message came through loud and clear.

Deciding on a dime to leave a message, Cassie said, "I really was hoping to see you since I haven't seen you in a while. You promised you would come out with us, Sam. Please call me back." Cassie hung up more confused and more hurt than ever.

Sam had been missing in action a lot lately. She hardly ever called and no one had seen her in months. Cassie was distraught, wondering what the hell was up with her friend, and made a mental not to go and find Sam's ass if she didn't show up tonight. She would hunt her down and one way or another, she would get to the bottom of whatever was going on.

Hopping in the shower, she bathed herself in her favorite sensual scent and complimented that with the lotion and the perfume of the same scent when she exited the shower. She then dressed her body in a nice pair of deep blue jeans, a blouse, a blazer, and a nice pair of pumps. She applied her makeup sparingly as she didn't want a full beat face that night. When she approved of her looks, she added her jewelry, approved of that look, and was ready to go.

When Lathom arrived, he took one look at her and said, "You look good. Please tell me that you're ready and that you're not going to change a thing about what you're wearing."

"Yes, I'm ready. And I'm not changing a thing," she assured him.

"Good," he smiled at her. "The other's made it yet?"

"Lakara and Denise haven't, made it yet, but they're on the way and I haven't heard from Sam at all."

"You're surprised?" Lathom asked, looking at her as if he was disappointed in her naivete.

"That's our friend, don't be like that," she chastised him.

Lathom stared at her with a blank face. "That's your friend."

"You slept with her, Lathom," she shook her head, "she's your friend too."

"I can assure you there was no sleeping involved."

"Eww, TMI!" Cassie turned up her nose at him. The last thing she wanted was details about her brother and her friend's sexual adventures.

Lathom laughed at her before he said, "You sure nobody is in here but us?"

"Just us," she assured him.

That was when he handed her a backpack filled with the fifty thousand. "Here you go. It's all there." Then he pulled out a money counting machine from another bag. "Let's count this money real quick."

Fifteen minutes later, all the money was counted and Cassie had taken the money and hidden it. Just as she was walking back into the front room, Lathom was letting Lakara and Denise in. As usual, he was pouring on the charm and flirting with both ladies. Most of her friends had fallen for that charm and had slept with Lathom, so there was nothing unusual about him flirting with them.

"Everybody ready to go?" he asked.

"Yes," was the consensus.

"We're riding in the truck instead of my car," he informed them.

"No," said Denise.

"I'm not riding in the pussy wagon," Lakara told him.

He laughed at their protests. I'm not driving that truck tonight," he said, speaking of his Pearl Caddy Escalade with the wood grain interior and the plush velvet seats.

"What is it, the tricked-out Tahoe?" Cassie questioned him.

"Yes," he spoke as he ushered them out of the door while Cassie locked up.

"Well, at least that's a little more respectable," Lakara said and made them all laugh as they headed toward Lathom's truck.

Chapter Twenty-One

Throughout the drive, Lathom continually flirted with both ladies. Denise paid him no mind, while Lakara, in her freak ass zone, entertained him. By the time they made it to a new spot called Shai's Bar and Grill, Lathom had Lakara hot in the pants and in the mood to fuck. They had originally planned to spend the evening at Club Noise, but it was prebooked, so they settled for the next best thing. Lathom dropped the ladies off at the door of the club while he want and found a place to park. He made it back to the club just as the ladies were about to enter.

Inside, they quickly found the area that had been reserved for their coworkers. After entering the area, they greeted everyone then began to make their rounds and mingle. When that became too boring for them, Denise and Cassie snuck off and hit the bar moments before they hit the dance floor and tore it up. While they were partying like rock stars, Lathom grabbed Lakara by the waist, took her back to his truck and fucked her so good she almost passed out. When they were done, the two of them snuck back into the club like nothing happened, spotted Denise and Cassie on the dance floor having fun, and joined in.

Unbeknownst to Cassie, Mazoo was in the club and he was watching her like a hawk. He loved the way she moved to the music, the way she smiled, enjoyed herself. He really wanted to approach her, but he wasn't sure if the guy she with was her husband. He'd seen her go to lunch with him, had seen them interacting with one another, but still couldn't tell if they were married or not, especially since he'd just seen the guy creep out and back into the club with the other girl. So instead of approaching her, Mazoo chose to stay put and keep watching to see what he could learn about Cassie and that guy.

As the night went on, Cassie finally spotted Mr. Martz. The moment they made eye contact, the smiles they exchanged were genuine and instant.

Cassie played it cool as she told Denise they should find a table outside of the overcrowded V.I.P. section. They were tired from dancing and didn't want to go back to the V.I.P. section and stand there with nowhere to rest their bodies. Denise agreed and they quickly located a table near the action but not too close to it. Before their butts were fully on the chairs, the bartender came over with four drinks.

"These are for you and your guest," she looked at Cassie. "They're from the gentleman over there," she said as he pointed to Mr. Martz. Cassie looked over, smiled, and mouthed, "Thank you," as they accepted the drinks. Mazoo was quick to return her smile with one of his own.

"Damn! Y'all on y'all second drink already?" Lathom said as he approached the table.

"No, Mr. Martz bought us this round," Cassie filled him in as she pointed to Mazoo.

Lakara and Lathom both looked in the direction of where she was pointing. "Oh, that guy? He's actually a cool dude."

"Wait! You actually know him?" Cassie asked her eyes big and surprised.

"Not personally. I just heard a few good things about him."

"That's good," Cassie responded, looking in his direction and seeing that he was still watching her. In fact, Mazoo kept watching Cassie as the entire night went on, until it was time to leave.

"I had a good time," Cassie said as she thought about how good it felt to be away from her husband and out with friends who didn't try to control every move she made.

"Me too," Denise said with a yawn. "But this alcohol got my ass sleepy."

"Alcohol always makes your ass sleepy," Cassie chimed in with a laugh.

Laughing at her girls, Lakara added, "I had a great time." Her smile was big and wide and she was secretly hoping that Lathom would take her home and break her off again, but he didn't. Instead, he dropped everyone off at Cassie's house, waited for Lakara and Denise to get in their ride, and he left. He had other things he wanted to get into.

Carrie was up early the next morning having the hardest time of her life. She was pissed off, hurt, angry, and confused about every aspect of her life. She was a mental wreck and her emotions were all over the place. She was so hurt about losing Terrail while at the same time she was pissed about Charles. She knew he had to have been fucking his assistant, otherwise, why would the man have felt that it was okay to answer his phone that time of night? And why was the man even in the same place as Charles that time of night?

"Shit never changes," she said as tears of hurt and anger fell from her eyes and burned her cheeks. Then, in an emotional shift, she asked herself, "But what if nothing was going on and it really was an innocent situation? What if I'm jumping to conclusions because of my past relationship with him?" She stood from her bed and began to pace. "Didn't he tell me that his wife didn't want him with any more female assistants? And how do I know if his assistant was even physically with him?" She shook her head as she realized that the possibility of her being wrong was strong. "What if he was in a different location than Charles and just had his phone? What if Charles' calls had been transferred to his assistant's phone?

So many other scenarios began to run through Carrie's mind that she calmed down tremendously. Then, deciding on a dime that she would give him the benefit of the doubt, she went into the kitchen to eat something, and then she would call Charles and see what he would say about the situation.

Charles woke with an epic hangover. It was so bad that before he could even open his eyes, the room was spinning and his stomach felt as if it was going to revolt and spew out its contents at any moment. Jumping from the bed, he raced to the bathroom and threw up his guts for almost ten minutes. When his stomach had finally calmed down, he washed his face, brushed his teeth, stepped into the shower, and washed the previous nights' sins off of him. Feeling much better than he had forty minutes ago, he stepped his naked body back into the bedroom and was startled to see Demetri there.

"What the fuck, Demetri?" he snapped. "How the hell did you get in here?"

"I helped you in here last night," Demetri smiled at him.

"What?" Charles' brows furrowed together in complete confusion.

There was no way Demetri was going to tell him anything about practically stalking him, so he went with a partial truth. "Apparently you drove home very drunk last night and was outside of your door struggling to get that keycard in the slot so you could get in. I had to open the door for you, practically drag you in here, and then get you into bed."

"Oh," Charles said as he sat on the bed, getting the sheets wet. He had no memory of any of that. In fact, Charles had been so high and inebriated that he didn't even remember how he'd gotten back to the hotel. But he remembered Sin City and a lot of the things he'd indulged in while he was there. "Fuck!" he said as he lay back on the bed, disappointed that he'd started those old habits again. "Fuck!" he said again as disgust ran through him.

"You okay?" Demetri asked when he saw how distraught he was.

"No," he was honest. "But I will be."

"You feel like talking about it?" Demetri hoped Charles was willing to tell him what the hell he was doing in Atlanta and what was going on with him but was highly disappointed with the next words that came out of Charles' mouth.

"We don't do personal, Demetri," he reminded his assistant.

"Each time we fuck, we're doing personal, Charles." His feelings were hurt, but there was no way he would tell Charles that.

"That's physically personal. We do that. We don't do mental or emotional personal. So, no I don't want to talk about it." Charles gave Demitiri a look that said drop it or else.

As much as Demetri didn't want to drop it, he did. He didn't want to get fired and lose the access he had to Charles, so he knew when to play Chess and when to play Checkers. This was a Chess moment and he needed to make a Chess move. He simply moved on to the next topic as if he and Charles had never even had that hurtful conversation. "I took the liberty of ordering you some soup for breakfast. It should be here any minute now. You received a phone call last night from a Carrie," he said as he handed Charles his cell phone. "She said to tell you that the services have been changed to tomorrow at Rhymes at twelve-thirty in the afternoon."

"Okay," he shook his head up and down, looking at the phone and absorbing the information from Carrie. "And thanks for ordering the soup. I really need it." Then he dropped his phone on the bed and offered his assistant a semi-smile.

Almost as if room service had heard him, there was a knock on the door and his soup was delivered. Demetri set it up on the table for him and Charles sat to eat it.

"That soup is hot, you don't think you need to put some clothes on before you eat it and possibly spill some of it on you?"

"I'm a grown ass man, I can eat hot soup without spilling it," Charles snapped.

"Your hands are shaking," Demetri pointed out and pissed Charles off even more.

Realizing that he was being an asshole for no reason, he looked to his assistant and said, "I'm sorry. I'm just not feeling my best. I need a few minutes to get my bearings, relax my mind and body, and I'll be okay. I'm just overloaded right now." Then he took that first sip of soup and his body shook as it thanked him for it. The heat hit his stomach and immediately began to settle it. After the first few bites, he no longer felt nauseated. "This is good," he replied as he gulped down the rest of it so fast that he was surprised when he put his spoon in the bowl and it made a tinkling sound. There was nothing there but the white bottom of that bowl. "Well, fuck," he said with a surprised laugh.

"Would you like me to order more?" Demetri volunteered.

"Yes," he told him. "And while I'm waiting for the soup, I'll lie down for a few more minutes and relax my body."

Demetri walked over to the phone, ordered another bowl, and walked into the room where he found Charles lying on the edge of the bed, eyes closed, feet hanging over and on the floor. Without saying a word, he walked to his boss, kneeled in front of him, spread his legs, and said. "I know how to relax you." Then he proceeded to take Charles into his mouth.

"Aaaaahhhh," Charles let out a deep, long, and satisfied sigh. Demetri did indeed know how to relax him.

Just when Demetri had taken Charles to the edge and had him gripping the sheets, almost ripping them, his phone began to ring. "Fuck," he said both in irritation and in pleasure. Turning his head toward the device, he looked at his screen and saw that it was Carrie. He almost sent her to voicemail so he could keep enjoying Demetri's superb dick-sucking skills, but he knew the call had to be important and he had to take it. Holding up a hand so that Demetri could stop, Charles answered the call. "Hello?"

"Good morning, Charles" Carrie spoke in a voice that sounded like she had been crying.

"Good morning, Carrie," he replied. "Are you okay?"

"Not really," she said. "But I'll manage." There was silence on the line for a brief moment before Carrie said, "I have an itemization of the cost of the services. I've emailed it to you so we can go over everything right now if you have time."

"Okay," he said as he opened his email and began to peruse the document.

Because he was so focused on the email and the conversation with Carrie about costs, Charles didn't see when Demetri dropped the hotel robe he had been wearing. And by the time Demetri had climbed atop Charles, quickly straddled him, and mounted him, it was too late for him to say anything because it would all come out as one long pleasure-filled moan. So, Charles proceeded to fuck his assistant while he went over funeral arrangements with his ex-wife.

For five good minutes, Charles was doing fine and he was able to keep the conversation with Carrie going without her knowing a thing. Until his mind gave all the way in to Demetri and the magic he was working on him.

"Do you hear me, Charles?" Carrie asked when he didn't respond to her question.

Charles hadn't heard a word Carrie had said, he was too busy fighting like hell not to moan, too busy doing his best not to let Carrie know that he was in the middle the best fuck of his life.

"Mmm, hmm," he moaned and responded to her simultaneously.

For the briefest of seconds Carrie paused and Charles heard papers being shifted around. "And you're okay with the blue casket instead of the black one?"

"Mmm, hmm," he replied again, biting his tongue to keep from groaning in extreme ecstasy as he looked at Dimitri.

"Okay," Carrie went on. "Now that we've settled that, do you mind if I come over in a few minutes just to have some company for a little while?"

"Mmmm," Charles grunted when Demetri made a move that should have been illegal. "Uhhm," he spoke breathlessly, trying to think, trying to stop his brain from frying.

"Charles?" Carrie called out to him.

"Ungghh," Charles grunted once more. There were no words he could give her as a spectacular orgasm ripped through him and shredded him to pieces. Before he could cry out and let Carrie know what was going on, he hung up in her face and tossed the phone across the bed. Then, "Fuuucckkk!" he shouted as he gripped Demirti and fucked him hard through one of the best orgasms of his life.

Carrie was pissed. She was so pissed than she screamed and scattered every one of those papers off of the table and onto the floor beneath her. She had been right, absofuckinglutely right. Charles was fucking his assistant. "Do you think I'm fucking stupid?" she screeched and wailed. Huh?" she screamed as she paced and stalked her living room. Her heart was pounding so hard it felt as if it would leap out of her chest. "I hate you, you son of a bitch!" she shouted and cried. "I fucking hate you! I hate that I ever let you touch me again!"

Charles may have thought Carrie had no idea what was going on, but from the first moan, she knew. And she hated him for doing it. Not only for doing it, but for doing it while she was on the phone. Her heart broke in her chest, just broke and disintegrated as she collapsed on the floor and bawled like a newborn.

The sounds the assistant was making were running through her head on repeat, driving her into an insanely jealous rage. Whatever Charles had been doing to that man had him making sounds of absolute ecstasy even though Charles had been doing his best to be as quiet as possible. But she'd heard the assistant and she'd heard Charles' grunts and groans. She knew those sounds, knew what his voice sounded like when he was fucking. So, Carrie lay on that floor and cried her eyes and heart out for the man she still loved and really hated at the same time.

"Feel better?" Demetri asked Charles when he stepped out of the shower for the second time that day.

"I really do," Charles said as he went to the closet and grabbed the guest's robe. That was all he planned on wearing for the day. "Still a little shaky, but better," he confessed.

"You just need a little more sleep and you should be fine," Demetri told him. "So, I'll just go back to my room and let you get your rest."

"Yeah," Charles spoke absentmindedly, his mind somewhere else as he made his way back to that bed, got in and covered himself.

"Don't forget there's more soup in there when you wake up. Call me if you need me," Demetri said, and with no more words, he left. Keying his way into his own room, a huge, malicious smile spread wide and deep across his face. "Serves that bitch right," he said to himself as he stepped into his room and closed the door behind him.

Even if Charles was unaware of it, Demetri knew that rude ass Carrie woman knew what was going down in that hotel room between him and Charles. His full intention when he saw her name come up on Charles' phone was for her to know. That's why he'd done what he did to Charles, and that's why he'd gone out of his way to make it feel as good as it did.

Charles had been so focused on her not hearing him that he hadn't even heard Demetri's soft moans of pleasure. Demetri made sure Carrie heard them though, and he knew he'd been successful when he heard her shuffling and ripping up that paper. She was pissed and he'd been happy.

"The bitch was rude to me last night, so I returned the favor."

Only his rudeness felt really good, especially when he'd served it to Carrie so fucking cold.

Chapter Twenty-Two

Romel slipped out of Kelly's apartment sometime in the middle of the night and went home. He'd spent the better part of the evening comforting her to the best of his ability and he was exhausted. He needed to get home and get some rest, especially since she'd asked him to attend the funeral of the girl his son had killed.

Keeping that information from Kelly was exhausting and he wondered how long he could keep it up before he grew too tired and had to leave her alone altogether. He didn't know, but he sure as hell had to think of something before she found out that his son was responsible for her niece's death. As a new level of tired rushed through him, he yawned loud and hard just before he drifted off into a deep sleep.

Kelly woke bright and early and looked around, Romel was nowhere to be found. Right then and there she grabbed her phone and quickly dialed his number.

"Yo," he spoke in a semi-groggy voice.

"You still coming, right?" There was fear and sadness in her voice.

"Yeah," he promised, hearing how worried she was. "I'm jumping in the shower right now. I'll be there soon as I get done."

She let out a deep sigh of relief. "Ok, see you soon." Feeling much better, she hung up the phone and prepared for Tee Tee's funeral.

After showering and getting dressed, Kelly looked at her reflection in the mirror. Her long hair that flowed midway down her back, her lightly done make-up, and her pure white dress all came together to make her look like an innocent angel. She felt anything but. Her eyes were swollen and puffy from crying for days and there was a scowl on her pretty face.

She was a little irritated that Carrie had called her the previous afternoon to inform her that the plans they'd previously had for the funeral had been changed. Everyone was supposed to wear blue to match the blue casket and the blue suit she had chosen, but out of the clear blue sky Carrie decided that she wanted to change things up. So Kelly decided to change things up as well.

She was tired of all of the changing emotions and decided then and there that she was going to do what the hell she knew Tee Tee would have wanted her to do. Carrie could stay indecisive, but Kelly was done with that.

Charles was sitting on the side of his hotel bed fully dressed in a navy-blue suit, a baby blue shirt, and black Stacy Adams. He was still reeling from his night at Sin City, but overall, he was much better. Looking at the watch on his arm, he saw that the time was now eleven a.m. There was only a little time left before he needed to get going and he needed to have a serious talk with Demetri before he left. Locating his phone, he called his assistant. Less than two minutes had gone by from the time Charles had called his employee until the time the knock came on the door of his suite.

"Sit down," he told Demetri the minute he stepped into the room and Charles had closed the door behind him. He immediately did what Charles told him to. "I know I told you that I wanted to keep personal, personal, but right now I really need your support."

"Okay," Demetri said as his itchy ears started ringing.

"What I'm about to tell you, you cannot repeat to anyone, Demetri, do you understand me?"

"Have I ever betrayed you in any other way?" he asked.

"No," Charles admitted.

"Then I'm not about to start betraying you now."

Believing what Demetri told him, Charles let out a deep sigh and then told the man he was having a hot affair with every detail of everything about what was going on with his son. "I have a son," he began, and left nothing out. Up to that point, he'd only spoken to Carrie about things and that was why he'd gone to Sin City. He'd needed an outlet and that seemed the best place for him to let some things out. That hadn't been a wise decision, though, because now he was craving the things he'd done in Sin City like an addict craved his addiction. Shit had become too real and Charles wanted someone to share some of that burden with.

"Well, okay," Demetri replied when Charles was done. He'd wanted to be all up in Charles' business but he had no idea that Charles' business was as deep and as crazy as it was. Still, he was going to support the man because he loved him. "What do you need me to do?"

"I need you to come to the funeral with me. I need you to be my rock right now. So, go get changed and meet me back here in half an hour."

"Okay," Demetri said as he shook his head yes. "I've got you."

Thirty minutes later, Charles called Demetri and said, "Let's get going."

Two minutes after that, Demetri stepped into Charles' hotel room ready to go. Taking one look at Charles, he fully understood why the man needed him. The man was a clear wreck and doing a terrible job of hiding it. Other people may not have been able to see it, but as someone that had seen Charles in the most intimate of settings, Demetri could see it just fine.

Walking up to his lover, he fixed Charles' tie and smoothed down his suit jacket. "Now we can go," Demetri said, and they left the hotel room to go and pay their last respects to Charles' son.

Romel arrived at Kelly's house fully prepared to support her through her difficult time. He was wearing funeral black with a pair of black Mauri's.

"You ready to do this?" he asked Kelly the moment she opened the door.

She didn't say a word, she just stepped outside of her home, locked the door, and headed to bury her niece.

The entire ride to the funeral, Romel thought it was pretty fucked up that the father of the man that had murdered that child was going to be at that child's funeral, but there was no way in hell he was going to back out of it now. Besides, escorting and supporting Kelly wasn't the only reason Romel wanted to be there. He had ulterior motives. And Kelly was the perfect excuse to exercise those motives. So he rode with her to that funeral in complete silence and hoped for the best.

***

Demetri and Charles pulled up to the funeral home, parked, and exited the car. Together they walked inside where there weren't too many people. There were a few faces Charles recognized from his former life with Carrie, those that already knew who he was and what role he played in Terrail's life. That surprised Charles because it was only supposed to be family and a few of Terrail's closest friends in attendance. Still, Charles greeted everyone, spoke to everyone, and proceeded to the casket.

Carrie was there sobbing uncontrollably. Charles was just about to reach for her to comfort her when all of a sudden, he noticed his son in that casket dressed like the daughter he never wanted. He was immediately taken aback to see Tee Tee instead of Terrail like he and Carrie had agreed. Instead of wearing a blue suit and nice shoes, his son was wearing a pure white dress, a bob that was obviously a wig, pink nails, female jewelry, and a fully made-up face. Carrie had told him one thing and had done something else completely. Charles was thoroughly disgusted and hurt and a look of sheer devastation covered his face.

Peering into the casket, Demetri looked to see what had devastated his man and was just as surprised to see a girl in that casket instead of Charles' son. Offering the support Charles had asked him for, Demetri began to rub Charles back. "It's okay," he said to Charles. "That's your child and you love him, remember that."

Hearing a male voice, Carrie looked up through her tears to see Charles and another man standing there looking down at her child. Charles had on the navy-blue suit with the light blue shirt he'd told her he would wear. The man with him had on a light blue suit and a dark blue shirt. Because they were matching, Carrie quickly surmised that the man Charles was with had to be his assistant and lover.

Seeing the hurt on Carrie's face when she looked up at him, Charles assumed it was because of their son. Putting his own hurt and anger aside, he reached for his ex-wife, the mother of his child, in his attempt to comfort her.

"Don't touch me!" she screamed at him loud enough to wake the dead, loud enough to wake Terrail.

Everyone in that funeral home stopped and looked around to see what the commotion was about. That was Demetri's cue to go to his seat. As much as he wanted to grab Charles and pull him away from that psycho, he didn't want to draw attention to them and give people any clue what their relationship was. If that were to happen, he was going to let Carrie do it and piss Charles off enough to make him never want to see her again. His mission would be accomplished and he would have Charles back to himself and Cassie again until he could get rid of Cassie too.

"What?" he was surprised at her reaction to him.

"I said don't touch me!" she shouted at him again, glared at him with furious eyes, and moved her body out of his reach.

Charles knew then that she wasn't just crying about their son. There was something else, something deeper going on with her, but he didn't know what it was.

"What's wrong with you?' he asked, genuine concern crossing his face.

"You are what's wrong with me!" she hissed at him before she began to sob hard and move farther away from him.

"Carrie," he spoke gently, soothingly, "Let's not make a scene," he told her as they both stood there grieving the loss of their son.

At that exact moment, in walked Kelly and Romel. Kelly, in a daze, spoke to no one as she made a beeline for the casket. The moment had come for her to see her niece one last time before she was buried. Her heart raced and she felt as if she would pass out. Tee Tee was her favorite person in the world and someone had ever so brutally destroyed the bond she'd shared with her. Drawing closer to the casket, Kelly breathed deeply, clenched her fists, and braced herself. Once there however, before she could even get a look at her niece, her gaze shifted to the man standing in front of her niece. Charles! It was her own fucking twin brother and she was instantly disgusted and enraged.

Kelly hadn't laid eyes on that sadistic monster in years and wasn't happy about doing it now. He'd stolen money from her, her inheritance, and then he'd casually walked out of her life when he realized she was pissed. Had it not been for her trust fund, Kelly would have been broke and destitute. But what he'd done to her was nothing compared to how he'd abandoned his own child. She was contemplating how she would confront him later about not being there for Tee Tee and then showing up at the last minute, when she noticed the tension between Carrie and Charles. Immediately, she sided with Carrie without even knowing what was going on. Somehow, she knew her brother had done something and she wanted to whip his ass right where he stood. But she was there for her niece and not her niece's evil father. Turning her focus away from her brother, Kelly turned her eyes toward her beloved Tee Tee and lost it.

Kelly's sobs were loud and harsh and just as gut-wrenching as Carrie's. Reaching out to comfort his sister, Charles began to rub her back and just as Carrie had done, Kelly snatched away from him as well.

"Get your damn hands off of me!" she said in a hushed but firm and angry tone.

Charles slowly removed his hands from her and placed them in his pockets. The tension was so thick at the casket that it could be cut with a knife. It appeared that everyone at the casket had a problem with Charles, to keep things from becoming any worse, Charles quietly excused himself and went to sit next to Demetri instead of on the front row next to Carrie's seat.

I hate him so fucking much! Carrie thought.

This is all his fault, Kelly thought.

I hate this dude, Romel thought, I should kill that mothafucka right now.

Everybody hated Charles, everybody except Demetri.

Finally going to her own seat, Carrie glanced at Charles and the man she assumed was his assistant and rolled her eyes. She wanted to claw his eyes out for bringing his lover to his son's funeral after the way he had fucked her just two days ago. She loved Terrail though, and would never disrespect his funeral that way. So, instead of focusing on her anger, she focused her attention on her son and the preacher that had just entered the room and asked for everyone to take their seats.

Chapter Twenty-Three

Back in buffalo, Mazoo woke up in a hotel room to the sound of his alarm beeping. Tired as hell, he grabbed his phone and shut the alarm off. He was pissed and rightfully so. He'd returned home from the club the night before only to find his wife that had been missing for three days in bed with her face buried between some chick's legs. There was liquor, pills, and coke on the nightstand, and those two were going at each other like they were in love.

"Tameka, what the fuck is you doing?" he yelled at her.

She was so damn high that all she did was stop, turn around, and say, "Hey, baby. Come have some fun, she's for both of us." Then she turned to the woman she was pleasing and said, "Say hi, Sam," before she buried her face right back in Sam's pussy.

"Hi," Sam said with a giggle that quickly turned into a long and intense moan.

Mazoo was so disgusted that he told his wife she had until the next day to be out of his house. He then turned, left, and headed to a hotel for the night.

Now, he lay there knowing that Tameka was beyond help. She probably didn't want any help. Reflecting on past conversations with Tameka, he wondered how the hell he could have missed the fact that his wife didn't want any help or wasn't ready for help. Tameka was happy on drugs and clearly wanted to stay that way. The more Mazoo realized that, the more upset and hurt he became.

"Fuck!" he said as wished he was in any other situation than the one he was currently in. "Why couldn't my wife be more like..." his words trailed off when he realized he was about to say Cassie. He didn't even know her, he'd only seen her a few times and interacted with her even less than that. Yet she had made an impression on him that he couldn't seem to shake. He was so enamored with her that he was having a hard time giving a damn that she was married. He wanted her, wanted her so bad at that moment that his dick shot up hard and long. "Fuck!" he said again as it began to throb at just the thought of her.

Closing his eyes, Mazoo gripped his shaft and began a slow stroke to ease the tension. The minute his eyes closed, the erotic fantasy began.

It was a warm summer day when he decided to call her.

"Hey, beautiful," he said the second he heard her voice. "How are you?"

"Fine, and you?" her voice was sexy, erotica to his ears.

"I'm ok, just thinking of you. Can I see you?"

"Yes, when?" She was as anxious as he was.

"Maybe around noon."

"That's fine."

"Great, I'll pick you up then."

"Perfect."

Wasting no time getting to Cassie, Mazoo hit the shower, then threw on a pair of black Nike joggers with a black matching t-shirt. A pair of crisp new white Nike socks with black Nike slide-ins. He sprayed himself with Gucci Guilty and as he was already wearing a gold pinky ring, he added a chain on which hung a cross filled with diamonds and a nice pair of diamond earrings.

Pulling up to Cassie's house, Mazoo called her.

"Hello?" she said in that voice that drove him crazy.

"I'm outside."

The vision in his head of Cassie exiting her house had Mazoo gripping his dick tighter, stroking himself harder. "Mmmm," he groaned as he spread his legs wide while he pleasured himself at just the thoughts of her. "Cassie," he called her name when his fantasy became more interesting.

Cassie emerged from her house wearing a short, fire, blonde bob, a black fitted t-shirt with rhinestones that said, 'Then who?', a big, oversized tutu, and a pair of black Converse sneakers with rhinestones on them. She had a small pair of diamond earrings in her ear and a silver chain with a diamond letter C pendant on it. Her makeup was feather-light, and she smelled amazing.

Mazoo, being the perfect gentleman, got out of his car and opened the passenger door for her. Once she was safely tucked inside, he got back in and headed straight to Glen Falls. When they arrived, they walked and talked and enjoyed the waterfall. It was a simple date with more mental connecting than anything else.

As Cassie moved, Mazoo couldn't help but to stare at her. To him, she possessed the sexiness of a stripper but the classiness of a professional woman. She was kind of classy and kind of hood. The more they maneuvered and talked, he found that he loved how extra she was and the way she seemed to command respect and attention. As Cassie stood close to the rail, just staring at the beauty of the scenery, Mazoo stood behind her with his arms around her neck, both of them lost in their own thoughts.

Drawn to Cassie's perfume, he couldn't help it when he lowered his mouth to her neck and snuggled his nose in the curve of it. He then began to plant soft kisses there, turning her on like crazy. Wanting more of him, she turned to face him and placed her arms around his neck. It wasn't long before they engaged in a passionate kiss.

Mazoo, aroused to a painful degree, broke away from the kiss and walked over to a nearby bench. Cassie stared at him as he motioned for her to come and sit on his lap. She walked over to him seductively, knowing exactly what time it was. The moment she stood in front of him, Mazoo turned her around, lifted her huge skirt and pulled her onto his lap and directly down onto his fully erect penis. She straddled him and dry humped him through his pants as he fought like hell to slide his manhood out of them. When he was fully free, Cassie guided herself all the way down on him and let out the slightest moans as pleasure inundated her.

"Mmmm," Mazoo moaned softly as she took him deep inside of her.

Slowly, Cassie began to move up and down, back and forth, round and round. Mazoo could feel her pussy heating up around his dick, Cassie could feel him swelling and thickening inside of her.

"Fuck me," she whispered when she leaned her back onto his chest while gyrating her hips.

Doing as she asked of him, Mazoo gripped her hips and began to raise and lower his hips from the bench just slightly, just in time enough to meet her every time she sank down onto him. People walked by, closer and closer to them. Each time, Cassie pulled out her phone, held it up, took pictures of them. The faces they were making showed the lust and the pleasure they were feeling, while the snapping sound of her phone made passersby think they were simply a couple taking sweet pictures.

"Fuuuuck meeee," Cassie's voice was now thick and lazy and husky and sexy as fuck.

"Fuck, baby," Mazoo said as he pressed her hips into him and held her still while he plunged deep into her hot, wet abyss.

"Aaahhhh," Cassie moaned when Mazoo stroked her so good her blood began to heat and boil out of control.

She rode him and he pumped her. Their adrenaline was up, their breath was becoming more and more shallow. They were close, closer, ready to bust. "I'm cummin', baby," Cassie said after a few long, hard, and discrete strokes.

"I'm cuimmin' with you," Mazoo told her.

They were both at a point of no return.

"Oh, shit!" she mewled as she squeezed her pelvic muscles together and released all over Mazoo's lap.

"Fuuuuuuuccckk!" Mazoo growled long and deep the moment he felt Cassie's juices drench him. "Fuuuccck!" he said again as his balls tightened and released, tightened and released and his seed shot out of him and plowed straight into Cassie's inner chamber.

"Fuuuccckkk!" he yelled when his fantasy ended and his dick erupted so hard that he shot cum all over his chest, almost reaching up to his neck. The fantasy had felt so real that he erupted rope after thick rope all over himself, his breathing so hard and so deep he almost lost consciousness. He'd never cum that hard from a dream or a fantasy or a *fuck* in his life. "What the hell is she doing to me?" he questioned as the last of him shot forth with power. "Fuck, Cassie, baby!" he moaned again as his orgasm hit him hard like a punch to the stomach. When he was finally done spewing all over himself and all over those hotel sheets, he sighed deeply, feeling relaxed and almost drugged. Then he fell into a deep coma-like sleep that lasted for another two full hours.

When he woke, the first thing he did was hit the shower to try and clear his mind as he had a lot to deal with that day. The bullshit back at home with Tameka, the meeting.

"Oh, shit!" he said when he remembered, "the meeting for Tameka!"

Pissed that he had to leave the hotel earlier than he was ready to, Mazoo checked out and headed home. Once there, he rushed in the house looking for his wife. It was really quite in his home except for the sound of a television playing in the bedroom. Bracing himself for whatever he may have found on the other side of that door, Mazoo opened it only to find a naked Tameka in a drunken and high stupor from the night before. Her company, thank God, was gone.

"Tameka?" Mazoo called her name to wake her, not even trying to hide the disgust in his voice. When she didn't respond, he called her name once more while he shook her body none too gently.

"Why are you bothering me, Mazoo? What the hell do you want?" she snapped at him. "And cut that damn light off with your loud ass."

"Get up and get it together," he snapped right back at her. "We got a meeting at the facility today."

"I'm not going anywhere," she told him as she turned over. Then, "Leave me the fuck alone and go see your bitch by yourself."

Mazoo looked at her, fury and annoyance all over his face. "Don't worry Tameka, I'm going to do just that." Then he changed his clothes, walked out of his house, and headed straight to the facility to meet with Cassie, the woman that had him cumming hard as hell just a few short hours ago.

Cassie jumped up late. After that long night of partying with everyone, she'd slept through her alarm and needed to get out of her house as fast as she could.

"Damnit!" She raced to her shower, practically tripping all over herself.

She remembered the last intake meeting she had scheduled with Mr. and Mrs. Martz. She wanted to smile because she would be seeing Mazoo, but her face automatically went to a frown when she remembered that Tameka would be with him. Cassie was feeling tired today and wasn't up for the bullshit antics of a drug addict that didn't want to be rehabilitated.

Quickly deciding on a pair of dark brown slacks, a tan and dark brown cami, tan and brown Gucci loafers, and a matching headband and bag, she was dressed for her day. A gold watch, tiny hoop earrings, and her favorite perfume, My Life by Mary J, added that little flair to her attire that she loved. In no time flat, she hit the door and was racing toward her destination of Tim Hortons to grab her usual XL coffee double, double with a shot of hazelnut, her strawberry cream cheese bagel, and the usual for the office.

It was only minutes later that she arrived at the office on time and the first thing she noticed was that everyone at the office felt the same as she did. Hungover. Handing Denise a jug of coffee and two dozen donuts to stick in the breakroom, she asked, "Where's Lakara?"

"In the bathroom where she's been all morning."

"I know the feeling, girl," she said as she rubbed her stomach. "I'll be in my office hoping I don't have to hide out in that bathroom with her today."

Inside of her office, Cassie sat her things down and checked her messages as she did her best to get settled in. Deciding that it was time to play the dutiful wife, she called her husband and was grateful that there was no answer. Although she thought it was weird that he didn't answer her that time of the morning, she didn't care to think any deeper into his actions since he'd been gone.

"Hey, just calling to check on you since I haven't heard from you this morning. Hope all is well. I know you're probably in a meeting or something, but hit me up when you get a free minute. Talk to you later, bye."

Now that she had completed that duty, she hung up and just sat at her desk for a few minutes, unable to do anything but try to get her shit together. Last night had been fun but partying the night before you had to go to work was a stupid idea at best and idiocy at worst. Even though she didn't regret her decision to attend the office party, she did regret how that hangover was kicking her ass. Before she realized it, twenty minutes had gone by and her phone was ringing, letting her know that she needed to snap out of it and get to work.

Irritated, she hit the speaker button, "Yes," she tried not to snap.

"Mr. Martz is here to see you," Denise said, sounding just as messed up as Cassie felt. "He's all done on our end."

"Send them in, please," was all she managed to say. There was no way in hell she was going to allow Mazoo to see her looking as if she had been dragged through every ring of hell, so Cassie reapplied her lipstick and ran her hand over her clothes. Then she popped in a breath mint just in case the alcohol from last night had her breath smelling like death, and she walked over to the door.

Confusion ran through her mind and across her face when she saw that Denise had walked Mr. Martz to her door and only Mr. Martz. "Come in and have a seat," she said as she walked back to her desk and tried to stop the room from beginning a lazy spin. That hangover was trying to kill her and she would be damned if she would let it make her die. "Thank you for coming in. Where is Mrs. Martz?"

"She won't be accompanying us today," his voice expressed just how pissed he was. "She's decided that she's not ready for any help, I'm sorry to have wasted your time." Mazoo stood up, embarrassed and ready to leave.

Cassie stood up and grabbed his arm, "No, wait. Stay, have a seat," she gestured to his chair. "Talk to me, please." She looked up at him as Mazoo looked down at her. Her eyes were penetrating, as if she could see all the way through to his soul. Damn, this woman's got me, he thought as he took the seat. "I'm sorry to hear your wife is not ready. I know you want her here, but if she's not ready, even if she is here it won't work. She has to be ready and want this for herself or the program will never be successful for her."

He sighed, knowing she was right, hating that she was right. "I really want to help her, and she promised, you know. She promised," he spoke defeatedly.

Cassie explained the different levels of addicts to him, explained which level of addict his wife was and what all it detailed. "Just give her time, eventually she'll come around, but she has to hit rock bottom first."

"Well, in case she does come around, you keep the money. That way, whenever she's ready, the help she needs will be available to her."

Those words touched Cassie like nothing she'd ever felt before. Her heart swelled for him and she fell just a little deeper in love with him. And even though he made her heart feel good, she was about to break his. "I'm sorry, but it doesn't exactly work that way," she spoke sadly. "We don't hold any money. It's all used for treatment and only when the client is in the facility. I'm sorry, Mr. Martz," she apologized again, "but we have to refund your money."

Mazoo looked down and let out an exhausted sigh. He was just so tired of all things Tameka. For the longest time, he didn't say anything, there were no words he could even think to say. He hated the position he was in and just wanted a way out.

Seeing how hurt he was, Cassie changed the subject to something that was lighter. "Well, to give you a mental break for a few minutes, I'd like to thank you for paying for my dinner the other night and for the drinks last night."

Mazoo looked up at her and smiled. "Don't forget about the time I helped you pick up your papers."

That actually made her laugh. Seeing the calm cover Mazoo's face made Cassie relax. Thank you for that," she laughed, "and thank you for this hangover I have today. You and the million drinks you sent me last night has me feeling like I need to be in the ER getting an IV."

That made him laugh hard. They spent the next hour and a half chatting, talking about everything from important topics to jokes. It wasn't until Lakara buzzed her line stating that it was lunch time and asking what they were eating, that Cassie even remembered she was at work.

"I'm sorry, girl. I lost track of time. Give me five minutes and I'll be out." She then looked to Mazoo who was looking at her and a blush covered her entire body from the tip of her toes to the crown of her head.

"I'm sorry for taking up so much of your time," his voice was sincere.

"It's okay," she continued blushing. "I enjoyed talking to you."

"I enjoyed you as well," his voice was deep, suddenly sexy as hell, and Cassie somehow had the feeling that he was talking about much more than talking to her.

He had been talking about more than their conversation. While Cassie had been on the phone with her coworker, Mazoo had been watching her, staring at how gorgeous she was. His mind instantly took him back to his masturbation session that morning. His dick shot up in his pants and ached for her. The intensity in his eyes changed and when Cassie looked at him, she could clearly see that there was more in that look. Mazoo had intended for her to see it, had intended for her to feel what he felt for her. He needed to transfer some of that energy to her as it was way too intense for him to handle alone.

Cassie, swallowing audibly, licked her lips and felt a sudden rush of desire for Mazoo. Not wanting her thoughts to go where they were going, she hurriedly wrapped things up with him before she said and did the wrong thing with him. The sexual tension in her office was suddenly so high that she could imagine herself riding the shit out of Mazoo on her desk. The blush that was running through her body made her entire face red and hot.

She cleared her throat to disguise the fact that she needed to clear her head. "I hope everything works out for you and Tameka. And I'll have a check for you to pick up next week." She risked looking at him, saw that he was still giving her that intensely sexy gaze, and her throat dried. Suddenly she felt as if she swallowed a bag of chalk. "I'm really sorry about everything," she told him as she stood up and handed him a card that had her number on it, her direct line and cell, unlike the first one.

"Thank you for your time and for being so understanding," he stood, still watching her.

Together, they walked to the door where she opened it, turned to him, and extended her hand for him to shake. Instead, Mazoo grabbed her hand and kissed it. The electricity that shot through her at that kiss almost dropped her where she stood. Cassie smiled and blushed, very taken back.

"I'll call you sometime next week when the check is ready," she said as she fought like hell to get herself together.

"Okay," he said as her hand burned at his touch and her core throbbed for his touch.

"But if you need anything before then, please don't hesitate to call me. That's my direct line and my cell phone." He released her hand and her entire body shook from the loss of contact.

"Thank you, and again and enjoy the rest of your evening," he told her as he walked out of her office.

Cassie shut the door behind him and let out an internal scream. "Damn, he does something to me," she whispered as she sat back at her desk and tried to figure out why that man had such an effect on her.

Chapter Twenty-Four

Jinx was pissed. He'd gotten word that Romel had been in town and that he'd reached out to Cassie.

"What do you know about Romel hitting Cassie up?" Jinx asked Lathom.

The two of them had been hanging out a lot more in recent days. He was pissed with himself for not knowing the answer to that question, but he had been so busy lately that he slacked off on the tabs he'd been keeping on Cassie over the years.

"It was about their son," Lathom began, then proceeded to tell him all about what happened with RJ and why Romel reached out to Cassie. Every internal antenna Jinx had risen, but he didn't say anything, he just let Lathom finish. "So she ended up borrowing the money from me to give to Romel for their son," he finished. Jinx had gone from pissed to furious. He was doing his best to keep his cool, but he was so mad that he was struggling to keep from running his fists through a wall. "I promised her I wouldn't say anything, but I don't know this guy and I damn sure don't trust him, so I've been trying to do some research on him."

"Well, I'm glad you told me, I needed to know. Now, I'm about to check into it as well. Whatever you find out, let me know. I'ma handle it."

"Fo sho," Lathom replied, "because if we don't look out for her, nobody else will. Especially not Charles' old bitch ass. Man, I really don't like that nigga."

"Me either," Jinx said as a hard look crossed his face. "That's why we have to do better about looking after her. I slacked off, but apparently, I need to pick up the pace again."

"I'm with you on that one. And if I find out anything, I'll definitely let you know about it." Lathom said.

Jinx was pissed with himself for not killing Romel right along with Romel's father all those years ago. That's what I get for leaving loose ends, he thought as he wished Lathom would have told him about Romel before he gave Cassie that money. But he couldn't be mad at the dude for being an older brother to Cassie. He was there for her in a way her other friends had never been and Jinx respected him for that. No matter what had gone down with Cassie, if nobody else had her back, Lathom always did. For that, Jinx would forever be grateful. Cassie was too naïve to be left unattended in this cold-ass world, so where he had slacked off, he was more than happy to know that Lathom had tightened the grip. Cassie would be protected no matter what.

"I'm going to get you the money she owes you," Jinx said to Lathom.

"I didn't tell you this for you to give me the money, I told you 'cause I feel like this guy is up to something."

"You can bet he is," Jinx said. "Romel is always up to something, and now I want to know what."

"Ditto," was Lathom's aggravated reply.

When the two parted ways, Jinx made a phone call. He was going to give Lathom that money back whether that dude wanted it back or not.

***

Charles was devastated.

"I can't believe she had him cremated after we specifically discussed having him buried," Charles said to Demetri as they sat in his hotel suite having lunch. "And what's worse is that she got me to pay for what I'm firmly against." He was pissed. Even though the funeral had been the day before, he was still reeling from how Carrie had behaved at the funeral and what she had done following it. "It's almost like she has some fucking vendetta against me," he spoke through clenched teeth as he clenched and unclenched his fists.

Demetri knew that woman had a vendetta against Charles, and he knew why, but he wouldn't dare say that to him, not at such a sensitive moment. "Just focus on the fact that you've funeralized your son," he offered his unsolicited advice. "The hardest part is over and now you just have to focus on getting through the grieving process."

Although Charles knew Demetri was right, he was still pissed. "That's why I told her to have a nice life and didn't attend the repass. I don't do crazy, Demetri. I just don't have the tolerance for it."

Demetri fought like hell to hold his smile back. That was exactly what he hoped would happen. He wanted Charles to ditch the ex that was clearly trying to get him back and he got his wish. "You did what was best for you. You have to heal and you have to do it in as peaceful an environment as you can. Besides, she's just hurting about losing a child and taking it out on you. When she starts to heal, she'll get in touch and apologize."

"Hmmm," was all Charles said as he walked to the bar and poured himself a strong drink. His emotions were all over the place and he was feeling extremely triggered. Suddenly he began to crave his addictions. He knew he shouldn't indulge in them, but those cravings were hard and he wasn't in the mood to resist them. Besides, they always made him feel better when he fed them and he damn sure needed something to make his feel better. So, he would feed them, each and every one of them.

"Are you sure you want to have a drink this early in the day?" Demetri asked.

"I'm just as sure about that as I am about you relaxing me," he said as downed the shot and looked at his assistant. "Come," he told Demetri as he walked into his bedroom and began to undress.

Wasting not a second, Demetri did as he was told.

***

Cassie tried to call Charles one more time. As the phone rang repeatedly for entirely too long, she was just about to hang up when she heard, "Hello, Mr. Charles Baxton's phone. How may I help you?"

The minute Cassie heard Demetri's voice the hairs on the back of her neck stood on end and she was instantly pissed. "No, you cannot help me. Where is my husband?" she snapped.

"Oh, hi, Cassie," Demetri spoke in a voice that was relaxed and satiated.

"That's Mrs. Baxton to you, sweetie. Now where's Charles and why are you answering his phone?"

The more Demetri spoke, the angrier Cassie became. Something just didn't feel right. "Mr. Charles is in a meeting, he told me to answer the phone and tell you that he'll call you back."

Before he could finish speaking, Cassie said, "Whatever!" and hung up in his face.

She was seriously pissed, but wasn't quite sure why she was pissed. She'd had no clue Demetri was in Atlanta with her husband and she wondered why Charles hadn't bothered to say anything about it any of the times she had spoken with him. That was odd and it grated on her nerves, that and the fact that something about Demetri just didn't feel right to her. In fact, the whole thing disgusted Cassie and she just couldn't put her finger on why.

Just as she was trying to figure out what was going on with her husband and why he was all of a sudden keeping secrets, her phone began to ring. It was Charles, almost like she had conjured him up.

"Why is Demetri answering your personal phone? When did he get there? And why didn't you tell me anything about it?" She was so pissed she hadn't even bothered to say hello.

"I'll be on a flight first thing in the morning," was his casual response.

"Okay, thank you for telling me that." Her brows creased and a frown formed on her face, "But that doesn't answer any of my questions."

Just then her line beeped, it was Sam calling. Now she was torn. As much as she wanted Charles to explain what the hell was going on, she hadn't really heard from Sam in months and didn't have a clue what was going on with her friend. She'd been worried and needed to make sure Sam was okay, but she also needed to know what was up with her husband.

"Shit!" she mumbled under her breath.

"What did you say?" Charles asked in a very authoritative tone.

"I need to take this call, Charles. I'll have to call you back," was how she replied to him. She didn't have time to sit around and wait for him to correct her language.

"At which time you can explain to me why you think it's okay to use that kind of language with me," he admonished.

"Hmph," was all Cassie said. Then, "I'll talk to you later." She hung up before giving Charles a chance to say a word.

"Hello," Cassie spoke with extreme concern.

"Hey, girl hey!" Sam spoke in a chipper tone.

"Don't hey girl me, where the hell you been, Sam?" Cassie was sincerely worried and slightly pissed. "You been ditching me lately, not hanging with the crew, what's going on with you?"

"Girl, I been trying to get my life together."

"Sam," Cassie was confused now, "when did your life fall apart? The last time we spoke and all the other times before that your life was great. You're a stay-at-home mom with a husband and children that love you like crazy. Your husband just built you a new house in that new community. Your kids are doing great, you were doing what you wanted to do and everything was fine. So, when did your life fall apart?"

"When my mother-in-law threatened to tell my husband that she thinks my twins are for his twin brother and not him," Sam answered honestly. "Shit fell apart right around then."

"What?" Cassie asked, shock and confusion in her voice. "Where did she get a stupid ass idea like that?" Cassie was pissed that anyone would think those things about her friend. At that moment, she wanted to slap the taste out of that old ass woman's mouth.

But what a surprise Cassie got when Sam said, "She got it from the fact that I really did sleep with Mitchell," Sam told the truth.

"What?" Cassie said as she jumped up, her jaw slamming onto the floor. "You did what?"

"I really slept with him," she went on speaking a truth that was blowing Cassie away.

"What the hell, Samantha? Why the hell would you do some shit like that?"

Sam let out a deep sigh. Since she'd told Cassie that she figured she may as well tell her the rest of the truth. "Because I'm tired of being alone. All Michael does is work, work, work. He wakes up, goes to work, stays there all day, comes home, eats, and then goes straight to sleep. He doesn't talk to me, he barely fucks me, he doesn't do anything with me or the kids. All he does is work and eat and sleep. I'm single in this marriage."

"So you just slept with his brother?" was all Cassie could say as she sat down again, she was too stunned to form any other words.

"It was more than sex, Cassie. We had an actual affair. For almost a year."

"The fuck?" Cassie said, not sure she could take any more of what Sam was telling her. "This is some messy shit."

"You're telling me," Sam replied in a defeated tone.

"But the twins are three now, that means all of this went down four years ago. Why are you just telling me this?"

"Because shit just hit the fan now. Mitchell is pissed with me because I broke things off with him when he started catching feelings," Samantha began to weave a tale that had Cassie on the verge of a stroke. "The point of the affair was never to leave Michael, I love my husband. But I was missing my husband like crazy because he was never around. Mitchell was my other half of Michael. Whatever needs Michael wasn't meeting for me, Mitchell was more than willing to meet them. And it was like my husband was actually doing those things for me because Mitchell looks just like him."

"Shit, Samantha," was all Cassie could say.

"So to me, it was never like I was cheating. I mean, how can you think you're cheating when the man you're fucking looks, sounds, acts, and feels just like the man you married? When he has the same parents, grew up in the same house? Hell," she said with frustration in her voice, "when he fucking smells just like your husband?"

Cassie said, "Damn," as she struggled to process everything.

"But Mitchell caught on to what I was doing and he didn't like it at all. He told me that if I was going to use him to fulfil some of the duties of my husband, I may as well make him my husband so he could fulfil all the duties of my husband. That's when he told me he wanted me for his own and that he was tired of playing second fiddle to his brother." She paused for a moment, remembering that conversation like it was yesterday. "I told him that I loved my husband and didn't want to leave him. That's when he told me that I was going to be his one way or the other."

"Well, Damn, Sam," Cassie replied, feeling sorry for her friend and angry with her at the same time.

"I was a little freaked out at first, but when we found out I was pregnant after that and Mitchell did nothing, I figured what he'd told me was just an empty threat. Then the twins were born, and still nothing. I just knew I was in the clear. Then they had three whole goddamn birthdays and his ass didn't do anything. Until three months ago." That was right around the time Sam had disappeared and stopped answering her phone, Cassie realized. "The twins spent the week at Michael's mom's house. While they were there, she let Mitchell take them to get some ice cream and to the toy store. His ass snuck off and got a paternity test done. It turns out that Devin is his child and Devine is Michael's."

"What in the entirety of fucks?" Cassie shouted as she jumped to her feet again. "How in the entirety of fucks?"

"Exactly," Sam said.

"Does Michael know?"

"Not yet. But Mitchell told me that if I don't get with him, he's going to sue me for custody of his child. If he does that, Michael is going to know everything and I'm going to lose my husband and probably all four of my children when Mitchell takes Devin and Michael takes Devine and our other two."

"What the hell are you going to do?" Cassie wanted to know, she was seriously invested in Sam's soap opera life.

"That's the thing. I have no clue what I'm going to do, but I've been spending time with my new friend and she's been helping me through everything. She's been giving me some good ass advice and just helping me to forget most of the time until I can make up my damn mind. I'd really like you to meet her. Her name is Ta-Ta."

"Okay," Cassie agreed, "I can do that. But do you need anything from me? Do you need my help with anything?"

"No," Sam's voice was sad and tired.

"Well, if you do, you know I got you, right? With anything. I mean anything, Sam."

"I know, Cass," she replied. "But look, can we just change the subject? I don't want to deal with this anymore. I need an escape with Ta-Ta right now, her crazy ass always helps me to escape this crazy shit."

"Okay, then what do you want to talk about?"

"How's Charles?"

As much as Cassie wanted to tell her everything that had been going on with her and Charles, it was just not the time. The last thing she wanted to do was add on to the shit Sam was already going through, so she kept her mouth shut about her marital issues. "He's fine, still being a workaholic. "He's actually out of town on a business trip as we speak. You know how those are."

"Yeah. How's Uncle Jinx and your grandparents?"

"Everyone is fine, same old same old. Jinx, Lathom, and I just had dinner with them this past Sunday."

"Shit, I'm mad I missed it. I know Momma Edmonds tore the whole kitchen down," Sam laughed.

"Girl, you know she did. You gon' have to come to the next one."

"Fo sho," Sam greedily agreed and laughed again. "Besides, I miss everybody, and I really can't wait to see y'all and for you to meet Ta-Ta. She really is amazing."

"Well, I can't wait to meet her then," Cassie replied sincerely. "But yo ass gon' have to answer the phone to set it all up."

"I will," Sam assured her. "I promise I'll do a better job of keeping in touch."

"That's all I need," Cassie said just before they said their goodbyes.

Chapter Twenty-Five

Deciding that she'd had enough drama for the day on top of a hangover that had only gotten slightly better, Cassie opted to leave work early. She wanted to go home, gather her thoughts, rest her mind, and put something hot and soothing into her stomach.

On the way home, she decided to make a quick stop and grab a couple of cans of soup to soothe her stomach. As soon as Cassie walked into the store, she saw Sam. Her eyes lit up and her heart began to race.

"Hey, stranger," she called out to her dear friend with a huge smile on her face. She was excited to see Sam after the wild talk they'd just had. Sam turned around and smiled just as big and wide at Cassie,

"Hey!" she said as she ran to her friend and embraced her." Oh, my God! Cassie! I am so happy to see you!" she screeched. "Hey, Ta-ta, come meet my best friend!" she shouted out.

When Ta-Ta turned around, all of the color drained from Cassie's face. The amazing Ta-Ta was actually the one and only Tameka Martz and Mrs. Martz eyed Cassie up and down. "I know her," she said with a roll of her eyes toward the ceiling. "My husband is in love with her."

"Excuse me?" Cassie said as she looked at the woman like she was crazy.

"Naw," Sam said with a shake of her head. "You must have the wrong person. Cassie is married to the one and only Charles Baxton."

Tameka was absolutely unimpressed. "Yeah, whatever," the woman clearly had an issue with Cassie.

Cassie eyed Tameka hard for a moment, then she looked at Sam and eyed her as well. It was then that Cassie saw all of the signs. Sam was on drugs and she knew in a heartbeat that Tameka was the one that introduced her to those drugs. Her heart broke in her chest and Cassie saw the moment Sam knew that she knew Sam was snorting Coke.

"Sam?" Cassie said as she kept staring at her friend, tears filling her eyes. "Why? You ain't gotta do this."

"Then this bitch is nosey too," Tameka said with a smack of her lips and another roll of her eyes.

"I'll talk to you about it later," Sam promised. "I just need to escape for a little while and then I'll be okay."

"You ain't gotta explain nothing to her," Tameka opened that reckless mouth of hers and let hot garbage fly out.

It took all Cassie had not to whip those raggedy ass sleeves off of Tameka's marked up arms. "Sam, I love you. I really love you. And I got you whenever you're ready. But right now, I'm out before I trip and shit get bad. The last thing I want to do is make things worse for somebody I love." Then she stepped to Sam and gripped both of her hands. "And anybody that's really your friend won't want to make things worse for you either, remember that." Cassie hugged her friend and said. "No judgment, no drama. I'm here for you whenever you're ready. I gotchu for real. Okay?"

"Okay," Sam said as she shook her head yes and her own eyes filled with tears.

Cassie was so mad that she raced to her car and jumped in like the cops were after her. Then she scratched off and damn near violated every traffic law on her way home.

"How do you know Cassie?" Sam asked Ta-Ta when Cassie was gone.

"My husband took me to the facility she works in to try and get me a bed in their program. The whole time she was talking about the place and the process, he was staring and fucking drooling. He was so interested in her that I said fuck him, her, and that bed, and left."

"That's my childhood friend, she's not like that," Sam told Tameka. "She's married and she's good people."

"Mmm, hmm," was all Tameka bothered to say.

"How do you know he's interested in Cassie anyway? Did he do anything or was he just staring at a woman that was talking to both of y'all?"

"I thought that at first, but it was the way he looked at her that got me. He was looking at her the same way he used to look at me."

"Girl, you trippin'," Sam laughed. "That man was just looking at a woman that was talking to him. "Did she flirt with him? Did she give him any looks? Did she say anything inappropriate?"

"No. He was just looking at her like that. I'm not crazy, Sam," Tameka defended herself as they paid for their stuff and left the store. Once inside of Sam's ride, Tameka spoke once again. "I know what my husband looks like when he's falling in love and I'm telling you that he's falling in love with your friend."

"Well, just because he might be falling in love with her doesn't mean she's falling in love with him," Sam told her.

For the longest time neither of them said a word until they pulled up to the trap to grab some coke. Drinking, sniffing, and freaking were their plans for the day, it had been their plans for the day every day for almost three months. That was how Sam escaped and that was how she wanted to keep escaping. At least for the moment. After that, she had no idea what the hell she was going to do about anything.

***

Early the next morning, Cassie woke feeling better than she had the day before. After running into Sam yesterday, she'd been mad, pissed, furious was more like it. She'd stopped at another store to get what she needed since she'd stormed out of the first one and then she went home. When she got there, all she did was eat the food and went to sleep while sincerely promising herself that she would never party that hard and drink that much again.

Now it was morning and she felt good. She stretched long and hard and luxuriated in the good feeling that flowed through her. Then she sat up on the side of the bed and was just about to stand up and head to the bathroom when she heard a sound. Turning to look behind her, she saw her husband lying in their bed sound asleep. He looked hard in the face, like life had beaten the fuck out of him while he was in Atlanta.

"That's what your ass gets," Cassie whispered to him as she eased out of bed as quietly as she could walked into the bathroom to begin her morning routine. Because she didn't want to wake Charles and actually have to talk his controlling ass, Cassie moved as quiet as smoke through the house while getting dressed. The moment she was fully clothed, she went to the living room, grabbed her things from the table and left. "Bye mothafucka!" she whispered before closing the door, that way, when his controlling ass asked her why she didn't say bye to him before leaving, she could honestly say that she did.

The minute she got to work, she got busy catching up on all the things she was too sick and distraught to complete the previous day. She had been so caught up in her work that the ringing of her phone shocked her.

"Mrs. Baxton," she spoke quickly.

"Mr. Martz's refund is here. I scheduled him to come in at one to pick it up," Denise told her.

"Oh, damn!" she'd forgotten all about that. "Thank you, Denise."

"You're welcome. You okay in there, girl? You've been locked up your office ever since you got here."

"Yeah, I'm good. Just catching up on what I didn't complete yesterday."

"You feeling better?"

"Definitely. I swear I will never drink like that again."

"Me either," Denise said as Cassie's cell began to ring. Then "Go ahead and answer that, I'll talk to you later," her coworker told her.

"Hello." Was her annoyed greeting when she saw that it was Charles.

"You left without saying goodbye," Charles' deep voice came through the phone.

"I said goodbye," she told the truth as she rolled her eyes. "You were sleeping too hard to hear me."

"Next time make sure I hear you, Cassie," he reprimanded her as if he was her father.

"Like you made sure I heard you come in this morning?" she went back at him.

"You were asleep and I didn't want to wake you, especially since I knew you had to be at work in a few hours." His response was sharp. "I was taking you into consideration."

"I did the same thing for you," she replied.

"What's going on with you?" he asked her after a few seconds of silence. "Who were you hanging with while I was gone?"

"Don't do this, Charles," her voice held the sheer annoyance she felt. "Now is not the time."

"Okay, I can respect that," she could hear the angry bite in his voice, but she ignored it. "But we will discuss your new behavior tonight over dinner. At home. Seven o'clock and don't be late."

"Yep," was all she said before she hung up. "Uuggghhhhh!" she screamed in disgust when she was sure her line was completely dead. "Why did this raggedy muthafucka come back?"

The minute she hung up with her husband and calmed herself down, she called her grandmother. She needed to talk to someone that would soothe her nerves and not fry them to a Cajun crisp.

"Hello," Momma Edmonds answered, "we are blessed and highly favored. How about you?"

Cassie chuckled, her nerves already calming at just the sound of her grandmother's voice. "Hi, Momma."

"Hi," Mrs. Edmonds said, "but I asked a question, child."

"Yes, Ma'am, I am blessed and highly favored." The gentleness and familiarity of their conversation always made her feel good.

"Good, now how have you been?"

"I been good, nothing much going on besides the fact that Charles is back home."

"Then why do you sound as if things aren't good?" her grandmother asked.

"I don't know, something is different about us and I'm not sure what it is."

"Marriages come with different problems, and different challenges, and different seasons. Sometimes you're in love, sometimes you're out of love. Sometimes you argue, fuss, and cry, and then again sometimes it's great."

"Yeah, I understand, and I guess you're right." As much as she wanted to give her grandmother details, she decided against it. This was something she wanted to work out on her own. "How's poppa doing?"

"He's pretty much the same as always, nothing much really going on with either of us."

"That's good," Cassie said as they began a chat that really made Cassie relax and feel much better. After the conversation began to die down, Cassie told her grandmother, "Well, it's time for me to get back to work, but I really enjoyed talking to you, Momma."

"I enjoyed talking to you too, baby. I love you."

"I love you too, and I'll talk to you later."

"Bye, baby."

It wasn't until she had hung up that Cassie realized she'd been on the phone with her grandmother for an hour. That brought a big smile to her face. She loved that woman and felt truly blessed and highly favored to have her in her life.

When she looked at her office clock, she saw that it was almost time for Mr. Martz to come in and get his refund check. She began to finalize all of his paperwork so that he wouldn't have to stay in her office too long. The last time he'd been there, things got heated. She didn't want that to happen again because she wasn't sure if she could or would stop that heat from going wherever it was going to go. Just then, her phone rang and Denise was letting her know that Mazoo was there. As much as she knew she shouldn't have done it because it was just asking for trouble, Cassie fixed her hair, reapplied her lipstick, and then stood to greet him when he walked into her office and shut the door behind him.

Damn, damn, damn. He is so damn fine and he smells so amazing, she screamed in her head just before she told herself to shut up and stop acting like a nutcase. Hello," she spoke in a voice that was much calmer than the one playing hopscotch in her head. "Come in and have a sit-down." Mazoo complied, giving her that look that made her clit jump. Cassie bit her tongue to keep from screaming out loud and then jumping his bones.

She took her own seat and looked back at him with sheer desire in her eyes. "I'm just finishing up your paperwork and the release forms for your check." Then she took a look at her computer screen and pretended to be searching for something, anything to get those sexy thoughts about him out of her head. "Let me look and see something here," she damn near gnawed her tongue off as she hit a few buttons on her keyboard.

"So how are you?" he asked and damn near killed her with that deep, sexy voice, "and how have you been?"

She swallowed hard before speaking. "I'm fine," her voice squeaked out.

"Oh, I see that," he said, his tone more sensual than it was before. "Now, really, how are you?

Cassie smiled and pushed the wrong button causing her computer to make a weird humming sound. "Damn!" She was so embarrassed that her face turned bright red.

Mazoo instantly apologized. “I’m sorry. Am I distracting you?”

“No,” she lied.

“Look at me and tell me that lie again,” he spoke so softly she almost couldn’t breathe.

She turned her eyes in his direction and opened her mouth, but no words would come out. His eyes held so much desire for her in them that she couldn’t think or lie to him again.

When she said nothing, Mazoo hit her with his heart-stopping smile and said, “Would you like me to stop talking and let you finish up?”

“Yes, please,” she spoke barely above a whisper. “I can’t think with you looking at me like that.”

“I can’t stop looking at you like this,” he was honest with her. “You do something to me, Cassie.”

Cassie cleared her throat, then she crossed and uncrossed her legs to stop her core from throbbing. “How are you, Mr. Martz?”

“I’m good, really good,” he told her, still looking at her like he wanted to blow her back out.

She cleared her voice once again and said, “Well, it’s good to hear that. How’s your wife?” She hoped the reminder that he was married would distract them both.

Mazoo shifted in his seat, "I think she's ok, but I'm really not sure."

Cassie's look went from aroused to puzzled. "It's complicated. We're separated as of yesterday."

"Oh, I'm so sorry to hear that." Her words were sincere.

"Don't be. It's been over for some time now. I'm the one that was trying to hold on and make it work. I really wanted to honor my vows, but sometimes we have to face reality, and the reality is that my wife loves those drugs more than she loves me."

"I'm sorry," Cassie said as she picked up a folder and began shuffling papers.

"No need to be. It is what it is and it's time for me to move on. No more putting off the inevitable."

"Okay," she shook her head up and down in agreement. "Well, I need you to sign a few papers, Mr. Martz." She handed him a pen.

He took the pen and looked at her with those eyes again. "Please, call me Mazoo."

She blushed hard. "Here you are, Mr. Mazoo."

It was his turn to chuckle. "Okay, but you can drop the Mister."

"Okay, Mazoo," she said and couldn't help the big grin that took over her whole face. Mazoo signed the paperwork releasing his check and stopping Tameka's process into the facility. "Just a few more signatures and you'll be all set," she handed him another stack to be signed. When he was done signing those, he handed them back to her and once again the two of them got caught up in staring at one another. The sexual tension was back and thicker than ever.

Chapter Twenty-Six

When Cassie couldn't take that look anymore, she breathed deep and asked him in all seriousness, "What are we doing, Mazoo?"

"I think we're fighting to keep from having an affair," he was honest and just as serious with her.

"Shit," Cassie said as she acknowledged the truth of his words. "I think you're right."

"The real question is why are we fighting it?"

"Because I'm married and you're married."

"You're married, I'm separated," the look in his eyes intensified.

"Until you have divorce papers, you're just as married as I am."

"I'm attracted to you," he caught her off guard by admitting it.

"That's why your wife wants to kick my ass," Cassie admitted and caught him off guard.

"So, what are we going to do about it?" He was very blunt with her.

"I'm going to fight her ass back. I'll put that bitch in a headlock and two chokeholds—"

Mazoo laughed hard and the sexual tension instantly left the room. Cassie could breathe again. "Seriously," he told her when he was able to talk again.

"I am serious. She'll get two to the body and one to the head."

Mazoo laughed again, she was really funny and he realized he loved that about her. "Cassie," he said her name in a tone that told her to stop avoiding the question.

She inhaled deeply, exhaled deeply. "Well, Mazoo," she began, "we should—" and her phone rang, stopping that conversation in its tracks.

"Saved by the bell," he said as he stared at her with that sexy gaze again.

“I’m sorry,” she apologized with sorry eyes. Then, “Excuse me.” She looked down at her phone and saw that it was her brother. “Hello?”

“Hey, Cass.”

“Hey, Lay.”

“We still on for the gym later?”

“Sorry, but no. I can’t because I forgot. Plus,” her voice had gone from soft to slightly angry, “I told you I was going to find a personal trainer because you’re trying to either kill me or turn me into a dude. And ain’t nobody got time to be walking around here looking like the damn hulk,” she huffed.

Mazoo raised a curious brow and Lathom laughed his ass off. “Ain’t nobody trying to kill you,” Lathom told her. “I’m just trying to toughen you up and tone up your body.”

“How tough are you trying to make me? Is prison tough? I’m not going to the pen, Lathom. The fuck?” she spoke incredulously. Lathom laughed even harder. He laughed so loud that Mazoo heard him through the phone as he too laughed at her. “You play too much and you’re not helping me at all. Now, I have to go, I have a client. Love you. Call me later, bye,” she told him just before she hung up in his face and turned her attention back to Mazoo and the paperwork.

"Don't you even say a word," Cassie said to Mazoo as she calmed herself down and handed him another stack of paperwork. Keeping his mouth shut, Mazoo only chuckled as he finished signing everything.

"Damn, I feel like I just signed my life away," he said as he let out a deep breath.

"No," Cassie told him. "We just stopped the process of you signing your wife away."

Mazoo laughed so hard that he could barely breathe. "You are something else, woman," he told her as she shook his head and cracked up.

Cassie looks at him and said, "You might not find it so funny while you're signing these last six pages." Then she sat another small stack of papers in front of him and pointed to what needed to be signed, dated, and initialed.

Mazoo signed everything and handed it all back to her. "I'm not trying to be in your business, but I'm a personal trainer and I can help you if you like. And I promise I won't try to turn you into Thor or The Hulk or anything like that. Would you like me to train you?"

Cassie sat silent as her mind screamed, You can do whatever you want to do to me. Here's your check," she said as she handed it to him. "Yes, I'd like you to train me."

Mazoo took the check and smiled at her. "When do you want to start?"

"When do you want me?" she looked at him, her eyes smiling sexily at him.

"I have my own spot, a few workers, nothing big or fancy at all. So, it's up to you. Are you really interested?"

"Yes, I am serious because my brother is playing," she pouted and Mazoo found that pout to be so damn cute. "He's trying to train me to be tier rep of cell block B and I don't want that. I just need to keep up with myself a little better. Besides, working out always makes me feel good and I need that right now."

"It should make you feel good," he told her.

"Working out is for so much more than physical appearance," they both said at the same time. They both stopped and stared at each other in disbelief at how in tune with they were with each other. The energy they shared between them was refreshing to them both.

Mazoo broke the odd silence by saying, "Take my card and give me a call when you're ready." He reached into his wallet and pulled out that card. "I'll give you a tour first, show you what I do and we can go from there."

Cassie looked down and saw that the card read, "M&M's Workout Wonders." Then she looked back up at him and smiled. "Okay, and thank you."

"Make sure you call me," her gave her that intense look again. "Whether you want that training or not."

"I will," she said as she slicked her lips sexily at him.

Mazoo saw that lick and his dick shot out so hard he almost dropped to his knees where he stood. "I'm a grown-ass man, Cassie," he warned her. "You better stop playing with me before you find yourself in a position you're not ready for." When her eyes widened in surprise, he licked his own lips and said, "Don't be scared, you'll like the positions I put you in." Then he walked out of her office and closed the door behind him.

"Well, shit!" Cassie said as she clutched imaginary pearls while her heart hammered, her pussy pulsed, and she fell into her desk chair amazingly aroused.

A few weeks had gone by and things were pretty quiet in Cassie's life. She still wasn't hearing from Sam as much as she would have liked to, but that was expected when someone was in the beginning stages of becoming an addict. She hated the fact that her friend was going down that road, but if Cassie had learned anything working in a rehab facility it was that if you tried to make them stop using, they would only use more. The last thing she wanted was to be the reason Sam used more drugs.

Surprisingly, Charles had been quiet himself, almost as if he had some serious things on his mind. He'd left her alone about the talk they needed to have and as long as he was quiet and wasn't harassing her, Cassie left well enough alone. She did notice that he had started drinking even more and was staying at the office later and later. He was still going to his monthly meetings with the fellows though, and after those meetings, he would be great for a few days. Then he would start to brood and sulk and keep to himself and his job again. As much as Cassie didn't like the person she saw her husband becoming, she found that she preferred him like that than like the controlling and abusive beast he'd been before.

Poppa Edmonds' health was quickly deteriorating. This go round the doctors said there was nothing they could do about it other than let nature take its course. As much as that hurt Cassie, she decided not to let it get her down. What she did instead was start spending as much time as she could with her grandparents, and she made it a point to have dinner with them every Sunday. Choosing to do the same thing, Jinx and Lathom were always there as well.

Because of Poppa Edmonds' illness, Jinx had started to become more like a father to Cassie than an uncle and Lathom was being more of an older brother than before. They were both keeping a close eye on her and making sure all of her needs were being met even when her husband wasn't. The three of them had grown even closer and Momma and Poppa Edmonds approved of that a lot.

Cassie was now speaking to Romel on a regular basis. He'd been keeping her updated about RJ and his case.

"Does he want to see me?" she asked Romel one day during one of their long conversations.

"He's still reeling from how harsh that judge was during the arraignment, and with preparing for his case, he's dealing with a lot right now," Romel began, trying to let her down easy. "I've been discussing you with him, but right now he's just not ready to meet you."

"Okay," Cassie spoke sadly. As much as the rejection from her son hurt her, she was willing to give him the time he needed to come around if he ever came around. "But he does want you at his trial," Romel said the words that put a big smile on Cassie's face and made her heart leap for joy in her chest.

"Thank God!" Tears stung her eyes. Up until that point, she hadn't realized how much she really wanted and needed to have any small part of RJ's life. "When is it?" she asked and Romel gave her all of the information she needed to attend.

It tore Jinx up to watch Cassie watch her grandfather die slowly. She had been spending a lot of time at her grandparents' house and her punk ass husband never once showed up to offer her or Poppa and Momma Edmond's any kind of support. So he decided to step up to the plate and take care of Cassie. Hell, if Poppa Edmonds passed, Jinx would be the head of the family anyway. There was no way in hell he was going to let Momma Edmonds struggle alone without her husband and there was no way, absolutely no way, he was going to leave Cassie without any support because her no-account husband was neglecting her and her emotional needs. He hated the fact that she was married to that political piece of shit.

In addition to getting the scoop on Romel and the bullshit he was up to, Jinx added Charles to that list. If his ass wasn't paying attention to his wife, what the hell was he paying attention to? So far Jinx had found out that Charles was more of a problem than any of them realized. That muthafucka was an addict. He was smart enough to always send his assistant to get his package so that no one would know what he was into.

"But, shit," Jinx spoke aloud to himself, "who do they think that shit comes from? Me, that's who! Every drug that comes to and through this city comes through me. I'm the silent partner in these streets. Everybody knows about me but nobody knows about me. But I know about Charles and I'm going to know even more before it's all said and done."

Going up the ramp of the interstate toward his destination, Jinx shook his head in anger. He may not have done a good job of protecting Georgia, but he wasn't going to fail Cassie. After all of those years, he was still pissed with himself for letting Georgia die. And he was just as pissed with himself for not protecting Cassie from Romel when she was younger. So he vowed to protect Cassie now at all costs. From both Charles and from Romel.

After Lathom told him about what Romel was doing to Cassie with that money, Jinx made an important phone call to his peoples in Atlanta. All he'd said that night was, "Reopen the case," and he hung up. Now that he realized Cassie's husband was too busy to be where he was supposed to be when his wife needed him, he was in the process of making another important phone call, and this one was going to a woman he trusted with his life.

"Mills Investigative Service, how may I help you?" she said when she picked up.

Jinx smiled at the sound of her sweet yet strong and feisty tone.

"Hello," He said as his smile grew bigger, "I see you still have that fire."

She instantly recognized the voice and softened her tone. "Hey there. To what do I owe this call?"

"Hello, Angela, How have you been?"

"I've been good, and you?"

"I'll be better when I get your services."

"Tell me more," she purred through the phone.

"I need the best of the best, Ang."

"That's why you called me, right? Because I'm the best of the best?"

"Yes, and I may need a whole team for this one," he stated, then he explained in greater detail what he needed from her. "His name is Charles Baxton and ..." Jinx gave her everything he had on the man.

"Okay," she let out a long, low whistle. "You really do need a lot, but I got you. And you know this is going to cost you," she said in a very seductive voice.

"Has money ever been an issue?"

She chuckled. "This may cost you a little bit more than money."

"As long as it don't cost me my life I think we can handle it."

"You are still cocky," she spoke the truth.

"Confident," was all he said.

"Well then, let me get this started for you, Mr. Confident."

"Just remember that he's very powerful like you and me. He has connections to people that can make things disappear."

"Good thing we have the power to make them reappear."

He chuckled, "That's why I called you. Let me know any and everything there is to know on him, dead or living, family members or pets."

"Will do."

"It's been a pleasure."

"I haven't pleasured you yet," she teased.

Jinx Chuckled again. "I'll be waiting to hear from you."

"I'll be in touch, now let me go and have my fun."

Lathom was in the kitchen of one of his spots counting money and talking to one of his workers, when all of a sudden he heard a commotion coming from the front hall. He made his way to the hall to see what was going on, only to find Sam and some lady giving Wild Tony a hard time.

"Yo, ladies, what's all the noise for?" he spoke in his deep, smooth as butter voice.

Sam looked up in total shock. "What are you doing here?"

"I could ask yo ass the same thing, but unfortunately," he shook his head in disgust, "I already know. The fuck is you doing, Sam?" Lathom was pissed.

Ta-Ta was intrigued. "Who is he?" she asked Sam before Sam could respond to Lathom.

"Nobody. Let's go, Ta-Ta. Lathom, stay out of my business," she snapped.

"This is my business and you strolled up in here. So what I should be tellin' yo ass is to stay out of my business. All the way out of it," he told her as he gripped her arm and forced her to look at him. "This shit ain't for you, Sam."

"But it is for me," Ta-Ta said, "and I want it."

"Well, you damn sure ain't getting it from me," Lathom assured her. "Not as long as you got one of my friends hanging with you," he told Tameka. Then he turned back to Sam. "Like I said, my business ain't for you so get yo ass back home to yo husband and them seventy-six kids you got."

"It's only four, muthafucka!" she tried to snatch her arm away and found that Lathom's grip was like steel.

"Well, they bad as fuck, and the way they was tearing your house down, I could've sworn it was seventy-six of them lil muthafuckas. Now get yo ass on out of here and don't let me see you around here again, Sam, or on everything, I'ma whip your ass and take you back home my damn self! Get yo life, man!" He was infuriated with her, but he had to keep his cool before he snatched her up and put a hurting on her for trying to fuck up her life.

"Whatever," she said as she turned and left. Sam was nowhere near stupid and she knew that if Lathom said he was going to whip her ass, he was definitely going to do it if she didn't get ghost asap. So she grabbed Ta-Ta by the wrist and pulled her out of there. They could score Coke anywhere, just not from there.

The minute Sam and her friend walked out of the door, Lathom made a few phone calls. He'd recognized Tameka instantly and was seriously wondering how her husband let her end up on drugs like that. And if old dude couldn't keep his wife together, how the hell could Lathom trust him with Cassie? Now Mazoo was on Lathom's research list and as far as Lathom was concerned, if he found one bad thing out about that dude, he was going to eliminate his ass to get him out of Cassie's life. Nobody was going to run her life down the drain. Nobody. Not even that sorry ass husband of hers.

Chapter Twenty-Seven

Poppa Edmonds had been in and out of the hospital no less than five times in the last two months, it was safe to say that his health was declining. Cassie was working and trying to help her grandmother take care of her grandfather, but there was really nothing anyone could do except pray. The whole situation was overwhelming for Cassie, so after serious consideration, and deep conversations with both Jinx and Lathom, she decided to take a little time off work to just focus on Poppa Edmonds.

She had been spending more and more time at the house with her grandparents so that she could be there in case anything happened and she was needed. Charles hadn't put up any objections whatsoever, in fact, Charles didn't seem to care about anything anymore except his political career, drinking, and those stupid ass meetings he attended once a month. Cassie's marriage was so strained that she found it a relief to spend most of her time at her grandparent's house helping her dying grandfather.

It was on one of those nights at her grandparents' place, after Cassie had just helped Momma Edmonds get him into bed, that her phone rang. She had just said goodbye to her grandmother and was telling her she would see her tomorrow when she reached into her pocket and pulled out her phone.

"Hello," she said without looking at the screen as she got into her car.

"Hey, beautiful. How are you?"

Cassie recognized the voice instantly She lit up before saying, "Hi, and I'm fine. What about you?"

"I know you're fine," Mazoo told her, "now tell me how you are."

"I'm okay," her smile was bright and warm.

"So you finally decided to call me, huh?"

"Huh?" she said. Then, "Oh, yeah. I'm sorry, I had a lot on my mind today and forgot I'd called you earlier."

"Really?" his voice had deepened, expressed concern.

"Yeah, I'm super stressed and I definitely need to get back on some kind of workout schedule. It'll help me relieve some of this stress."

"Do you mind if I ask what's wrong?"

"My grandfather is sick and it's kind of like we're just sitting around watching him die." The pain in her voice was crystal clear.

"I'm so sorry to hear that," Mazoo's first instinct was to soothe Cassie.

"Thank you. I was trying to figure out ways to cope and I figured working out would give me a little relief. I need to come in and get myself back on a regular workout schedule."

"We can do that. When are you free? I mean, I know you have a lot going on, but are you able to squeeze some more time in there somewhere?"

"I can, I definitely need something to distract me so I'll make the time." She was quiet for a few seconds before saying, "I can be free for these next few days. How's that?"

"How does tomorrow at one sound?"

"It sounds great. I'll see you then."

***

A startled Cassie was awakened at almost ten at night to the sound of her phone ringing. In a heartbeat she grabbed the phone, praying that it wasn't her grandmother telling her that her grandfather had passed.

"Hello!" She rushed that single word into the phone, scared to death of what she might hear on the other end of that line.

"Don't wait up for me," was what she heard coming from her husband.

Cassie was so pissed with Charles for scaring her like that she didn't even bother to ask him why or anything, she simply said, "Okay," and hung up. Unable to sleep now, she began to watch television, something she hadn't done in a long time. At that point, she was willing to do anything to calm herself down.

Charles had been out of control ever since learning about the death of his son. Carrie had gone out of her way to hurt him and it had been very effective. Now he was spiraling out of control and there wasn't a damn thing he could or even wanted to do about it. He had remained in contact with Carrie, but barely. The only reason he even bothered to speak with her was to stay informed about the trial for his son. He promised himself he'd be there for that and he would keep that particular promise even if he never kept another one in his fucked up life.

The downside to attending the murder trials was that Kelly would be there. His sister hated his guts and he was only a step away from hating hers. Everything in his life had seemed so perfect until everything with Terrail happened. Now nothing was right. Things were so bad for him that Cassie's grandfather was dying he couldn't even bring himself to be there for her like he should've been. He was either too drunk or too loaded most of the time, and since he was so busy trying to hide his addictions from Cassie, there was no way he could be around when she needed him the most.

He was way more affected by Terrail's death than he thought. He blamed himself and the state of depression that settled over him had him doing everything he could not to have to face reality each day. Charles sat in White's Lounge on his fourth shot of Grand Marnier. He was trying to cope the best way he could and was failing miserably. The only time he didn't fail was when he indulged and that was just what he was getting ready to do.

"I'm ready for you, Sir," the young hottie said to him when he stepped into the foyer of the club. "Follow me this way."

***

"I'm sad, I'm scared, and I'm not ready for you to leave me," Cassie said to Poppa Edmonds the next morning.

"It's ok," her grandfather told her. "If the Lord is ready for me, who am I to ask him to pick someone else?"

"Yeah, but—" she began to protest but he cut her off.

"I promise you you'll be ok, baby girl," Poppa Edmonds told her.

"I'm not so sure if I'll be ok," she was fighting back her tears. Not only was she crying for her grandfather, but she was also crying over a marriage that she knew was over. Her husband had never come home that night. Cassie had woken, dressed, and left, and still, Charles hadn't walked through that door. She was pissed and heartbroken and had no idea how she would cope with anything going on in her life at that moment.

"You'll be okay," he told her as he looked into her eyes, letting her know that he knew there was more she wasn't saying. "You'll be okay about everything. Plus, God has some work up there that only I can take care of, so you have to be okay down here so I can do what I need to do up there," he said as he started to laugh. "It's probably your mother that He needs my help with."

"Poppa, you ain't right," she said as they shared a good hearty laugh.

"You know it's only right I go be with your mother. God is probably saying I'm tired of watching this child, come get her," he began to laugh even harder. "That girl was always daddy's girl, so it's only fit for her daddy to go and be with her."

Cassie wasn't trying to hear what he was saying, but she understood. When it was time it was time, and her Poppa had to comfort himself with whatever would help him to accept what seemed to be his fate.

After a while, Poppa Edmonds fell asleep and Cassie got up and took the dishes into the kitchen.

"Is he all done?" Momma Edmonds asked.

"Yes, ma'am. He's sound sleep."

"Well, I'm going to turn the covers back myself while he's down."

"I figured you'd say as much, that's why I washed the dishes for you. Now you can just go to bed and get you some rest. I'm going to go."

"You don't have to leave, baby, you just got here."

"I know," she looked at her watch, "but I have a one o'clock appointment at the gym."

"Oh," she said with a warm, smile, "when did you start back?"

"This is my walk through; I'm thinking about joining this new gym. Something small, not a big busy gym."

"You seem excited," her grandmother noted, staring into Cassie's eyes.

"Yeah, it's something different, something I might be able to stick to."

"Then go, it'll be good for you, especially since you love working out," Momma Edmonds told her as the made their way to the living room where Poppa Edmonds was knocked out in his recliner. Seeing that her husband was comfortable and looked like he would be sleeping for a while, she focused her attention back on Cassie as she walked her to the door. "I'll see you later, baby. I love you."

"I love you too and if you need me, call."

"Okay, I probably won't need you anymore today since a few of the sisters from the church are stopping by. But if anything arises, I call."

A short time later, Cassie pulled up outside of M&M's Work Out Gym and sat in her car for about five minutes trying to pull herself together. She was losing her grandfather and she was losing her marriage. One would devastate her, the other would only shake her a little, but both of them would hurt. Deciding that she didn't want to become too emotional before she walked into the presence of others, she put those thoughts on the back burner of her mind and got out of her car to head inside of the gym.

As soon as she reached her hand out to open the door, out came a very pissed Tameka saying, "Fuck you, Mazoo! You can't just put me out of the house. Where the fuck am I supposed to go?"

"I don't know, Tameka, but you need to stop coming by here showing out and causing a scene," his voice was irritated and Cassie could tell he was refraining himself from tossing his wife out on her ass. Then Mazoo's eyes lifted from his wife's and landed on Cassie's.

Seeing the expression that suddenly came over her husband's face made Tameka turn around to see what caused it. The minute she made eye contact with Cassie, she was shocked and pissed at the same time. Now she is yelling louder, "Fuck you and this high-priced bitch!" She turned back to her soon-to-be ex-husband and said, "You can't afford her, you fucking ex-con!"

Mazoo simply said, "Tameka, what I really can't afford is you and your drug habit. That's why I want a divorce. Now get the fuck out and have a good day!"

Tameka was so enraged at his words that she stormed off, mumbling under her breath about how he would see.

Cassie looked at Mazoo as he stood there holding the door open for Tameka's dramatic exit.

"Bad timing?" she asked him when Tameka had left the building.

"I'm sorry. I'm so sorry," he apologized a million times for Tameka's behavior as he led Cassie into the small gym.

"No need to apologize. I'm very aware of what drug addicts do and how they behave when they don't get their way."

Once inside, Mazoo locked the door behind them. "Well, I might as well give you what you came for," he looked at her with that expression that pissed off his wife.

Immediately that look sent her mind into a sexual territory and Cassie's clit clenched. "The tour," she said as she licked her lips nervously, sexily.

"Right," Mazoo said, fighting to pull his mind from that sexual territory as he began to give her that tour.

The gym was a good size and very nice and clean, Cassie noted. "This place is actually bigger than what it looks on the outside."

"Yeah," he smiled at her, "that's what turns people off about it until they come inside. They think it's much smaller than it actually is at first." He made a few turns and then lead Cassie down a long hall. "Let's go this way," he said after one more turn. "This is my office." The room he'd taken her into was nice and cozy. "Have a seat," he directed her to one side of the desk while he sat on the other.

"Well, isn't this a change," she smiled. "Now you're the one behind the desk.

Mazoo chuckled. Then more seriously, he said, "I wasn't always behind a desk, once upon a time I was behind bars." Cassie looked up at him intrigued, and that look prompted Mazoo to tell Cassie all about himself. From his mom passing away, to being adopted, to his adopted parents passing away. He told her everything about him being a troubled youth, about his daughter, about his time being incarcerated, and even about his up and down marriage with Tameka.

Cassie's heart went out to him and she felt compelled to tell him that she had someone she loved that was in prison. Mazoo and Cassie talked for hours, neither of them aware of how much time had passed. It was so easy for them to talk to one another that they felt like old friends, like they had known each other for centuries. They shared information, the good and the bad about themselves until Mazoo's phone rang and made them realize that most of their day had gone by.

Because Mazoo was scheduled to work the midnight shift, he had to end their conversation so that he could begin getting ready.

"Wow," they said simultaneously at the thought of how amazing their conversation was and at the realization that the clock had advanced by hours. They looked at one another and the sexual chemistry between them could have fried their circuits.

"Uhhhm," I think I should go," Cassie said when her feelings began to get the best of her. She was aware that they hadn't set up a schedule for her workouts, but she wanted to fuck Mazoo so bad that she didn't care about that schedule. She needed to get away from him before she broke her marriage vows.

"Just let me lock up first and I'll walk out with you." Cassie waited, but she fought like a Viking warrior not to initiate the sex she really wanted with him. When Mazoo came back, he caught the look on her face and said, "Trust me, I want it as much as you do."

After he'd walked her to her car, Cassie met his eyes once more and said, "Thank you."

"No, thank you. And get home safely, beautiful. If possible, let me know when you make it." Then he shut her door and Cassie pulled off.

Chapter Twenty-Eight

By the time Cassie made it home, she was starving. It was nine o'clock at night and she had been with Mazoo for eight straight hours without eating a single thing. Not wanting to cook, she picked up her phone and ordered enough Chinese food for herself and for Charles. She then went to the bathroom, stripped, and showered. By the time she was done, the delivery person was at her door delivering their food. Because she wasn't sure when or if her husband would get home that night, Cassie dug into her dinner. When she was done, she put Charles' food in the microwave and went to bed, falling into a deep sleep immediately.

It was late when Charles finally came home. He stepped into their room, shed his clothes, and went directly to the bathroom. He was relieved that Cassis was asleep and hadn't yet awakened. He had fucked Demetri so hard that night that he was surprised Cassie didn't smell the sex the minute he walked into the house and woke up to accuse him of exactly what he had done.

"I need to get my shit together," he shook his head in shame.

As he bathed himself, he thought about how fucked up his life had become in the last few months. He was miserable and wished he could do anything to bring Terrail back. He wanted another chance with his son, a better chance with his son. He'd actually thought that he and Terrail might have developed a relationship once he was older and able to form his own opinion about Charles. He thought that by that time he wouldn't be ashamed of himself and Terrail would be too old for him to fuck up the way he'd been sure he would have done when his son was younger. He thought they'd had more time, but some coward had snatched that time away by killing his son.

Now, he would never develop that relationship with him. He would never apologize for being a fuck up and leaving Terrail to be raised alone by his mother. He would never get to say how sorry he was for hurting Carrie and for abandoning him. All because someone decided to play God and take a life they didn't have the fucking right to take. Charles was so angry that tears of rage ran down his face. His fists squeezed so tight that he damn near broke the bar of soap as he thought about how much he wanted to kill the bastard that killed his son.

"Fuuuccck!" he sobbed silently, letting the water from the shower wash away his tears. "Fuck!" he cried quietly again.

When he was all cried out and had thoroughly washed the scent of sex off of him, he dressed in bedclothes, went into the kitchen, and saw the note his wife left him telling him that there was Chinese food in the kitchen. He sat at the table, ate, and fought the urge to go back to Demetri's to fuck him again, or to go to his bar in the den and make himself several drinks. His anger had triggered his addictions and now he wanted to fill them. However, instead of giving in to them, Charles walked into his bedroom and crawled into his bed with his wife. That's when he noticed that Cassie was awake.

"Sorry," he said in a voice that was fake with normalcy. Charles felt anything but normal. "Did I wake you?"

"Yes, but it's okay," her eyes searched his face, searching everything about him. "I'm hungry again. You know how Chinese food is. You eat it and an hour later your starving like you've never eaten before in your life. Now I'm just trying to decide if I should go and make a pig out of myself."

That made Charles laugh. "Any updates on you grandfather?"

"Pretty much the same."

"I'm sorry to hear that." He lay down beside her and asked, "Is it okay if I just hold my wife tonight?"

"Of course," she looked at him, became instantly worried about him.

Immediately Charles grabbed her and pulled her close to him. Cassie lay her head on his chest, her mind processing how bad her husband looked. He was super stressed and it showed. He looked defeated and worn out, and even though he'd just showered, he somehow still managed to still look unkempt. Now she wondered what had him stressed to that degree. As much as she wanted to ask him, she didn't want that to lead to any arguments. So she lay still in his arms, listening to the sound of his heart beating like she did when they were first married. And she allowed the rhythm of his heartbeat to lull her into a deep sleep.

Three weeks later, Cassie got that four a.m. phone call she had been dreading. "Come to the hospital," Momma Edmonds said. "Something is going on with Poppa."

Cassie jumped out of bed in full panic mode, tripping over everything as she tried to get ready. She was so out of it that she didn't even bother to wake Charles. Even if she had, however, he would have been no use to her since he'd just come home three hours earlier, drunk and loaded out of his mind. Instead, she managed to get dressed and get to the hospital ten minutes after her grandmother had called.

Upon arrival, Cassie gave the intake registration nurse her grandfather's name and was directed to a waiting area where she found her grandmother alone praying. With no words, Cassie walked in and quietly kneeled beside her to join in that prayer.

"In Jesus' name, Amen," Lee Edmonds said as she ended the prayer.

"Amen," Cassie followed suit. Together, they got up and sat in the same chairs they'd been kneeling in front of. "What happened?"

"I think he suffered a stroke," her grandmothers' voice was sadder than Cassie had ever heard it. That caused a massive lump to form in her own throat.

The two of them shared no more words, instead choosing silence. Even though they had both already prayed, they continued doing so in their heads. They were putting their personal requests before God, asking him for what they each wanted and needed out of the situation. After what seemed like forever, a doctor finally came into the waiting room and spoke to them. They jumped out of their seats as if those seats were on fire.

"He suffered a massive stroke," the doctor began, "but we finally got him stabilized. We're running a few tests. His lungs are unclear so we're also testing to see what's going on with that. In a few minutes, they'll have him situated and in a room, you can go in and see him then. I'll come and fill you in with more detail as soon as I get those test results."

Both ladies told the doctor, "Thank you," as they headed back to their seats.

"There's something I need to tell you," Momma Edmonds broke the silence in the room. Cassie looked at her grandmother, concern, and confusion crossing her face. The seriousness in her tone had the hairs on Cassie's arms standing straight up. "Your grandfather has been sick for a lot longer than we've let anyone know." She could see the hurt look in her granddaughters' eyes but she kept going, kept telling her the hard truth. "We wanted to pray and talk to God about things first, we needed His direction in this matter. When we finally got it, we still chose not to say anything because we didn't want to worry or alarm anybody."

"I understand not wanting to tell other people, but I'm family. Why did you leave me out?" The hurt in Cassie's voice was loud and clear.

"What could you have done besides know, child? All knowing would have done was stress you out much longer than it did, and the last thing your Poppa wanted was to drag out stress for you. You already know he thinks your husband is an idiot that keeps you stressed already."

Cassie raised a brow and her jaw dropped. "What? I didn't know that!" Now her voice was shocked.

"Oh," Lee said, looking at her granddaughter and seeing that she really hadn't known. "Well, sorry to tell you this way, but your grandfather thinks you married a moron that wouldn't know a shoe from a shirt if there weren't labels on them." Cassie's jaw dropped lower and for a minute the room was silent. Then both Cassie and Lee began to crack up with laughter. The ladies laughed so hard that tears fell from their eyes. "Oh, child," Mrs. Edmonds said when she caught her breath, "I sure needed that laugh."

"Me too," Cassie replied truthfully.

"Well anyway," she got back to the serious topic, "Poppa was diagnosed with lung cancer a few years ago. We beat it the first time and it had been in remission for a long time. But it came back last year and this time it was more aggressive. That scared the mess out of us but wasn't nothing we could do about it." Silent tears began to roll down Cassie's cheeks. "I know it's hard to hear, it's hard to say it, it was hard living it, but I've had plenty of talks with him and plenty of talks with the Lord. We've come to peace with it. If it's God's will, we both understand."

"How can you be okay with it?" Cassie asked, confusion once again making an appearance on her face.

"The Lord giveth and the Lord taketh away. Now don't get me wrong, that don't mean I'm happy about it or that I agree with God's decision. Do I wish things could be different or better? Yes, that's my husband in there. Am I ready to part ways with your grandfather, my soul mate, my husband? No. But if God sees fit for him to go, what can any of us do but count the blessings of the time we were allowed with him. I disagree with it, but I understand God's will and His will be done. Do you understand?" She looked to Cassie, searched he eyes for the truth.

"I understand, but I don't like it at all," she continued to wipe at her tears.

When her grandmother heard her say that she understood, Mrs. Edmonds began to give God praise and Cassie followed suit. Then they fell into a comfortable conversation, reminiscing on old and fun times. After another hour had gone by, they were finally able to see Pastor Cleothis Edmonds.

Walking into the room, it broke Cassie's heart to see her grandfather lying there with all types of tubes attached to his lifeless body. Overcome with emotion, the ladies ran to the bedside, staring at him as they both began to weep.

"His vitals are strong, but we've put him in a medically induced coma so his body can rest, it has been through a lot," the doctor said. "Mrs. Edmonds, may I speak to you in the hall, please?" Mrs. Edmonds took a few seconds to get herself together before she followed him out. "Your husband is in rough shape right now and I must be honest and tell you that it's not looking good. The tests have revealed that the cancer has spread from his lungs to his other internal organs, including his brain. It's pretty bad in his brain as it's through his whole head. The only thing we can do is let him rest for now. The possibility is very high that he might not wake up again. The only good thing about this situation is that if he does go, it's going to be very quick. I think you should prepare yourself for that reality."

"Thank you for everything," was all she told him.

"If you have any questions, call me," he tapped her on the back of her hand and left.

When Momma Edmonds reentered the room, she found Cassie sitting in the chair silently rubbing her grandfathers' hand and crying. She walked over, rubbed her shoulders, and told her, "I'm going to run to the cafeteria and grab a coffee. You want something?"

"You stay here and spend time with him, I'll go." Cassie wiped her face and got herself together before turning to exit the room. Without giving her grandmother time to protest the way Cassie knew she would, she hurriedly exited the room, giving Momma Edmonds the time alone with her husband that she needed. Cassie heard what the doctor had said and as much as it shattered her, she knew that it had to be devastating for her grandma. There was no way she was going to let that woman spend what may be some of the last minutes of her husband's life away from him getting coffee.

The moment Cassie shut the door to her husbands' room, Lee Edmonds broke all the way down. Her sobs were uncontrollable as she cried for the husband she loved with everything in her. "Cleo," she cried out to him, "I'm going to miss you with everything in me," she told him. "I know this is God's will, baby, but I'd give anything to have more time with you." Then she buried her head in his chest and wept until she was weak. After she had gained some control over her emotions, she sat silently, wept silently, knowing that the life she'd known for many years would never be the same again.

On her way to get coffee, Cassie made the necessary phone calls. Jinx, Lathom, and her husband were the first three on her list followed by her friends and some members of her granddad's church. When she reached the cafeteria, instead of just getting coffee, she also grabbed sausage biscuit sandwiches and headed back upstairs. On her way, she made one more phone call.

"Hello, beautiful," he picked up on the first ring.

"Is it okay that I just want to hear your voice?"

"Of course, Mazoo told her. "What's wrong?"

"It's my grandfather. He's in the hospital and he's not doing good."

"Do you need me there?" were the first words that came from his mouth and they made Cassie cry. Mazoo had stepped up to the plate in a way that Charles hadn't in months. "I didn't mean to make you cry," his voice sounded cracked, hoarse.

"It's a good cry," she said. "You have no idea just what that one question has done for me. Thank you so much!"

"You're welcome," he spoke again. "But Cassie. You never answered me. Do you need me there?"

"I do need you he—" she started but was cut off.

"I'm on my way," he said and she could hear shuffling going on in his background.

"No," she picked up again, "my husband will stop by and I don't want any commotion. But thank you, Mazoo. You just made a tough time a little bit easier."

"And I'll do that from here on out if you let me," came his amazing reply.

"Someday I will," she spoke wistfully. "But for now, I'll just hold on to the memory of how great you are."

"Okay," he replied softly. "I lo—" he stopped himself, shocked at what he was about to say, at just how easily it was about to flow from his mouth. "Call me when you can."

Cassie was floored. She'd heard that slip, knew exactly what he'd been about to reveal, and was stunned in a good way when she finally stepped back into that room.

Mrs. Edmonds had gotten herself together by the time Cassie returned. Being a good granddaughter, Cassie sat the breakfast on the tray table and pushed it in front of her grandmother. She then grabbed the other chair and sat opposite her, next to her grandfather.

Momma Edmonds look oddly at Cassie when she saw that she wasn't eating. "Where's your food?"

"I don't have much of an appetite," she admitted.

"That's okay for now, but eventually I'm gonna see to it that you eat," the older woman spoke sternly. "You need the sustenance if we're going to make it through this together."

Chapter Twenty-Nine

The first to arrive at the hospital was Jinx. He walked into the room and was instantly saddened to see Poppa Edmonds in that state. He looked over at Cassie and Momma Edmonds and was equally as hurt to see how defeated they seemed.

"Y'all need anything?" he asked as he walked to each of them and kissed them on the cheek.

"No," they replied simultaneously.

He stepped into the hall, grabbed another chair and sat in silence with them as he did his best to take it all in. About thirty minutes later, in walked Sam and Lathom. They too greeted and hugged everyone, found chairs, and took their seats. Everyone had been sitting around talking in hushed tones for more than an hour when Charles finally strolled in. The room grew instantly silent as everybody stared at him.

"Hey, bae," Cassie stood and embraced her husband. Momma Edmonds stood up and did the same.

"Hello, everyone," he spoke to the entire room.

Sam gave him a bone dry, "Hey."

Lathom gave a, "What's up?"

Jinx just nodded his head.

The tension in the room was thick as everyone eyed Charles, taking in his disheveled appearance and his distressed look. He looked nothing like the GQ model everyone was accustomed to, but his arrogant demeanor was still enough to bring a bitter taste to everyone's mouth.

"Hey, Cassie, I have to go," Lathom said when his irritation got the best of him, "but I'll be back."

"Yeah, me too," Sam added. "I have to get home so Michael can go to work."

Cassie looked from one to the other and tilted her head to the side. It was clear that they'd slept together, but there was no way she was going to ask them in front of her grandmother, her husband, and Jinx. She was positive that Sam wouldn't say anything, but Lathom's answer may have been enough to snatch her grandfather from the clutches of death and wake him from that coma.

"I see you," Lathom said as he eyed Cassie eying them, "and yeah, I did," he said as he smirked at her. "Love you, lil sis, Momma Edmonds." Then he walked out of the door with a sheepish look on his face as Sam exited behind him.

"Did you have to tell her we fucked?" Sam asked, embarrassed when they were on the elevator and away from hearing ears.

"You lucky I didn't tell her it was a threesome with me, you and Tameka," he stared down at her. "But if you give me any lip, I might tell her everything."

Sam blew out a deep breath and rolled her eyes at him. "Do you tell her everything?"

"You ashamed of fucking me?"

"Don't everybody need to know my personal business, I'm married," she said when the elevator reached the first floor and they stepped out.

"I couldn't tell by the way you was eating the fuck out of old girl's pussy while I damn near fucked you to death last night." Lathom gave it to her straight.

Samantha blushed so hard she could barely think straight. "Damn, Lay!" she yelled at him when they were seated in his pussy wagon.

"That's exactly what you said when I had your ass cumming," he looked over at her, daring her to prove him a liar. "And what the fuck you doing using that shit, Sam? I should make your ass walk from this hospital for that dumb shit."

"It's a long story," she spoke sadly.

"Ain't no story long enough to make you Coke out," he was pissed with her. "You got thirty days to get your shit together or I'ma put a hurtin' on you. 'Cause what I'm not gon' do it is let yo ass turn into a junkie."

"Mind your fucking business!" she fussed.

"Long as we been friends, your business is my business. Thirty days," he warned her as he drove out of the parking lot.

***

"I'm going to run to Tim Hortons," Jinx said to everyone in the hospital room. "I'll be back." He knew Cassie hadn't eaten and it pissed him off that her own husband hadn't even brought her any food. Then it was time for Momma Edmonds to eat again as it was now around two o'clock. Jinx was already stepping into Poppa Edmonds' shoes. He was going to take care of those women even if Pops made a full recovery. They needed him and he would definitely be there for them.

Charles' presence had thrown the whole room off, everyone had bounced, leaving Cassie, Charles and Momma Edmonds to talk which was fine with Charles. He didn't give a damn if they didn't like him, he wasn't married to any of them. He was Cassie's husband, the rest of them could go straight to hell.

Even though he had managed to clear the room, Charles only stayed for about thirty minutes. "I have to get back to the office," he told his wife.

"Okay," Cassie said, pissed that he even showed up if he was going to run everybody off and then leave.

The least he could have done was stayed to make up for the fact that he made everybody else leave. However, he was too selfish to do that, so Charles left the hospital and headed back to his office.

"Demetri," he called his assistant the minute he was seated at his desk. "Get in here." Less than a minute later, Demetri was walking into Charles's office. "Close the door." When Demetri did as he asked, Charles said, "You have the package?"

"I do," Demetri pulled the packet from a pocket on his suit jacket.

"Set it up for me," he commanded.

When Demetri had the heroin in straight lines on a glass mirror on Charles' desk, he looked to his assistant and said, "I just had a rough afternoon, I need a massage."

Understanding what his boss needed and more than willing to give it to him, Demetri dropped to his knees, freed Charles' dick, and downed it while massaging his balls.

"Fuck, that feels good," Charles said as he snorted his heroin and got his dick sucked superbly at the same time.

***

Romel had just walked out of the jailhouse after visiting RJ, when his phone rang. He answered immediately, "Yo."

The caller replied, "Can you meet me?"

"Yeah, where?"

"Meet me at Fowkles and Main Street."

"Be there in ten."

A few minutes later, Romel parked his car and sat listening to music as he waited on his contact. Less than three minutes later, Sosa opened his car door and got in.

After they slapped one another up, Sosa said, "Yo, Mel, this nigga Charles is a busy man, and he's powerful muthafucka! That was his son that neph and them killed. He was a transgender named Tee Tee, his real name is Terrail." So far Sosa was telling Romel things he already knew, but Romel kept quiet and kept listening for anything that he might not know about. "Charles was married to his mother, that's the lady we saw at the airport with him. Her name is Carrie Baxton. Shit went bad and the ex-wife kicked his ass out and divorced him."

"You know what went bad?"

"Naw, but I'm digging for that as we speak. Anyway, the shorty you been kicking it with is named Kelly, that's his sister, his twin sister. Her real name is Kaleya and those two got some kind of beef. Like nobody likes this nigga. Oh, yeah, nigga's into nose candy, heroin. There's a few more things that aren't adding up, but I'm on it. It's like somebody is protecting this nigga hard and uncovering the truth about him is hard as a muthafucka."

"Somebody like who?" Romel was curious as to who would be protecting Charles that hard.

"I don't know, but I'll damn sure find out."

"Thanks," Romel said as they slapped each other up once again.

Sosa jumped out of the car. "I'll be in touch."

Romel drove off, his mind in a whirl. Who the fuck is this nigga?" he asked as he lit a blunt and just drove, taking in everything he'd just heard about the most mysterious muthafucka on earth.

Poppa Edmonds' condition had worsened. Three full weeks had gone by and his body was rapidly deteriorating. They had tried to bring him out of the coma, but he never woke and never responded to them. Cassie and Momma Edmonds were exhausted, but the church had come through for them, showing up and staying with their pastor while those two went home to shower and rest and eat. When a church member couldn't make it, Jinx was there. When Jinx needed rest, Lathom was there. There was so much love and support that had been shown by everyone that Cassie and her grandmother were more than grateful.

Then the doctors said what Cassie knew would eventually come. "It's time to prepare yourselves to take him off of the life support machine. There is still no brain activity and his lungs are about to fail him completely."

Those were the hardest words Cassie had ever heard in her life. She was in a serious funk and wasn't ready to have to make funeral arrangements. But she knew her grandmother needed her help and she was determined to not let her do something so difficult alone.

"You ready to do this?" Cassie asked her grandmother.

"Ready to do what?" Momma Edmonds looked at her curiously.

"Make the funeral arrangements," Cassie looked at her grandmother like she had horns or something,

"There's no arrangements to be made," Lee told her. "Poppa had a decent life insurance policy and he withdrew some of it to pay for his funeral plot, his headstone, and his service. He already wrote his own program and already made all of his own arrangements with the funeral home of his choice for both himself and me. We're to be buried next to one another when the time comes. You know your Poppa was always prepared."

Cassie was dumbfounded and simply stood there with her mouth hanging open as she shook her head in amazement.

Once again, Charles was out of town. When Cassie called to let him know that tomorrow was the day they would be pulling the plug on Poppa Edmonds, Charles was a little irritated that he would have to change his plans in the middle of them. However, he didn't show that irritation to his wife. All he said to her was, "I'll be there as soon as I can get a flight."

"Okay," was Cassie's only reply.

When Charles ended the call with his wife, he turned to Demetri. "Book a flight, we're going home."

"What about the—"

Charles cut Demetri off sharply. "Book it now."

"Yes, boss," Demetri said, disappointed that he wouldn't get to follow Charles to Sin City again.

He loved watching that man overindulge in behaviors that were too sinful to mention. He loved it, even more, when Charles indulged in him when those sinful activities were over and he didn't really remember anything. Those fucks were the best fucks. Charles would do everything, even the things he would never do with Demetri when he hadn't been to Sin City first. And the next day he wouldn't remember a damn thing. Demetri made a mental note to get Charles to Sin City as much as possible from here on out.

Despite the things going on with Charles, he did love Cassie. He knew he wasn't being a husband to her at the time she needed one the most, but his old demons had resurfaced again, this time much worse than before. And those demons were hungry, starving, in desperate need of being fed. Those demons had proven that old saying to be true. When demons left, they were gone, but when they returned, they came back with more friends than before.

Charles' demons had come back with greed. He wasn't just drinking now, he was using too, snorting every chance he got. They also came back with gluttony, sexual gluttony. He was fucking up a storm, as much as he could. He was an addict in every sense of the word and feeding that addiction took a lot of time and money, both of which he had. There was no shortage of drugs for him, no shortage of sexual partners for him. Demetri took great care of him and if his assistant ever got tired, which was a rarity, that assistant knew just who to call to keep Charles satisfied. Cassie couldn't compete with that. So Charles neglected her needs and nurtured his demons and there was no way in a sinful hell he was willing or able to do anything different.

"Demetri," he called out to his assistant when he was done with the arrangements.

"Boss?" Demetri replied.

"We have three hours until the flight. Since I can't get to Sin City for a few hours tonight, you're going to be my Sin City right here in this room. Get my heroin, the throat numbing spray, and the ass numbing cream. I need to fuck your holes deep until you go blind and pass out."

"Yes, Sir!" Demetri wasted no time doing exactly what Charles asked of him.

It was going to be a beautiful few hours.

Lathom finally got the calls he'd been waiting on. What he'd found out about Charles made him want to kill that nigga on sight. Dude was powerful as fuck and into some seriously bizarre shit. But he couldn't kill him just yet, not when he Cassie was already about to go to one funeral. He didn't need her burying her grandfather and her husband in the same week, but she was definitely going to bury his bitch ass.

When it came to Charles, Lathom's trigger finger was itching like a muthafucka, but he couldn't use it to pull anything just yet. He had to play his cards right. The last thing he wanted to do was harm Cassie in the process. He would lay low on Charles for a minute, but not too long a minute. It was time for his ass to stop walking the earth and take his place under the map.

Mazoo on the other hand turned out to be harmless. His stint in jail was on some bullshit. He'd sold to an undercover FED and got sent away for eight months. That was the most dirt that dude had ever done, so Lathom was cool with him fucking around with Cassie. As far as his wife, it seemed nobody could put a lid on her. Tameka was a wild one, the only way Mazoo could control her was by abusing the fuck out of her. Since old dude wasn't into laying hands-on women, he tried his best and then turned her ass over to the streets. Word was that he'd already filed for divorce.

Lathom had much respect for Mazoo's control because the few times he'd fucked Tameka he wanted to choke her ass to death. Her mouth was good when it was on his dick, but when she was using it to talk, Lathom wanted to snatch her vocal cords cleanout and fry them bitches in catfish grease. The woman was a mess, but her pussy was so damn good. Lathom had decided that as long as she didn't look like a coke head and as long as she kept serving him that fire mouth and ass, he would keep fucking with her. But if things ever went south in any way with her, he would divorce her ass too, and he wasn't even married to her.

As far as Mazoo and Cassie were concerned, if things ever got serious between those two, he'd pull up on him and check Mazoo's temperature, but for now, he'd leave well enough alone.

"But that Charles nigga..." Lathom said as he drove toward his destination.

Chapter Thirty

The day arrived for Mrs. Lee Edmonds to pull the plug on her husband. Cassie had stayed at her grandmothers' house overnight. She didn't want her to spend the night alone when she was going to have to face the equivalent of hell the next day. Surprisingly, she had slept very well and woke to the smell of bacon, scrambled eggs, toast, oatmeal, and freshly brewed coffee. In a heartbeat, she was up and, in the bathroom, washing her face and brushing her teeth.

When she was done with her grooming, she almost fell down the stairs in her rush to the kitchen and all of that food. Her appetite was back and mad as hell with her for not feeding it in a few days. Stepping into the kitchen, Cassie found Momma Edmonds cooking and listening to gospel music.

"Good morning, Momma," she called out.

"Good morning," she turned to Cassie and offered a warm smile. "I was just about to come wake you to eat."

"The smell of the food woke me up. Apparently, my appetite is back," she looked in the pots and inhaled deeply. That kitchen smelled like whatever Cassie was sure Heaven smelled like.

"Good, because I didn't want to have to force-feed you," her grandmother told her. "I would have, but I didn't want to."

"You seem like you're in good spirits," Cassie noted.

"Not good spirits, just better able to accept what I believe God is willing for Cleo." She let out a deep sigh. "I guess you can say I'm more agreeable today than the days before. I don't want my husband to leave me, but I don't want him here suffering anymore either."

"I'm so sorry, Momma," Cassie's eyes filled with unshed tears.

"Me too," Momma Edmonds said as she put a plate in front of Cassie and one in front of for herself. "Bow your head." Cassie did as she was told. "Heavenly Father," she began, "I come to you in the most humble way to say thank You. Thank You for this day, thank You for this food, thank You for the situation I now find myself in, and thank you for trusting me with it. If I had a million tongues, I couldn't thank You enough." Momma Edmonds felt herself about to get carried away in the Spirit and quickly ended the prayer with, "In Jesus' Name, Amen."

"Amen," Cassie added and together they ate their breakfast and talked about the giant elephant in the room.

The moment breakfast was over and Momma Edmonds exited the kitchen to shower and get dressed, Cassie burst into tears. She had come to accept what was happening, but that didn't mean it didn't hurt like hell. She was so proud of her grandmother for being strong, but she was struggling with it. She didn't want Poppa to die even though she had to let him go. She was trying to get herself together while she cleaned the kitchen, trying to keep quiet because she didn't want to upset her grandmother. However, that was proving to be hard. The tears just wouldn't stop, so she grabbed her phone and dialed the only number she could think to dial at that moment.

"How are you, beautiful?" he asked the moment he picked up.

"I neeeeed yooouuuu!" Cassie wailed the second she heard Mazoo's voice.

While Cassie was in the kitchen getting emotional support and comfort from Mazoo, her grandmother was in the tub breaking down herself. Both ladies were doing their best to be strong for the other, but secretly they were sharing the same pain. The difference in their grieving process was that Momma Edmonds always ended her breakdowns with a breakthrough. She went from weeping to worshipping. Cassie just stopped crying with no breakthroughs to speak of.

A short while later, Mazoo had Cassie feeling better and God had Momma Edmonds feeling better. The ladies were both dressed and ready to be on their way to the hospital. They were quiet leaving the house, quiet on the ride there, and quiet when they arrived and proceeded to Poppa Edmonds' room. Lee took one look at her husband and knew that he was ready to be gone. The machine may have been breathing for him, but she knew her husband was ready to be out of that body and to get on with his eternal journey with the Lord. There was a small comfort in knowing that.

Because the room was cold and dark, she walked in, sat her purse down, and opened the blinds. She wouldn't allow the room to look like gloom and doom, so she let the sunlight in and turned on the radio she'd requested from the hospital. Gospel music slowly played as the sunlight filled the room and brought in a different type of energy. Lee Edmonds took a seat beside her husband's bed and began to rub his hand and talk to him as if nothing was wrong, as if they were the only two in the room.

Cassie had always admired her grandparents' marriage, everything about it. The way they loved each other, took care of each other, and acted as if they were the only two people in the world made her long for that kind of love. Feeling sad and sorry, Cassie took a seat on the other side of Poppa Edmonds and took that hand in hers.

"I love you," she whispered to her grandfather as tears fell down her face. "And I'll see you on the other side."

Only a short amount of time had gone by when the knock came on the door. It was the doctor, letting them know it was time. Both ladies looked at one another, not yet ready to let him go but understanding that they had to.

"I'm sorry for disturbing you," the doctor said, "but it's time. Are you ready?" he asked when he had walked fully into the room.

"Yes," Momma Edmonds spoke.

"Will there be anyone else joining you?"

"No," she responded again. "No one else will be joining us and we're as ready as we can get."

"Remember I explained before that we will shut the machine down and take all the tubes and other machines off of him. That does not mean he will go immediately, it can be minutes, hours, or days. It just all depends on him."

Both ladies said, "Okay," and grabbed each other's hands.

Tears began to flow as the doctor and two nurses shut the machines off and removed every tube from his body.

"Okay, ladies," all there is left to do is wait. We'll leave you to your privacy, but if you need anything, please feel free to let any of us know and we'll assist you. I'm sorry again," he said and they all exited the room.

Both ladies sat again and just stared at Poppa Edmonds. After a while, another knock came on the door and Charles entered the room. Cassie got up and greeted him. He greeted Momma Edmonds with a sincere hug as Cassie filled him in on everything that had happened thus far.

"Now we just wait," she told him.

"Are you both okay?" he asked, genuine care and concern in his voice.

"As good as we're going to get," Momma Edmonds responded.

Just then there was another knock. "Come in," Cassie called out and in walked a nurse wheeling a cart that consisted of Danish muffins, cakes, cookies, teas, waters, and coffee.

Momma Edmonds looked, her mouth opening in surprise. “What’s all this?”

“It’s a bereavement cart,” the nurse spoke so low her voice was almost a whisper. “It’s in case anyone gets hungry or thirsty but don’t want to leave the room.”

“That’s very kind of you, thank you,” Lee smiled briefly before turning her gaze back to her husband.

“You’re welcome, Mrs. Edmonds. Do you need anything else?”

“No, ma’am,” Cassie replied, seeing that her grandmother was focused on her last moments with her grandfather.

As quiet as smoke, the nurse exited the room, leaving the family to their loved one. A few minutes later, Lathom walked in and immediately felt his temperature rise when he saw Charles. Because that was not the time to act a fool, he maintained his cool and greeted Charles the same way he did Momma Edmonds and Cassie. He kissed Momma Edmonds on the forehead, kissed Cassie on the cheek, and shook Charles’ hand. He then walks over to Poppa Edmonds and looked down at him, finally coming to grips with the fact that this was it.

Unable to take the loss of one of his father figure, Lathom broke down. He hadn’t realized how hard it would be for him, his only concern had been for Cassie and Momma Edmonds. He sobbed as he held Poppa

Edmonds' hand. "Thank you for teaching me how to pray," he said as his voice broke. Cassie stood and went to him, wrapping him in her arms as she and Momma Edmonds wiped tears away from their eyes.

To everyone's surprise, Momma Edmonds stood up, went to Lathom and rubbed his back. "It's going to be ok, son," she comforted him.

Just then Jinx walked into the room. "Am I too late? Why is everybody crying?"

"No, son," Momma Edmonds said, "we're just comforting one another. He's yet alive."

Jinx visibly relaxed, relief flooding him like never before. When he was over the shock that had punched him in the throat when he'd first walked in, he began to greet everyone, even Charles. Then he walked over and hugged Momma Edmonds. For the longest time they all sat and talked and eventually started laughing, reminiscing on the crazy and sometimes funny things Poppa Edmonds had done or said over the years. Even Charles relaxed enough to participate in the conversation.

When the coast was clear and everyone was calm enough, Jinx asked Lathom to take a walk with him. With no protest whatsoever, Lathom rose from his seat next to Cassie and walked out of the room with Jinx. Once they reached Jinx's car and got in, Jinx lit a blunt and passed it to Lathom.

We gotta stay calm for them," Jinx told him. "We're all they have now and if they see us break, they're going to break. So me and you," he gestured his fingers between them, "we break in the private company of one another. I got you and you got me and together we got them."

Lathom inhaled deep and let the smoke out slowly. "Seeing him so lifeless and weak almost took me out. I wasn't expecting it to hit me that hard," he confessed. "I'm so used to seeing him strong and full of life, man."

"Listen," Jinx told him as tears clouded his own eyes, "there's strength in a man who dies peacefully. You may not understand it now, but later you will. Trust me, I know." Lathom shook his head up and down and took in a few more pulls. Jinx continued when he got his own emotions under control. "We can cry, but let's do it later. Now finish up this blunt so we can get in there, them ladies needs us."

"You're right, plus we left them in there with that clown."

"Yeah, that nigga is a fucking character," he frowned hard and deep at just the thought of Charles. "But spray this on you and let's go."

Cassie and Momma Edmonds were still laughing and sharing memories when Jinx and Lathom returned. Charles was laughing, starting to seem semi-normal. Jinx and Lathom joined in, willing to do anything to make and keep the ladies happy. Together they all spent the next few hours sharing stories and cracking up. The doctor came into the room from time to time to check on the family and Poppa Edmonds. The last time, it was a nurse that came in.

"Visiting hours are over," she said. "However, you guys are more than welcome to stay."

Everyone had lost track of time and was surprised to learn that it was eight o'clock at night.

"I'm staying," Momma Edmonds told her.

"I'm staying," Cassie chimed in.

The doctor walked in just in time to catch that conversation, "I'll bring you, ladies, some pillows and blankets," he added.

The guys all stood and said their goodbyes, giving the ladies hugs. Charles was the first to leave as he was smart enough to know that it wasn't a good idea to walk out with the fellas.

He hugged and kissed Momma Edmonds and then his wife. "If you need anything, I'm just a phone call away."

After he left, Lathom and Jinx stayed a few minutes longer, giving him time to be all the way gone. Just because they were going to kill him didn't mean they had to do it then and there. Jinx made his way over to Poppa Edmonds to say his final goodbyes as Lathom spoke with the ladies.

"Hey, Pops. I know you told me to be strong and I promised I would, but it's hard seeing you like this," he admitted as he wiped tears away, hoping no one saw him. Then he gave Poppa a kiss on the forehead. Rest up," were the last words he said to the only man he'd ever known as a father. Jinx then gave love to the ladies just before he and Lathom finally left for the night.

Shortly after the exodus had been made, the nurse returned with pillows and blankets for the ladies. Cassie and Momma Edmonds got settled into their chairs, one on either side of Poppa's bed. Before long both ladies were sound asleep.

Momma Edmonds woke from her brief nap to find Cassie napping. She took that opportunity to grab Cleo's hand and talk with him one last time. "Cleo," she began just above a whisper, "I love you so much. I know you want to be with the Lord and to see Georgia. You've always been crazy for that girl. I know that when she died a piece of you died that day too. I didn't say anything, but I noticed it. I've spent the best years of my life with you, Cleo," she said as hot tears rolled lazily down her face, "and I just want to thank you for loving me. I'll always love you and carry you in my heart. I know you've been holding on for me and Cassie, but you can let go now. We'll be alright, we've got God and you know He'll never let us fall. I love you, I always will," she told him as she never once let go of his hand.

That's when she felt it, a slight twitch of his hand, almost like he gripped her hand. She wasn't sure if it was in her mind, but it sure felt real. Immediately she smiled as more tears ran down her face. She knew that was her husband's way of letting her know that he was listening. "Go on and rest now. I'll be alright." For a short time, she sat in silence, holding his hand. After a few minutes, she felt her husband's grip loosen and knew that Cleo was no longer among them. Silently, she sat with his hand still in hers as tears of sorrow rolled down her face, the clock displayed 2:22 a.m. as she cried herself to sleep.

Around 4:23 in the morning, a nurse entered the room to check on them. "Excuse me, Mrs. Edmonds," she called out, waking her. Lee jumped as the nurse startled her. "I'm sorry for startling you, but I just wanted to tell you that your husband is gone."

"Yes, I know. It happened at 2:22."

"Okay, the nurse said as she wrote on her pad.

"I'm sorry I didn't inform anyone, I just wanted to spend a little more time with him. But we'll get going now. Don't want to be in your way.

"You can take as much time as you need, there's no rush."

Lee looked over at a sleeping Cassie and then back at the nurse before saying, "Yes, I'll take a little more time. I really don't want to wake her." She looked back over at Cassie.

"I understand," was all she said as she quietly exited the room.

Cassie finally woke at 7:35 that morning. She took one look at her grandmother and instantly knew. Immediately, her gaze went to Poppa and she began to cry.

"He's been gone for a while now; I just didn't want to wake you. 'Specially when you was sleeping so good."

When her granddaughter broke, Lee made her way over to Cassie and held her, letting her release all of her pain and sorrow. After a good ten minutes of crying, Cassie was finally able to pull herself together. She and her Momma spent another few minutes saying their goodbyes. Then they prayed and kissed Poppa Edmonds as they prepared to leave. The clock now read 8:00 a.m.

Chapter Thirty-One

They got to the house a little after nine a.m. It had been a really long week and they were exhausted. Both ladies hit the kitchen, washed their hands, and got a pot of coffee started. Cassie sat at the table reflecting, processing as Momma Edmonds went to her bedroom and dug out a small box. She then returned to the kitchen and sat back at the table.

"I have to make a few calls and inform everyone of what's happened and of what's about to happen. Everything is pretty much taken care of, so there's not really much to do."

"Momma, I'll call this set of people and you call that set," she said as she looked at the list. "You're not doing that by yourself."

As a unit, they both sat there and called every number on their list until they were done. Then it was time to set a date for the funeral. Cassie rummaged around the house and found an actual paper calendar.

Momma Edmonds looked at it and said, "Tuesday for the wake and Wednesday for the funeral."

"That's the old-fashioned way of doing things, Momma," Cassie told her grandmother. "Nowadays most people do everything in one day."

Nothing Cassie said would convince her grandmother to do it all in one day. She was old fashion and some things she just wasn't willing to compromise on. When they finished setting that date, Lee got in touch with the assistant pastor who was about to become the head pastor and informed him of the plans she'd made. The ladies finished up with the arrangements and the calls and people started showing up.

Momma Edmonds took the box and stuck it back in her room when people start rolling in. The time would come to discuss the contents of that box with her granddaughter, but for now, it would have to wait. Stepping back downstairs, Lee was genuinely surprised to see just how many folks came calling. Some came with comfort and hugs, many came with dishes of food. Everyone came to show support for the man that had been a pillar in that community. That's how it began and that's how it remained from that day until the day of the funeral.

After three weeks of being in a severe depression, of which Momma Edmonds firmly yanked her out of, Cassie woke at her grandmother's house to the sound of her phone ringing.

"Hello," she said in a sleepy voice.

"I have an emergency trip to take," Charles informed her.

"Another one?" she asked in a still sleepy voice.

"Yes," he volunteered very little information.

"Well, what's this one for?"

"A business convention. I'm trying to get out of it because I know you really need me here," he began but she stopped him.

"No, it's okay. You should go. I'll be okay." She sat up and threw her feet over the side of the bed. "I'll be here helping Momma like I've been doing until you get back."

"I'll probably be gone for a week or so, I'm not sure," he was unsure of exactly how long the trial would last, but he knew it had to have lasted at least a week.

"It's okay," she assured him. "Do what you need to do for your career. Your life doesn't have to stop just because I'm letting mine stop."

There was a deep sigh on the line before Charles said, "I'm sorry I have to leave you when you need me, but I'll stop by to see you on my way to the airport, okay?"

"Okay," was all she said and hung up.

Deciding not to lay around again and have her grandmother come up those stairs and give her another talk, Cassie got up, dressed, and pulled out her cell phone. She really wasn't in the mood to talk to anyone, but she had to get back into the real world and get her life back on track. As much as she hated life without her Poppa, her grandmother had been right, he would be really disappointed at her giving up on her life after he'd fought so hard to keep living his.

Reluctantly, she looked at her cell phone and was stunned at all of the calls and messages she had missed. For the first time in weeks, she read her text messages and listened to her voicemails. Some text messages she responded to, others she didn't. She chose not to return a single phone call. She just wasn't ready for that level of communication yet. Lying back down in that bed fully clothed, Cassie shook her head.

"Life is not fair, God," she said as she closed her eyes to the world around her and fell sound asleep.

The next time she woke, it was to the sound of her name being called by her grandmother. Still sort of groggy, she got out of bed, took her medication, and walked down the stairs saying, "Yes, Ma'am?"

"Charles is here."

"Hey," she said to her husband when she walked up to him and allowed him to kiss her on the cheek.

"How are you doing?" his baritone voice sounded in her ear.

"Much better than I was. Momma got on me and helped me to pull out of the funk I was in. I still want to stay with her a few more days, but overall, she got me right."

"Well, I'm glad she helped," he spoke quietly, feeling that it should have been him that helped her. "I'm really sorr—" he began but Cassie quickly changed the subject.

"Do you have everything you need for the trip?"

At first, he was caught off guard by her abrupt change of subject, but when he saw in her eyes that she too was disappointed in him for not coming to her rescue when she needed him the most, there was really nothing he could say. She was right, he hadn't been her husband in a long time and she had come to accept that. Charles knew then and there that if he didn't get his shit together, it would only be a matter of time before Cassie decided that she wanted a divorce.

With that heaviness on both of their minds, Cassie and Charles talked to one another for about ten more minutes before he said, “I have to get going.”

“Call me when you get there,” she smiled weakly up at him.

After they said their goodbyes, Charles said goodbye to Momma Edmonds and left.

Once in Atlanta, Charles made into the hotel and checked in. After getting settled, he called his wife like he promised he would and informed her that he had arrived safely. When he was done with that obligation, he called Carrie to let her know he’d made it. Her response to him was both dry and angry and he still had no idea why she all of a sudden hated him so much. Choosing not to focus on her and her new kind of crazy, he made up his mind to get to Sin City as fast as he could. His addictions were hungry and he needed to feed them before the trial started tomorrow.

Demetri was due to fly in early tomorrow morning, so Charles had plenty of time to engage in the debauchery before his assistant got there and began to hog up all of his time. If Charles didn’t know any better, he would believe that Demetri was trying to take ownership of him. “That’ll never happen,” he chuckled to himself. “I own people, people don’t own me.” But that didn’t stop him from making a mental not to keep a closer eye on the very possessive Demetri.

All shined up and ready to go, Charles left his suite and headed to the underbelly of the city to get all of his fixes.

Romel had been trying to get in touch with Cassie for weeks. He knew her grandfather died and he wanted to offer her his condolences as well as update her on what was going on with the trial. However, he hadn't been able to reach her for three straight weeks. Deciding to call her yet again, he dialed her number and still got no answer. This time he opted to leave a message.

"Hey, Cassie. I heard that your grandfather passed. I know this has to be really hard for you so I'm calling to offer my condolences. I've been calling you, but haven't been able to get in touch. Just wanted to let you know that the trial starts tomorrow and I hope you can make it. RJ really wants you to be there and honestly, so do I. Call me when you get this message or whenever you can. One," he ended his message and hung up.

Cassie made her way back upstairs after Charles left. It was her intention to call Mazoo and see if she could spend some time with him, could maybe get some comfort from him since her husband didn't have the time or the inclination to give her those things. She knew it was wrong to seek those things from another man, but what was she supposed to do? Keep waiting on a man that clearly had things going on that were far more important than her. What sense did that make?

Grabbing her phone, she put in the code to unlock it and was just about to dial Mazoo's number when saw that she had a new voicemail message. After punching in the code to listen to it, she was surprised when she heard Romel's message come through relaying important information. Immediately she started to panic. There was no way she was going to make it to Atlanta for a trial that started tomorrow.

Her first thought was to call Lathom and ask him to book her a flight and hotel room.

"Why?" he asked, his suspicions very high. Cassie told him what was going on and the message she had just received. "Alright, sis. I gotchu," he assured her.

She then went back downstairs and told her grandmother that she had decided to go home. There was no way she was going to tell her that she'd been in contact with Romel and that the son Lee had made her stay away from was on trial for murder, a trial she planned to attend. So she lied. "Momma, I'm going to head home so I can clean up and get a few things together. You're right about me getting back among the living, so I may as well start now. That way, by the time my husband comes home, I'll be close to back on track again."

"I'm glad to hear it, because I was going to kick you out at the end of the week and force you to go home."

Cassie's mouth dropped and she chuckled. "Are you serious?"

Momma Edmonds looked at her granddaughter with serious eyes, "Whatever it takes to get you healthy and keep you healthy is what I'm willing to do. I already lost one love of my life, I'm not trying to lose the other one."

"Awwww, Momma," Cassie said as she walked to her grandmother and embraced her, tears rolling down her face. "I love you, too!"

"I know you do, child. Now get on out of here and go live your life. And if you feel it's too much and decide you wanna come back here and rest up a little more, my door will be closed and locked."

"Momma!" Cassie was shocked out of her mind.

"Don't Momma me, Cassie Lisa Edmonds Baxton! You're not allowed to spend anymore nights here until you're able to stop using this house as your crutch. No more hiding out here, young lady. I will not let you feed that depression demon that's trying to destroy your future. Now I really do love you, but get out!"

The smile on Cassie's face was big and bright. "Yes, Ma'am," she said as she hugged the woman that raised her again.

"But before you go," Momma Edmonds said, and went to retrieve that box, "here." Then she extended the box to Cassie. "I've been trying to give it to you, but I just couldn't do it until I knew you were ready. Now, you're ready."

"What is it?"

"It's from Poppa." Cassie's heart melted. "Open it when you have time and when your mind is calm. He's been saving it for you for years. I used to check it every now and again, but I stopped a few years ago. So, there might be some new things in there that I'm not aware of."

"Okay," Cassie shook her head as she accepted the box.

"Are you sure you're going to be ok?" Momma Edmonds asked Cassie. "You're in a mighty big hurry to get home all of a sudden. You in a rush to hid out in that big old house because I won't let you keep hiding here?"

"No, Ma'am. There will be no hiding anymore, I promise."

Momma Edmonds took a good look at Cassie one last time, almost as if she was searching her eyes for the truth. When she saw what she needed to see, she walked her granddaughter to the door, hugged her once more, and locked that door behind Cassie. She meant what she said about making sure Cassie was not hiding out at her house as a crutch anymore.

Cassie got in her car and started it, feeling as if she hadn't been in it in forever. It had only been a few weeks, but it felt like much longer than that. As she sat there letting it run and warm up, she reached for the box and was just about to open it when the ringing of her phone stopped her in her tracks. Moving her hands away from the box, she reached for her phone instead.

"You got a late flight out," Lathom said. "It was the earliest flight I could get for you at the last minute. I got you a room at the Loews Atlanta so I know you're safe while you're out there."

Cassie let out a long low whistle. "You didn't have to pop for that, a regular hotel would have been fine."

"Nothing regular for you, sis," he let her know. "I'm going to text and email you your itinerary in a few, along with your car rental reservations. You'll arrive in Atlanta a little after nine tomorrow night, but you'll get there."

Cassie knew she'd miss the first day of trial, but better late than never she thought. "Thanks, Lay," she told him and they ended their call.

Lathom, immediately after talking to Cassie, called Jinx.

"Yo," Jinx answers.

"I just booked Cassie a flight to Atlanta. Apparently her son's trial starts tomorrow and he wants her out there. Romel just messaged her about it," he told Jinx. "I'm not comfortable with her going to Atlanta by herself, but there's no stopping her. I'm about to book my own flight and follow her out there."

"Naw," Jinx told Lathom after taking it all in. "Don't do that. You stay here and look after Momma Edmonds, I'll look after Cassie."

"You sure, man? Because I can be on the next thing smokin'," Lathom assured him.

"I'm sure. Give me her flight, hotel, and car rental info. I got this one." When Lathom relayed the information to him, Jinx wrote it all down and hung up. Then he called and made his own reservations.

Once Cassie's bags were packed and she was ready to make her way to the airport, she shot Romel a text.

Cassie: Hey, I got your message. I'll be there. I won't be there for the first day as my flight doesn't get in until later tomorrow night, but I'll be there for the rest of it.

Romel: Cool. Me and RJ will be happy to see you.

Cassie: Once I make it there, I'll let you know. Bye.

Romel: One.

Putting her phone in her purse, Cassie carried her bags out to her car. Once inside, she saw the box sitting on the seat, she had completely forgotten about it. Deciding that she would take it with her, she stuck it in her carry on bag, buckled up, and made her way to the airport. It was time to meet her son and watch the trial that would seal his fate.

Chapter Thirty-Two

The next morning, Charles was awakened by the sunlight coming through the window of his suite. "Ugghhh," he said as he opened his eyes and a headache punched him in the eye.

He knew he should have stopped at just one drink last night, but when he really got in the swing of things, that one drink had turned into five. His only saving grace was the fact that he hadn't snorted like he really wanted to. Instead, he fucked and drank and still had a great night. Now, instead of having a really bad hangover, he only had a headache which he would remedy with two Aleve and something seriously spicy for breakfast.

He got out of bed and stumbled his way to the shower, thanking God that he had plenty of time to get ready for the trial. After he dressed, making extra sure to look like the old, impeccably dressed Charles, he ordered his breakfast, was ecstatic when he was able to get it down and keep it down. He popped two pills and waited patiently for them to kick in and rid him of the headache that reminded him of the night before. When he was feeling much better, he called for a car and made his way to the courthouse where he would finally be face to face with at least one of the men that killed his son.

Upon arrival, he could feel his blood pumping through his veins. Anger was eating him alive from the inside out. He was actually in the same building as the men that had changed his life forever and he couldn't wait to see what they looked like. No matter what the outcome of the trial was, Charles had plans for them, plans that would make them regret every decision they'd made that night. If they were set free, he would get them on the streets. If they were sentenced to jail time, he would get them in their prison. Either way, they would pay for what they did to his only child.

His thoughts were triggering him, making him want a drink, some snort, and a good long fuck. He needed to get himself under control before the trial started before he started going into withdrawals and let the whole world know that he was on that shit. Closing his eyes and taking one deep breath and then another as he counted to ten, he let his body relax and got his thoughts in check. Then he stepped into the courthouse lobby, went through the metal detector, and spotted Carrie. Debonair as ever, he walked over to her, greeted her with only words, and escorted the mother of his dead child into the sparsely filled courtroom where they took their seats on the very front row.

Romel made it to the courthouse on pins and needles. He hadn't been in contact of any kind with Kelly since the funeral and he was worried about how she would react when she saw him sitting on the side of the defendants. As of yet, she still had no idea that he was the father of the boy that had killed her niece. Her reaction, when she found out, would be crazy he knew, but there was no more stopping the train she and he had been on. The time was now to let her know that she had been fucking the shit of the enemy.

"Fuck it, it's game time. This is my boy's life on the line, I'll deal with whatever comes up accordingly," he pumped himself up.

Walking into the courtroom, Romel was not surprised to see that it was a little crowded. He had actually expected a crowd seeing as though it was a very high-profile case. Heading toward his seat, he instantly spotted Charles and Carrie but no Kelly. Then he made his way to the very front row on the side of the defendants and sat down.

The boys were escorted in and seated at the table with their lawyers as Romel and RJ made eye contact. As expected, they had all agreed to be tried together instead of separately. According to RJ's lawyer, by doing it that way, it would show that they all had the exact same reaction to being tricked into sex with a man. That would demonstrate that four different young men with completely different backgrounds had simply reacted the way most of society would have reacted under the same set of circumstances. With individual trials, it would have been harder to prove that one person behaved the way most people would have. The purpose of the trial was not to prove that they hadn't committed the killings, the purpose was to show that they acted understandably in a very shocking situation. The boys behaved as psychologically expected to unusual and provoking stimuli.

A few seconds later, the bailiff called out, "All rise," and everyone in the room stood. The judge walked in, took her seat, and the bailiff spoke once more. "You may be seated." Everyone sat and the trial began.

Opening arguments were compelling as each team of attorneys stated what they intended to prove with their cases. RJ's team intended to prove not guilty by reason of temporary insanity, an insanity that occurred when they realized they had been deceived into homosexual sex without their knowledge or consent. The prosecutors argued that they intended to prove that because the victims identified as female, there was no deception involved and the defendants were guilty of stone-cold murder. After the opening arguments, the judge called for a lunch break.

"You okay?" Romel asked RJ when he went into the defendant's suite to talk with his child.

"As good as I'm going to be under the circumstances. Is Cassie here?" he looked at his dad, nervousness on his face.

"Naw, her flight comes in late tonight, so she'll be here tomorrow."

"Okay," he said as he shook his head up and down. "Okay."

After a few more minutes of talking with one another, Romel headed back to the courtroom and waited for the trial to resume. After lunch, the prosecutors began to present their case. There was so much evidence presented on just the first day that Romel was stunned. Charles' ex-wife was a total wreck and Romel watched in disgust as the man did all he could to console the woman he used to be married to while the woman he was currently married to was nowhere near him at that moment.

"Dirty bastard," Romel mumbled as he shook his head, hating Charles with a deep-seated passion.

Finally, after a long and exhausting day, the court was recessed until tomorrow.

Charles arrived back at his hotel to find that Demetri had finally made it.

"How did everything go?" Demetri asked the moment he laid eyes on Charles.

"Everything went to hell," anger flowed through Charles' voice like fingernails on a chalkboard.

"I figured as much. That's why I have a few things set up for you," Demetri's smile was wolfishly big and wide.

"As long as it involves a massage, I'm up for it."

"Oh yes," Demetri cooed, "it definitely involves a massage."

Immediately, Charles sat back, removed his tie, closed his eyes, and indulged in everything Demetri had set up for him, including that exquisite massage.

While her husband was cheating on her once again, Cassie arrived in Atlanta. It was late and she was tired. She hadn't been out of her grandmother's house in weeks and the first time she finally ventured out she'd decided to take a flight to one of the busiest cities in the country. Overwhelmed was an understatement for how she felt and Cassie was ready to hide in her hotel room for a little while, just long enough to get her mind together before she looked for something to eat.

Once settled in, Cassie called Romel, but his phone just rang until it finally went to voicemail. “Hey, it’s me. I made it in and I’m at the hotel. I’ll meet you tomorrow at 8:45 outside of the court building since I don’t know my way around it. About to grab dinner and some shut-eye, talk to you then, bye.”

After calling Romel, she then called Lathom to let him know she made it. He sounded worried, but after she assured him that she was okay and that she would indeed call him if she needed anything, he let her off of the phone with a promise to check on her at sunrise. When she was done talking to him, she called Mazoo.

“Hey, beautiful,” was how he greeted her.

“Hey, handsome,” was her response.

“Long time no hear from,” his voice was so mesmerizing.

“I know and I’m sorry. I was really having a hard time with my grandfather’s death,” she felt compelled to tell him the truth.

“How are you doing now?” he seemed genuinely interested in her wellbeing.

“I’m better, actually I’m in Atlanta.”

“What? Why?” she could hear the concern entering her voice.

"Remember I told you about my son and what was going on with him?"

"Yes," his answer was cautious.

"Well, I'm here for the trial. He asked that I be here and since I never had the chance to be his mother with anything else, I decided to take this first step and try to be his mother for this."

"And you're okay with that?"

"No," she was once again honest, "I'm actually a nervous wreck. I'm so scared that he's going to reject me. Then I'm scared that he's going to spend the rest of his life in prison. Then I'm scared that if he goes to prison, I'll never get to show him just how much I love him and how much I really want to be a mother to him." She was quiet for a moment before letting out a worried sigh. "I'm just scared and stressed and worried and to top it all off, I'm still kind of fighting that depression."

Mazoo could hear her voice cracking, could hear how tired and distraught she was, so he decided to do what he could to help her from hundreds of miles away.

"Cassie," he called out to her in that sexy, deep voice of his.

"Yes?" her voice faltered, almost broke.

"Play a game with me," he requested of her.

"Huh?" now she was confused.

"I want you to play a game with me," he repeated his request.

"Uhmmm," she began but he cut her off.

"Have I ever hurt you before?" he asked when he heard her hesitation.

"No," she quickly replied.

"Then trust me, okay?"

"Okay," she agreed, shaking her head up and down even though he couldn't see her.

"Are you in bed?"

"No, I'm sitting at the dining table in the room."

"Turn off the lights and go to the bed. When you get there, let me know."

"Okay." She stood, did what he asked of her. "I'm in bed now."

"What are you wearing?"

"A button-up blouse and a skirt."

"Good. Now, I want you to close your eyes and listen to me. As you're listening, I want you to relax and do whatever comes naturally to you. Okay?"

"Okay," she agreed.

"Imagine that I'm in that hotel with you," is how he began. "You just got in and you're stressed and worried. I walk over to you, ask you how your day was and you tell me. When I realize that you're stressed, the first thing I do is tell you to let me take care of you. When you agree, I kneel down as you stand in front of me. Gently, I place my hand on one of your legs and begin to move up, up, up, caressing your legs until my fingers reach your pussy."

"Oh!" Cassie said, her eyes wide with shock. She hadn't been expecting that.

"That's exactly what you say when I begin to run my finger back and forth through your slit, making you instantly wet. You moan as I rub and rub and rub circles around your magic button. Light circles at first but then I apply slight pressure and rub you into a frenzy. Your breathing deepens as your legs begin an easy spread. Your hips gravitate in the direction of my hand, gyrating your core on my finger."

"Mmmm," a very small moan escaped Cassie's lips as she closed her eyes and listened to the sensual words coming out of Mazoo's mouth.

The sound of Cassie moaning made Mazoo's dick concrete hard. Slowly, he reached down, unzipped his pants, and began a long and slow stroke on his bone. On the other end of the phone, in that hotel room, Cassie was slowly raising her skirt, inching her fingers toward the exact place Mazoo was talking about.

"Your pussy is so wet for me," he tells her. "It's hot and it's juicy and it's throbbing. You've been waiting for this moment for a long time. To ride my face, to have me fuck you. Your pussy is soaked with anticipation. Slowly, I begin to ease my way up to your legs, kissing your claves and then your thighs, licking and nipping your skin along the way. Your legs begin to tremble as you spread them even more for me." In bed, Cassie spread her legs, sheer need making her tremble. "Then I reach your dripping pussy, French kiss your puffy outer lips. Teasing one, then the other. Sucking on one and then sucking on the other. Your head falls back as I torment you, as I make you wait for what you really need.

"You beg me to lick you, to suck you, but I don't. Not yet. Slowly, softly, I lick your outer lips, slip my tongue into your slit and tease your lips from inside. You start to ride my face, going crazy for my tongue. You grip my head, keeping me in place so that I don't stop the sensual assault on your tender pussy. You move faster and faster, press down harder to increase the pressure between your legs. And finally, when your clit is thumping and thrumming for me when you're panting like crazy, I slither my tongue out like a snake, stroking your pussy with one long, hot lick from clit to entrance."

"Aaahhhhh," Cassie moaned out loud when she heard those words, when she felt her own fingers mimicking Mazoo's words.

Hearing the sound of Cassie moaning for the first time had Mazoo on the edge of greedy insanity. He wanted more, wanted to hear more. His deep voice dropped even deeper, became even sexier as he said, "Just like that."

She rewarded him with another, "Aaaaahhhhhh." The exquisiteness of her moan made him grip his dick so much tighter.

"I lick up and down, around and around, bathing your pussy on my tongue, basting my tongue in your warm juices. Then I latch onto your clit like a baby latching onto his mother's nipple and I suck like I'm dying of thirst. I feed on you, drink from you, as if you alone are my fountain of youth."

"Mmmmmm," Cassie moaned again, her clit throbbing so hard it began a slow ache. "Ooohhhhh," she was lost in Mazoo's wonderful words.

"I suck and suck and suck, spreading your thighs wider and wider so I can have full access to all of you, so I can taste all of you. Your pussy is so hot now, so boiling hot that your juices are flowing and burning my tongue. And still, I keep sucking and sucking and sucking, latched on to you and sucking from you until you explode, pouring into my mouth and down my throat."

“Fuuuuuck!” she screeched as she reached the edge of a real explosion. “More,” she said, now desperate to hear more. “More!”

“Fuck, Cassie!” Mazoo groaned when her moan shot through him and made his dick twitch. He gripped it tighter, harder, his strokes firmer. “When you finally stop cumming in my mouth, when your body stops shaking, I quickly stand up, lifting you in my arms and I carry you to the bed and lay you on it. I’m so fucking hot for you, so fucking desperate for you that I swiftly release my dick, spread your legs once more, and plunge deep into your blazing abyss!”

“Maaazoooo!” she moaned as she plunged her fingers into her core. The sound of her moaning his name almost made him spill his seed all over his hands. His stroking intensified, every muscle in his body strained. “Please,” she begged him.

“Please what?” he teased her.

“Please, make me cum,” she sensually begged him, pleaded with him.

“Fuck!” he said again as the sound of her on the edge had him on that same edge with her.

“My dick invades your personal space, Cassie, filling you deeply, spreading your walls wide.”

"Ooohhhhhh, god!" she mewled, whimpered in ecstasy. He could hear that she was on the verge and he was right here with her on the razor-sharp edge of bliss.

"You wrap your legs around my waist, locking me between your sexy legs. You begin to moan and thrust your hips toward me so that I can give you more, give you all. I start to power drive into you, pumping and pumping, thrusting, and sinking into you so deep that your womb opens for me."

"Shiiiit, babyyyy," she hissed, her voice rose in both volume and pitch. He could hear the sound of her fingers plunging into her depth, could hear how turned on she was, how wet she was. She was so close that Mazoo could hear her heart racing through the phone.

"I sink into you, Cassie, over and over and over again. Sinking deeper and deeper each time. Marking you, writing my name in your pussy, making you mine. You beg me to cum, beg me to cum deep inside you, to saturate you with my babies. Your uncontrollable pleading turns me on so much that I give you what you want. I plow through you, groaning and growling and pumping and driving so hard that the bed shakes and the headboard bangs the wall. I drive into you with all of my might, force my way into the depth of you one last time before my cum shoots out of me so hard that it ricochets off of your back wall, stinging your center and saturating every part of your essence."

"Aaaahhhhhh," Cassie came so hard that she screamed. "Aaaahhhhh!"

The sound of her cumming was enough to shatter him, to obliterate him. His balls throbbed, clenched, spasmed, and then detonated, forcing his cum through him at lightning speed. "Fuuuucccck!" Mazoo's cum shot out so hard and so high that it actually stung his chest through his shirt. "Cassieeeee!" he cried out again when he skeeted out more of his heat, zapping himself of all strength. When their orgasms had subsided, their hearts had stopped racing, and their breathing had calmed, neither of them said a word for the longest time. Cassie was stunned into silence. Mazoo was stunned at the realization that he was seriously in love with her. "You okay?" he asked after a short while. "Do you feel better?"

"Oh, my god, Mazoo!" she breathed out in a long, lazy, relaxed breath, "I feel amazing!"

"Then I've done my job," he chuckled so deeply and so sexily.

"And what job was that? To make me weak for you?"

"To take care of you," his voice was serious, firm. "I just want to take care of you. In every possible way."

The smile that spread across Cassie's face was beautiful, Mazoo made her feel beautiful. "In that case, you did one hell of a job."

Mazoo smiled at her words of satisfaction as he and Cassie talked for a while longer, as they talked until Mazoo heard her voice grow sleepy and her speech slow down. That was the reason he'd done what he did for her. She needed rest and he knew that as long as she was worried about her son and that trial, her mind would race all night and she would never get any sleep. So, he helped her to go to sleep and wished with everything in him that he could be in that bed with her to tuck her in and sleep with her wrapped snuggly and securely in his arms.

"Good night, Cassie," he whispered when he heard her breathing even out and deepen, a sure sign that she was sound asleep. When she didn't say anything, but instead kept on breathing softly, peacefully, he whispered very quietly, "I love you," and hung up.

Thirty-Three

The next morning everyone was back up and getting ready for the trial. Cassie woke refreshed and feeling better than she had since before her grandfather had died. Her night with Mazoo had been just what she needed to get her mind right for that trial. Carrie was a complete mess, dreading another day of hearing the gory details of how her child had been slaughtered. Romel woke, fearing what new things he would learn about how his son had killed that kid. Charles woke with his dick firmly planted in Demetri's mouth, sucking him so skillfully that Charles orgasmed hard and wild as he ripped the hotel sheets to shreds.

Charles was the first to arrive at the court building with Demetri at his side. They proceed into the courtroom as Carrie had told him not to wait for her that day. Carrie arrived accompanied by Kelly, she hadn't told Charles that his sister would be there and she knew he would be pissed. But Kelly was Tee Tee's aunt and she had just as much of a right to be there as anyone else. The two ladies proceed into the courtroom as a duo less than five minutes after Charles and his assistant.

When Kelly caught sight of the man her brother was with, she asked Carrie," Who is that?"

"His lover," Cassie replied as deadly rage filled her. "He actually has the audacity to throw his lover in my face at our son's trial."

"I swear, I hate that muthafucka!" Kelly practically growled. "His ass will never stop being evil."

Romel and Cassie met up outside of the court building as discussed. Jinx watched them all from the corner of the court building's lobby, hiding in plain sight. Because he had done his homework along with Angela, his Atlanta connect, Jinx knew who everybody was. When they had all gone inside and taken their seats, Jinx made his way into the courtroom, remaining in the back where he would not be seen by any of the people he was now watching. As everyone waited for the judge to arrive and for day two to start, the courtroom filled with more and more people until there was standing room only. Jinx was glad he'd snuck in when he did because they had stopped allowing people to come in. It was the total opposite of yesterday.

Charles looked over toward Carrie and was very surprised to see his sister in the courtroom with her. He was even more surprised to see Kelly glaring at him for no apparent reason. Knowing that Kelly was present changed the mood for him and he was instantly and extremely uncomfortable. Yesterday, court had been bearable, today it was going to be hell. Looking at his sister, Charles could clearly see that she couldn't wait to bring the chaos and the drama she was infamous for. Kelly was going to make a scene, Charles knew. In fact, he was willing to bet good money on it.

"Why didn't you tell me it would be this crowded?" Cassie asked Romel.

"I promise you it wasn't nearly this crowded yesterday," he said, just as shocked as she was, especially when he saw that the aisles had been blocked by cameras and microphones as the judge had allowed the case to be televised. If anyone wanted to leave, they had to use the side aisles to exit instead of the center aisle. Romel was a little pissed to see that the cameras made it impossible for him to see Charles and for Charles to see him. He wanted that grimy bastard to get the shock of his life when he saw Cassie there, but he would have to wait until later for that.

Once again, when the boys were escorted into the courtroom, RJ made eye contact with his dad. This time he nodded his head in acknowledgment. Then he looked over to Cassie and made eye contact with her and when he smiled at her, Cassie could have jumped for joy.

Even though the noise in the courtroom was loud due to the personal conversations people were having, everyone heard the, "All rise," come from the bailiff's mouth. The entire room fell silent as they all did what they had been told. The judge entered the room and the bailiff spoke once again, "You may be seated."

The trial picked up right where it had left off the day before, with very descriptive details presented. Those details were horrific and heart-wrenching. The prosecutor painted a very clear picture and the evidence was helping them to make their case, a case that painted the defendants as monsters. The atmosphere was very stressful and very emotional as both sides sat listening in complete silence to the horrors that had occurred in that hotel room that night.

Carrie was fighting back tears of absolute anguish.

Kelly was on the verge of a nervous breakdown.

Charles wanted to kill the bastards that had killed his son.

Romel couldn't believe his son could have done anything like what had been described.

Cassie was unable to form a single word.

Jinx was watching it all.

After a long and emotional morning in the courtroom, instead of the judge dismissing everyone for lunch, she adjourned the trial until tomorrow. Cassie was very relieved because she didn't think she could stomach another detail about how those young people had been murdered. Everyone stood when the bailiff had dismissed them and began making their way out of the crowded court, sometimes only moving an inch just to stand still again. As a result of where they had all been seated, Charles, Demetri, Carrie, and Kelly all ended up standing together as they each waited for the room to empty enough for them to exit.

Carrie, extremely pissed at the sight of Demetri, looked at Charles and asked in a disgusted tone, "Why is he here?"

Demetri, with his ever reckless mouth, began, "Excuse me, but I'm here because—"

He was cut off by Charles' firm "Demetri!"

At the same time Charles verbally reprimanded Demetri, Kelly told Demetri to, "Shut up!"

At the sound of the one voice in the entire world that she absolutely hated, Cassie instantly looked up and in the direction of Demetri. It had indeed been his voice she'd heard over the commotion. "What the hell is he doing here?" she whispered to herself and she stared right into his face, but he was too caught up in some kind of drama to even notice that she was there and that she was staring at him.

However, it wasn't long before the crowd had dispersed a little more, leaving Cassie and Romel face to face with a group of arguing people. It was then that Demetri looked over and spotted a livid Cassie. Jinx stood at attention, ready to murder anyone that touched Cassie and ready to get her out of there if need be.

"Charles?" Cassie called out to her husband when she saw him standing next to his assistant while two women yelled and shouted at him. It was then that Charles finally noticed his wife's presence and the shock that plowed through him could have taken him out. "What are you doing here?" she asked, anger and suspicion all over her face.

Kelly, seeing the woman Charles had married for the first time in person, stepped forward across the center aisle and said, "Hello sister-in-law. I'm your husband's twin sister, Kelly." Then she pointed to Carrie, who had finally stopped yelling at Charles to get a good look at the woman Charles had married after their divorce, and said, "This is Charles' ex-wife and the mother of his child, Carrie Baxton. And that thing over there," she said as she pointed to Demetri, "is your husband's lover. We're all here for the trial of the four young men that murdered your husband's transgender son."

"What?" Cassie said as she looked at each person, astonishment and confusion running through her, showing clearly on her face.

"Baby," Charles immediately began as he plowed through the crowd of people to get to his wife, "I can explain."

Before Charles could say another word or even reach Cassie, Kelly saw the man standing next to Cassie with a satisfied smirk on his face and said, "What are you doing here? And why are you on that side of the courtroom?"

Romel, finally ready to admit the truth to Kelly, responded by saying, "My son is one of the defendants."

"What the fuck?!" Kelly shouted in a rage that had taken over her whole body and mind as she dove for Romel.

And the courtroom erupted.

People began running away from the chaos, trying to escape the melee. Some were pushing and shoving to be free, having no idea what was going on. Others were trampling over people in their attempts to exit the room before things got worse. Confusion ensued and before anyone could even process what was really going on, a massive number of deputies filled the room and began to escort people out.

Groups of people were escorted to different exits of the building, Charles and Demetri had been pulled in one direction, Kelly and Carrie had been yanked in another. Cassie and Romel had walked out of yet another with Jinx discreetly on their heels.

Pissed and confused, Cassie exited the courtroom and began looking everywhere for her husband. "Where the fuck is he?" she spoke angrily as she searched the crowd, looking everywhere for him, but she couldn't find him anywhere. Now in rare form, she decides to get the fuck out of there, forget about Charles for now, and get back to her hotel room. She was so pissed that she could barely breathe. As fast as her legs would take her, she made her way to her rental car as Romel chased after her.

"Cassie!" he shouted, trying to get her to slow down so he could talk to her. "Wait, let me talk to you!"

"Not now, Romel!" she shouted back at him as she reached her car, jumped inside, and scratched off, grateful that she hadn't told Romel what hotel she was staying in so he couldn't follow her there.

Charles was pissed and scared out of his mind. He knew that eventually, he would have to tell Cassie the truth about everything, but not there and not like that. How the hell had she found him? Who told her where he was? Had she been following him? If so, for how long?

How much did she know about him? What the fuck was going on? Nothing, absolutely nothing, made any sense.

When he made it back to his hotel room, he tried calling his wife, but got no answer. Every time he dialed her number it kept ringing before he was sent to voicemail. "How the fuck am I going to explain this?" he asked Demetri who was unusually quiet. "How am I going to explain why I've kept everything from her? My sister? My ex-wife? My son?" When Demetri still said nothing, Charles looked to him, saw the rage on his face and said, "What is your problem?"

"I don't like the way you spoke to me in that courtroom in front of everyone. Like I was your subordinate. Like I didn't have a right to speak." Demetri was furious.

"In case you've forgotten, Demetri, you are my fucking subordinate!" Charles rudely reminded him. "And you didn't have a right to speak!"

"That's not what you say when your dick is down my throat or when you're fucking the shit out of me!" Demetri's voice was razor-sharp and laced with fury.

The deadly transformation Demetri saw in Charles when those words were spoken scared the shit out of him. "I pay you good money to have my dick down your throat and to fuck the shit out of you whenever I want to. I do not pay you to get in my goddam business if I don't fucking invite you into it!" Charles was ruthless with him, showing no mercy. Demetri was quite as anger and hurt raced through him and had his adrenaline pumping hard. "I made the rules of engagement very clear from the beginning. We are not a couple!" he began to tick the points off on his fingers. "There will be no public displays of affection. You are to stay out of my business. You are my assistant, my errand boy, my fuck toy, and nothing more. You keep your mouth shut about any and everything that I do. The only time you open your fucking mouth is when I want my dick firmly planted in it! You do not tell my wife or anyone else about us. And you do not, under any fucking circumstances catch feelings because I will never, ever reciprocate them!" Charles was so mad that his breathing was shallow and hard.

"You signed a contract accepting the terms of your employment and you signed a nondisclosure agreement that obligates you to keep your fucking mouth shut until the day you fucking die! What you do not have, nor will you ever have, is a say in anything I do unless I ask you! Do I make myself clear?"

"Yes!" Demetri bit the word out through clenched teeth.

"Then get me a fucking drink and a goddamn massage," Charles ordered. "And make both of them a fucking double!"

"Yes, Sir!" Demetri snapped and got to work obeying his orders. He had finally been introduced to the monster in Charles that everyone had told him was there.

Romel knew that bitch Kelly was crazy, but damn, she'd put it all out there. He was shocked as shit to hear everything she'd said and he knew Cassie must have felt embarrassed and horrible. He kept trying to get ahold of Cassie, but she never once answered his calls. Her phone just kept ringing and ringing until a recording finally came on telling him that her mailbox was full.

"Fuck!" he said as he slammed his phone down and lit a blunt. He needed something to calm his shattered nerves. With court and then the chaos after court, today had been wild as fuck.

Kelly was mad as hell and happy as hell at the same time. She was happy because years ago she'd told Charles that one day she would get him back and today was the day she'd done it. She'd put his ass on blast and destroyed that marriage and that career that he thought was so damn precious. She was mad as hell because she couldn't believe Romel was the father of one of those boys that had killed her niece. That son of a bitch had been fucking the hell out of her, had known the whole time, and hadn't said a word.

"I'll get his ass just like I got Charles," she promised as she rolled a blunt and hit it so that she could calm down. One way or the other she was going to light into Romel's ass. As for Charles, "Fuck him and the evil ass horse he rode in on!"

Cassie finally made it to her room and the minute she did, she muted her phone, silenced all notifications, called room service, and requested a bottle of 1738. She didn't even drink dark liquor, but in lieu of everything that had just happened, she needed peace and quiet and something really strong to settle her mind and her nerves. The alcohol was delivered in what seemed like no time at all and she wasted no time opening it and taking a big gulp straight from the bottle. After a few seconds more, she took yet another big gulp. Then out of the blue that depression hit her again and in no time at all she had gone from silent tears to outright sobbing.

As she allowed the anguish to escape her in the form of tears, she reflected on what the hell Charles' sister said. She was his twin. He had an ex-wife. He had a child. Her husband actually had a kid that she knew nothing about. His son was one of the young men that had been murdered by her son. "What in the entire fuck?" she shouted, freaking out as she realized the gravity of her newfound situation.

She took another gulp of the hard liquor as her mind continued repeating the words of the woman that claimed to be her sister-in-law. "Then she'd said lover, as in Demetri." The man she knew as Charles' assistant was his lover. "Charles is gay?" she asked aloud as she hit that bottle hard enough to blur her vision. She had known something was off with Demetri, but there was no way he was her husband's lover. Or was he? "My husband cannot be gay!" she sobbed.

Steadily drinking and crying, her mind shocked and reeling from the shit that had gone down and the alcohol she was drowning her sorrows in, Cassie was slowly losing touch with reality. "Poppaaaa!" she began to cry. "If you were here, you would tell me what to do!" But he wasn't there, would never be there again, and the hard reality was that she was going to have to figure things out on her own. Without the safety, security, and wisdom of her Poppa. "Fuck!" she cried, sobbed so hard that her stomach ached. Then her eyes focused for a brief second and that was when she glanced over at the table and saw the box her grandfather had left for her.

Deciding that she wanted to escape the madness that was her life and spend time with her Poppa the way she had been doing for the past three weeks, she stumbled to the table where the box was, grabbed it, took it back to the bed, and finally opened it.

"It's just me and you, Pops," she spoke drunkenly as she took another gulp from the bottle and sat beside the now open box.

Peering inside, Cassie saw that there were pictures, papers, and lots of money. Her grandfather had always taken care of her and this time seemed to be no exception. One paper, in particular, caught her eye. She picked it up, examined it and saw that it was a birth certificate with her name on it.

"I already have my birth certificate," she slurred, the alcohol distorting her speech.

After examining the birth certificate, a little more thoroughly, Cassie noticed that, unlike her own birth certificate, the area that read father on that one wasn't blank. There was a name there. And when Cassie read that name and read that name and re-read that name, she screamed at the top of her lungs.

"I can't!" she sobbed uncontrollably as she dropped the document and it floated to the floor like a feather. "I just can't take anymore!" Her sobs were gut-wrenching, so much so that her head began to ache, she went into a full-blown panic attack, and instantly she felt ill.

That's when the knock sounded on her door.

Stumbling to it, she was struggling to even remain on her feet. Her mind was racing, her heart was racing, her blood was racing through her veins. Her vision blurred once again as her head began to spin. She was on the verge of passing out and began to hyperventilate to the point where breathing became almost impossible. "I just can't take anymore," she wailed through shallow breaths as she fought like hell to reach that door before she fainted and couldn't reach it.

She had gone from drunk to a desperate need of medical attention.

And the second she made it to the door, opened it, and saw who was standing on the other side, all she could say was, "Jinx." And, "What are you doing here?" Then she passed out cold as Jinx caught her in his arms just before she hit the floor.

To be Continued!

About The Author

R. Frazier is a correctional officer who fought her way to where she was told she couldn't go and became what she was told she couldn't be.

She defeated the odds.

Even though she conquered every battle that came her way, she is among the people who feels that she doesn't belong. While they and their negativity tried to make her uncomfortable, Rae Shanda stood and still stands unfazed and unbothered by the foolishness. She came a long way from the poor little black girl who grew up in the ghetto of Buffalo NY, Woodlawn and Kehr to be exact.

She always knew she was different, always knew she would carve out a different path. She went from high school drop out to bachelor's degree owner, from a young, single teenage parent to a proud mother of three and a wife. She journeyed from a quiet, timid little girl to a strong woman with a voice, from a renter to a homeowner, from a job to a career.

Rae Shanda went from a sinner running from God to a Christian who now chases God in the hopes of one day seeing His face. She's not perfect, but she's a child of God.

After years of doubting herself, she got the courage to write her first book, something she had always wanted to do ever since she was a little girl. She did it! With hard work and sheer dedication, she finally did it! It was her first, but it definitely won't be her last.

Rae Shanda has something to say, so pay attention!

Made in the USA
Coppell, TX
13 April 2022